Fast Break

Fast Break

Mickey Minner

P.D. Publishing, Inc.
Clayton, North Carolina

ISBN-13: 978-1-933720-40-1
ISBN-10: 1-933720-40-9

9 8 7 6 5 4 3 2 1

Cover design by Stephanie Solomon-Lopez
Edited by: Day Petersen/Medora MacDougall

Published by:

P.D. Publishing, Inc.
P.O. Box 70
Clayton, NC 27528

http://www.pdpublishing.com

Acknowledgements

I would like to thank the readers who take time from their busy lives to read my stories and write me with words of encouragement. And the members of my discussion group who generously support my writing yet keep my feet firmly rooted to the ground.

I would also like to thank Sherry Bovinet, PhD, ATC for her technical assistance on sports injuries and treatments. Linda and Barb at PD Publishing for the enthusiastic support of my writing. Day Petersen and Medora MacDougall for their editing expertise. And Jo Fothergill for being willing to proofread my manuscript as many times as I ask.

Fast Break is dedicated to all the talented women who play, coach, and enjoy the great sport of basketball — be it professionally, in college, high school, or on the playground.

And to my parents, Bob and Madelyn Minner.

CHAPTER ONE

Seated in a hole-in-the-wall restaurant located just off a downtown alley, Dawn Montgomery drummed her fingers on the tabletop. The dining room was a jumble of non-matching tables and chairs that seemed to occupy space with no thought or plan, and she had claimed a seat at the side of room, which was lit primarily by smoky candles in the center of each table. Stale air, flavored by smells of the food being prepared, circulated only because of the draft caused by overworked kitchen fans. She had deliberately picked the restaurant on account of its out-of-the-way location and poor lighting, and the cheap dinner fare didn't hurt since she would be paying for the evening's meal.

Dawn's nervousness was a stark contrast to her casual attire — matching gray breakaway pants and warm-up jacket. One long leg crossed over the other, the raised ankle resting on a knee and the basketball-shoed foot twitching nervously as she waited for her guest to arrive. Keeping her eyes on the restaurant door, she picked up a glass of water and took a long drink, sucking the cold liquid up through the straw.

Finally, to Dawn's relief, the door opened and a gust of fresh air accompanied a well-dressed woman into the gloomy room. It took only seconds before Dawn's eyes met the woman's and reflected recognition. "I was beginning to think you were going to stand me up," she said as her guest sat down.

"Your directions were a little sketchy." The woman pulled several napkins from the dispenser on the table and wiped the greasy surface in front of her, frowning when the results proved unsatisfactory. The waitress approached but was waved off by the new arrival.

"Why did you do that? I thought this was supposed to be a dinner meeting."

The woman's frown deepened as she studied her surroundings. "Maybe some other time. What I have to say won't take long."

"All right."

"I watched you last night and, to be honest, I wasn't impressed."

"What?"

"I wasn't impressed."

"I had a good game last night."

"You half-assed your way through it."

"That's not true. I put up good numbers."

"I wasn't looking for numbers, I was looking for effort; I saw very little of that. You couldn't be bothered to run the full length of the court. You missed easy rebounds because you were too lazy to jump. You played like you couldn't have cared less. Is that what you call a good game?"

"I played as good as my competition."

"If you want to play for me, you need to play better than your competition, and you need to do it every single time you take the court. I don't have lazy players on my roster." She stood, tossing the wad of napkins onto the table. "No matter how good they think they are."

"I *can* play for you," Dawn said angrily.

"You didn't prove it last night."

"Come to the game tomorrow night and I will."

The woman shook her head. "I don't have that kind of time to waste. But I'll tell you what I will do and only because I think you're a better player than you've shown so far. You get yourself on a team, any team, and prove yourself on the court, and I'll give you another look."

"It's a little late for that. Most teams have already filled their rosters."

"That's the best I can do."

"You said I had a shot. I turned down other offers so I'd be free—"

"Don't pull that with me. You're the one who limited your options. I never promised you anything but a look. You got that. Take my offer or not, it's up to you. Find a team; play a good year. We'll talk again."

Dawn slumped in the chair as the woman turned and walked to the door. A moment later she was gone.

The waitress returned. "You planning to order or just taking up space?"

"Do I look hungry to you?" Dawn snapped, pushing up from the table. "Here, this should cover the glass of water." She tossed a dollar bill at the annoyed waitress as she brushed past on her way to the door.

"Baby, what's wrong?" Mandy Christopher asked. They were lying naked on the bed in her hotel room, but all her efforts to engage the woman in sexual activity had been rebuffed. "I don't want to spend my last night in town just watching you lay there."

"I've got stuff on my mind." Dawn pushed away the hand inching up her leg. "Stop it. Damn, do you ever think of anything but sex?"

"Not when I have a naked woman in my bed." Mandy grabbed a breast and squeezed it hard. "I thought you wanted it, too. If you don't, what are you doing here?"

Dawn slapped the offending hand away from her body, then swung her legs off the bed to sit on the edge of the mattress. Looking over her shoulder, she saw Mandy glaring at her as she waited for an explanation. She stood and walked to the window to look at her reflection in the glass. Just shy of 6'-3", her body was toned from years of playing ball and hours spent in weight rooms. She was muscular, with broad shoulders and long powerful legs. Unruly sandy-colored hair, cropped short, stood out against pale skin that never tanned, no matter how much time she spent outdoors. Pale green eyes roamed over the body reflected in the window until they came to rest on the thatch of hair at the apex of her legs. She felt a sudden tingle and smiled, remembering how it felt to have Mandy's fingers playing in those curls.

What am *I doing here?* She turned to face the woman on the bed. "I do want that. It's just that I have a problem, and I can't concentrate tonight."

"You could tell me what it is," Mandy said, fluffing up a couple of pillows and shoving them against the headboard to lean against. "I might be able to help."

Dawn studied her lover. Unlike her own tall frame, Mandy's was petite, barely topping out at 5'-5". Brunette hair stood out against her lightly tanned skin and hung down past her shoulders. Her face was round, and she had a single dimple on the left side of her mouth that Dawn found very appealing. As she stood there, she realized she knew practically nothing about the woman except her name. "I doubt you can help with this."

"Believe it or not, I do have some connections. I'm not just a good roll in the hay."

Dawn grinned. "Well, you are pretty good in that department."

"I'm glad you noticed."

"Be hard not to."

They had met three nights earlier in the hotel bar where Dawn had gone hoping to pick up a good-looking woman for another in her endless string of one-night stands. Being a tall, athletic woman usually meant she had no shortage of women wanting to share her bed for a quick fling. That night had been no different, except that she had ended up in Mandy's bed instead of the bed of her intended conquest. As she was being led across the hotel lobby by a cute blonde wearing a miniskirt and see-through blouse, Dawn had found the way blocked by Mandy, who had boldly informed the blonde that her almost-night of romance was over before it had begun.

"You're a cocky bitch," Dawn said as she walked back to the bed.

"So I've been told."

"What made you think I'd give up the blonde for you?"

Mandy laughed, patting the mattress beside her. "Oh, you big dumb ballplayer. I've had my eye on you for some time now."

"You have?"

"Yes. Ever since I saw you play in the NCAA tournament last spring. I knew there was only one place you belonged."

"And that would be?"

"Right here, with me. You don't really think I'd let that bimbo get in the way."

"I could have told you to get lost."

"Yes. But you didn't. And I knew you wouldn't."

"How?"

"I just did."

"Think you're pretty smart, don't you?"

"I have my moments."

"That you do." Dawn knelt on the bed, straddling Mandy's legs. Placing her hands around the smaller woman's waist, she yanked her from her sitting position to lay flat underneath her. In one smooth movement, she stretched her body on top of her lover's and pressed their mouths together.

Mandy wrapped her arms and legs around Dawn, pulling her closer.

Dawn pushed up just enough to slip a hand between their bodies, reaching down until her fingers came in contact with Mandy's clit. "I love how wet you get," she breathed as her fingers slid along silky labia lips.

"Inside." Mandy thrust her hips up, emphasizing her need. "And hard."

Dawn adjusted her position so she could enter Mandy as forcefully as she knew her lover wanted. Cupping three fingers together, she slipped them just inside the vagina, then spread them to stretch the tight opening.

"Do it," Mandy demanded.

"Not yet." Dawn withdrew her fingers. "First, you earn it." She pressed herself back up onto her knees. Looking down, she inched her way up Mandy's body until she was poised above her head. Spreading her legs, she slowly lowered herself. "First, you suck me. If I like what you do…"

Mandy wrapped her arms around Dawn's legs. Opening her mouth eagerly, she darted her tongue out to circle the throbbing clit.

Bracing herself on the headboard, Dawn moaned as her clit was sucked into Mandy's hot mouth.

"So, what's the problem that almost kept us from having sex last night?" Mandy asked as she pulled her leg free from where it was trapped under Dawn's waist.

Dawn groaned. "Let me wake up first, will ya?"

"No time. I have a plane to catch." Mandy rolled to the side of the bed and stood. "I need a shower. So talk."

"I need to get on a team."

"Do you want to clarify that? I thought you were on a team."

"Not an amateur team. I need a spot on a pro team."

Mandy laughed. "Oh, is that all?"

"See, I told you, you couldn't help."

Mandy laughed again. "You joining me?"

Dawn thought the idea of a shower with Mandy sounded wonderful, but... "No. After last night, I'm not sure I'll ever walk again."

"Okay. You rest. I won't be long. Don't go anywhere."

"As if," Dawn mumbled as she wrapped her long body around the pillows and fell back to sleep.

"Why won't you tell me?" Dawn asked again, lifting Mandy's suitcase out of the trunk of her car.

"I told you," Mandy stood in front of Dawn, stretching up on tiptoes to kiss her lover's chin, "I need to make some arrangements. You just be ready to say yes when the offer comes."

"But if I don't know when or how it's coming, how can I be prepared?" Dawn wrapped her arms around Mandy's waist and lifted her off her feet to kiss her. "How will I know?"

"You'll know. Now put me down. I'm going to be late for my plane."

"All right." Dawn gently lowered Mandy to the ground. "But at least tell me who you know that can do this."

"Oh, didn't I tell you? My aunt is Martha Ann Christopher." She picked up her suitcase and walked toward the terminal, leaving her slack-jawed lover standing at the curb.

"*Mac* is *your* aunt?" Dawn called after Mandy.

"The one and only." Mandy waved over her shoulder as she walked through the terminal doors.

CHAPTER TWO

Patricia Calvin sat in the first row of the second tier of seats that ringed the arena, the location providing her with a perfect view of the action taking place on the court below. She wasn't happy to be in North Carolina on a last-minute scouting trip for the Missoula Cougars, the women's professional basketball team that she coached, but the owner of the team had insisted she check out one of the post players on the Charlotte amateur team. Pat was sure it was most likely at the insistence of the owner's niece, her administrative assistant and the woman sitting beside her, that she had been forced to spend most of the day cooling her heels in airport lounges while waiting out extended gaps between connecting flights.

"Well, what do you think of her?" Mandy asked excitedly. "Isn't she wonderful?"

Pat frowned, wondering if her assistant had been watching the player's lackluster performance or had simply been checking out her lithe body.

"Well?" Mandy insisted, interrupting Pat's thoughts.

"She doesn't put forth much effort."

"Why should she?" Mandy huffed. "Look at what she has to play with."

Pat had been looking. In fact, she had been having trouble keeping her attention on the intended player because of the spirited play of the point guard on the same team. Pat forced her attention back to the player Mandy was discussing. She had enough guards on her roster and wasn't looking to add any more.

"I'm not impressed."

"Doesn't matter." Mandy smirked. "Mac said to invite her to tryout camp. Come on, the game is over." Mandy leaped to her feet before the final buzzer had proclaimed the official end of the contest. "I'll go down and give her the good news."

"No." Pat stopped her assistant before she could leave. "You go get the car and pick me up out front. I'm tired, and the sooner I get this over with, the sooner we can get to the hotel and I can get some sleep."

"But..."

"I can handle this, Mandy." Pat's tone was sharp. "You go get the car."

Knowing better than to push her luck with the coach, Mandy sulked toward the stairs that led to the arena's main corridor and eventually to the exits.

Pat watched the young woman leave, wondering again why she had allowed herself to be saddled with the worthless assistant. Shrugging, she shoved the notebook she'd used to jot down her observations during the game into the soft-sided briefcase she carried. Then she stood and took the stairs, making her way down to the court's hardwood surface. Several of the departing fans recognized her, some waving or mumbling a shy greeting as they passed.

Patricia Calvin had enjoyed a stellar basketball career. After being named Montana State High School Player of the Year for three consecutive years, she had attended her hometown university and helped win national championships in her junior and senior years, earning the honor of being the tournament MVP and a Kodak All American in the latter. Fully expecting to continue her career on the professional level, she had seen her dreams came to an abrupt end during a weekend pick-up game a few days after graduation. While she was executing a spin move, her right shoe stuck on the asphalt court surface and, unable to withstand the pressure of the abnormal twist, her knee blew out. Reconstructive surgery repaired the damage to the ligaments and meniscus, but she had never returned to the court.

Dejected over the loss of her dream, Pat had spent her months of rehab struggling to come up with a plan for her future. She came home one day to find a message on her answering machine offering her an assistant coach position with the Cougars. She wasn't a fool and knew immediately what the offer was — a way to fill the empty seats for the Cougar games. Hometown heroes pulled in lots of fans, even if they were assistant coaches rather than players.

After considering her limited options, Pat accepted the offer and was subsequently surprised to discover she actually had a knack for coaching. Her playing experience gave her insight into how the players approached the game, and she was able to reach them in ways others hadn't thought of. Two years later, the Cougar head coach accepted an offer from another team and Pat was promoted into the position, to everyone's surprise. Pat worked hard and was pleased when the Cougars went all the way to the quarter-finals of the league championship. Now in her second year as head coach, she was set to begin tryout camp with talented athletes she had personally picked to mold into a team that would go all the way to the championship.

She sighed. Apparently she had picked all but *one* of the players who would start camp. And the one who wasn't her choice didn't appear to have the motivation to even survive the camp, let alone play when the season began in a few months.

Determined to put the distasteful chore behind her as quickly as possible, Pat marched across the hardwood floor to the passageway where she knew she would find her prospect. Still upset over the situation her unwanted assistant had forced upon her, Pat shoved open the door to the home team locker room, almost crashing into a tall brunette. Only the woman's quick reflexes kept her from being knocked to the floor.

"Damn, Pat." The woman grinned as she regained her balance. "I saw you up in the stands and expected you'd be stopping by to say hello. Just didn't think you'd try to nail me to the wall to do it."

"Hell, I'm sorry, Karen." Pat reached out for the coach of the amateur team she had just been watching. "Guess I wasn't paying attention. You okay?"

"Yeah, fine." Karen allowed herself to be pulled into a hug. She pushed back just enough to gaze at her friend.

Pat Calvin looked like a basketball player, with a lean but muscular body. Even though team programs had always listed her at an even 6'-0", Karen knew she was slightly shorter than that. Short reddish-brown hair framed an angular face with features that could appear harsh or soft, depending on the coach's mood.

To Karen, the face carried a sadness of too many long nights spent alone. "How are you?"

"Good." Pat smiled, releasing her college teammate.

"Little late to be scouting players. Who did you come to see?"

"Montgomery."

"You don't sound too happy about it." Karen motioned for Pat to follow her back out into the corridor and away from the locker room full of players.

"I'm not," Pat answered honestly. "It was Mac's idea."

"She could be a good player," Karen offered, having coached Dawn for the past few months.

"She's got potential," Pat agreed. "Unfortunately, she doesn't do much with it. I'm surprised you leave her in as much as you do."

"She's who the fans come out to see." Karen was resigned to having to play the lazy player in order to fill the stands. "Local girl made good. You know the drill."

"Not much of a reason." Pat smiled to take the sting out of her comment. She knew Karen was in a tough spot, coaching in an amateur league full of college stars and pro wannabes that depended entirely on fan support for its revenue.

Karen shrugged. "That's the game."

"Yeah." Pat was all too aware of how having a local girl on a team was a revenue producer that couldn't be taken lightly.

"You have time to grab a bite? Or is this just a quick turn-around for you?"

"Sorry." Pat smiled apologetically. "I've been up since four this morning, and all I want to do is get back to the hotel and bed. Wish I had the energy for dinner but—"

"I understand," Karen said. And she did. Being a coach of a professional sports team meant having little time for anything else. "Go ahead. They know you were in the stands tonight, so they're expecting you to show up," she said, referring to her players.

"Thanks." Pat nodded. "Rain check?"

"Sure." Karen grinned, then gave Pat a quick hug. "Count on it."

"It's nice to see you again, Karen," Pat said as she turned to the door, this time being more careful when she pushed it inward. "You're looking good. Debbie must be taking good care of you."

Karen was pleased that Pat had remembered to mention her partner, something that didn't always happen with her preoccupied friend. It probably didn't help matters that Karen and Pat had been dating when she'd met Debbie. It hadn't taken long for all three women to realize whose hearts belonged to whom, and Pat had been gracious when Karen officially broke the news to her.

Karen often wondered why Pat had never had a serious relationship after that; it surely couldn't be because of a lack of opportunities. There were many women who had made overtures to the graceful athlete, but all had been politely rebuffed. Karen asked Pat about it once and had received a shrug of the shoulders and a mumbled, "Guess I haven't found anyone worth the trouble" as an explanation. Hoping that someday someone would claim her friend's heart, Karen turned toward the other locker room to see if the visiting team needed anything.

Pat turned around, calling out to her friend, "Hey, Karen. What can you tell me about your point guard?"

"Gallagher?"

"Yes." Pat wasn't sure why she had asked the question. She didn't need a guard. Hadn't she already told herself that?

"Good player," Karen answered. "Quick hands and feet. Smart. Thinks ahead. Hard worker. Why?"

"Nothing really, just wondering. Don't think I've seen her before. Where'd she play?"

"Western Arizona. Graduated this year."

Pat made a mental note of the information. "Um, thanks," she said, turning back to the locker-room door.

"Far as I know," Karen added before the door shut, "no one has talked to her yet."

"Another wasted night."

Sitting on the bench in front of a row of lockers, Sherry Gallagher looked up to see her teammate standing beside her. "I wouldn't say that, Nancy. I thought we had a good game."

"*You* had a good game. I didn't do much."

"You had that nice 3-pointer to end the half."

"That's about all I did. I'm thinking of calling it quits."

"What are you talking about?" Sherry reached up and grabbed Nancy's uniform, pulling her down to sit beside her. "We agreed to play the full season. You can't just quit."

"Look, it's obvious I'm not good enough to play pro ball. Every team has scouted us, and not one even bothered to tell me to get lost. What's the point to keep playing?"

"To get better," Sherry said. "And to give the scouts a new look next year."

"No. I've given it my best shot, and I don't have what it takes. I'm throwing in the towel."

"What will you do?"

"Go back home and see if that college degree I earned is worth anything."

Sherry looked at her friend. They had been college roommates and teammates and had vowed to make it into the professional league together. "What about our plans to play together as pros?"

"It's not going to happen. All the teams have filled their rosters for the season, and I don't feel like prolonging the inevitable."

"But someone said Coach Calvin was in the stands tonight."

"If she was, she didn't come to see me."

"You can say that again." Dawn walked up behind the two players, towering over them, a confident smirk on her face. "You're definitely not who she came to see."

"I suppose you know why she is here," Nancy said.

"Sure. She's here to invite me to Cougar tryout camp."

"And you know that how?"

"Let's just say I've got friends in high places. Won't be long now before Pat walks in here and hands me my invite."

"Little late for that, isn't it?" Sherry asked. "Doesn't tryout camp start next week?"

"Yeah. But I've already got my flight booked to Missoula. I'll be there in plenty of time. I'll miss you." Dawn grinned. "In fact, I'll miss all of you." She raised her voice so everyone in the locker room would hear her. "Not!" Laughing, she walked back to her own locker.

"Do you think Coach Calvin is really here to recruit her?"

"Don't know. I suppose she could be," Sherry answered.

"Why don't you go back home with me?" Nancy asked.

"I'm not ready to give up yet. Basketball is all I've every wanted to do."

"But you'll have to sweat it out in amateur play for at least another year."

"That's okay. At least I'll be playing."

"You could come home, start a real life."

"There's nothing for me back in Arizona, Nance. I want to play ball. If I have to stick it out in the amateur leagues another year or two, I'm willing to do that."

"Okay, if that's what you want. But I'm telling Coach tonight that I'm done."

Pat walked into the locker room, not surprised when the talking came to an abrupt stop at her appearance. She looked around at the players who were looking back at her, their faces betraying the varying degrees of awe they held for the coach. Most would have given anything to receive an invitation to her tryout camp. The women in the room also realized that they weren't the caliber of player that Pat looked for. If they had been, they would have already heard from her or one of the other professional teams.

Dawn Montgomery stood in front of her locker, a smug smile born of certainty spread across her face. She knew the coach was there to see her, and she was enjoying the looks of envy she was receiving from her skeptical teammates.

"Hello, ladies," Pat greeted the players. "Good game tonight."

"Thanks, Coach," the players answered almost in unison.

"Thanks, Pat." Dawn leaned back against her locker.

Inwardly, Pat cringed at the use of her name by the arrogant player, but she didn't let it show on her features. "Montgomery." She acknowledged the player as she crossed the room to stand in front of her. "Cougar tryout camp begins Monday," she said, her teeth clenched together as she made her offer to a player she was sure would be more trouble than she was worth. "This will get you in the door." She held out an envelope. "The rest is up to you."

"Thanks, Pat." Dawn reached out, snatching the offered envelope.

"Doors are locked at eight sharp. If you're late, you don't get in. Period."

"I'll be on time."

"Be early." Pat snapped. "Oh, and one more thing."

"Yes?"

"My players call me Coach."

That had been the first lesson Mac had taught her when she became an assistant coach. Fearing she would be unable to be an effective coach to players older than herself, Pat had voiced her hesitation to the owner. "You have to let them know you're in charge," Mac told her. "How do I do that?" Pat asked. She had just graduated from college. How could players several years her senior take her seriously? "You tell them," Mac answered, as if the explanation should have been obvious. "You get in their face and you tell them."

"You call me Pat again and you won't play for the Cougars. Are we clear?" Pat's angry eyes narrowed to slits as she dared the player to protest.

"Yeah, Coach," Dawn muttered, her cheeks flaming when she heard the snickers of the other players. She bent down, snatched her sports bag off the floor at her feet and rushed out of the room.

Pat took a deep breath, attempting to rein in her irritation before she had to turn around and face the other players, who had again become unusually quiet. Pat shrugged, smiling sheepishly at the players. "Joys of being the coach."

The players laughed, grateful for the tension breaker.

Out of the corner of her eye, Pat noticed the point guard whose play had earned her attention. She was sitting quietly in front of her locker. Without thinking, she walked over to her. "You made some nice moves out there tonight."

Sherry smiled self-consciously. "Thanks, Coach."

"I, ah..." Pat paused momentarily while she dug around in her briefcase. "If you're interested," she pulled a crinkled envelope free and held it out, "I'd like to see you at tryout camp."

"Really?"

"Really." Pat grinned at the bewildered look on the player's face. "That is, if no other team has made you an offer. And *if* you *are* interested."

"No. I mean yes." Sherry blushed with embarrassment over her garbled response. The coach waited. "I'd love to come." Sherry finally forced the proper words out of her mouth. "And no, no other team has approached me."

"Their loss." Pat smiled. "See you at camp."

"Thank you," Sherry said as Pat walked away.

"Be on time," Pat called back over her shoulder.

"I'll be early," Sherry said, remembering the coach's advice to Dawn.

As soon as the door closed behind Pat, the other players rushed to Sherry's side, all talking at the same time. Sherry heard none of it as she stared at the envelope clutched tightly in her hands.

Pat quickly made her way to the front of the arena, cringing when she saw Mandy rushing across the vestibule in her direction.

"What took you so long?" Mandy asked from several feet away.

"Thought I told you to wait for me in the car," Pat muttered as she walked past her agitated assistant.

Mandy spun around and trotted to catch up. "I know it's been a long day, Pat." The coach stopped to glare at her assistant. "A nice hot bath will fix you up. Then..." Mandy said, reaching to brush the back of her fingers against the coach's cheek.

Pat slapped the hand away. "I'm tired, hungry, and in a rotten mood. You can't seduce me, Mandy, so don't even bother trying." She turned away from her. "Let's go."

A frustrated Mandy followed her outside where their car was idling at the curb.

CHAPTER THREE

Pat sat at one side of the conference table in her office. Occupying chairs on the opposite side were her two assistant coaches, Marcie Thomas and Kelley Stockley. The coaches were finishing their evaluations of the skills and weaknesses of the players who would be arriving for Cougar tryout camp the following morning.

"That's all of them," Marcie said, ticking off the last name on the list in front of her.

"There's one more." Pat passed a folder across the table. "Sherry Gallagher. Point guard, graduated from Western Arizona."

"Thought we had enough point guards," Kelley said as she picked up the folder and opened it.

"We do." Pat waited for the inevitable questions as to why she had invited another to tryout camp. She wished she had an answer.

"So what makes her special?"

"She was playing the night I went to see Montgomery. She's a solid player — smart, quick, and not afraid to take on her opponent."

"That describes most of the point guards in the league," Marcie said. "Including the ones we already have on our roster."

Pat glared across the table. "Look, we had an extra spot after that player from Australia backed out, so I offered it to Gallagher. What's the harm in trying her out?" she asked a little too angrily. She wasn't mad at her assistants; they were only asking the questions they got paid to ask. "Sorry." Pat smiled apologetically. "It's been a long day, and I'm sure you're as tired as I am. Let's just give her a look. Okay?"

"Sure, Pat." Kelley smiled back. "Fact is, I've seen Gallagher play. She's got some real talent. It's too bad her coach at Western Arizona didn't know how to draw it out."

"Yeah?" Pat asked. *Maybe my impulsive offer wasn't such a bad one after all.*

"Yeah." Kelley pointed at some numbers on one of the pages in the folder. "Good averages, over 14 points and 12 assists per game. She's a little short, but she's got good speed and quick bursts. I've seen her make opponents look like statues when she's put a step or two on them in the paint."

"We've still got too many guards on the roster," Marcie reminded as she read the stat sheet.

"We do," Pat agreed. "But Wendy has had knee problems the past two seasons, and Kinsey is..." She paused, unsure how to appropriately phrase what she wanted to say.

"Kinsey is getting old," Kelley provided. "Let's be honest about it — she's been in the league almost ten years. Not too many point guards play that long, especially on bad knees."

Marcie refused to let it go. "We've got nine, no ten, guards coming to camp." She was responsible for the guards, and she didn't like the excessive number of players she would be working with over the next few weeks. She would have help from the veteran players already signed for the season, but she still wasn't happy. "With Gallagher, that makes eleven. That's too many for camp. I can't work with that many and be effective."

"You're right," Pat told her assistant coach. "I'll help you out with the guards. And to make matters easier, as soon as any of them look like she can't cut our style of play, we'll send her packing. Okay?"

Marcie shrugged, shoving the folder on the unwanted point guard back across the table. She was a few years older than Pat and had been the other assistant coach when Mac had chosen Pat to take over as head coach. Marcie had argued with Mac about the decision, saying the younger woman was too inexperienced to handle the job. To her, the unexpected recruitment of a player they'd never discussed was just further proof that she had been right. "You're the coach."

"I'm the coach," Pat muttered, gathering up all the folders spread out on the table. She had hoped that because the Cougars had made it to the playoffs the year before Marcie would accept her as coach, but it was obvious her assistant wasn't ready to do that. "Let's call it a day," Pat suggested. "Camp starts early in the morning, and I don't want any of us to be late for the first day."

"Looks like it should be a good camp," Kelley said, trying to break the tension between the other two.

"Don't forget." Pat smiled at Kelley, grateful for her attempted conciliation even if it didn't seem to be working on Marcie. "I want you to work Montgomery hard. No slack."

Kelley nodded. "Gotcha." Her assignment was the post players, and Dawn would be in the group she worked with in camp. "See you in the morning, Coach."

"Goodnight, Kelley," Pat said as the assistant coach exited her office. She turned her attention to Marcie. "Look," Pat said softly, "I was kinda hoping we could put all the crap behind us this season."

Marcie took her time before answering, her eyes focusing on a rough spot in the table rather than looking at the coach. It wasn't so much that Pat was a bad head coach as much as that Marcie believed that Mac had all but promised the job to her if it should ever become available. She raised her eyes to look at the woman across the table and discovered anxious deep brown eyes studying her.

Marcie sighed, deciding to give the coach a break. "I'll try, Pat. But there are times I just don't agree with your decisions," she said honestly.

"I understand. I don't expect you or Kelley to always agree with me. I do expect that we keep the disagreements between us and that we don't carry them onto the floor. It's hard enough to coach some of these players. If they thought I didn't have the support of my staff, it would be impossible."

Marcie knew Pat was right, and if their positions were reversed, she'd expect the same consideration from her assistant coaches. "Okay." Marcie smiled for the first time all day. "Truce." She offered her hand across the table.

"Truce." Pat shook the outstretched hand. "Let's get out of here."

"You won't hear me arguing with that," Marcie said with a wry grin as she stood.

"What do you know about Sherry Gallagher?" Mandy asked Dawn. She had just met the player arriving at the Missoula International Airport, and they were waiting for her luggage to appear on the serpentine conveyor.

"Not much. Why?"

"I saw her name on the camp roster."

"Really?"

"You were there," Mandy snapped. "Didn't you see Pat inviting her?"

"No. Must have happened after I left. What's the big deal anyway? Sherry's an okay player but nothing special. She probably won't last camp."

"*That's* the big deal. Pat doesn't invite *okay* players to camp." She had noticed the coach seemed drawn to the play of Gallagher the night they had gone to Charlotte. At the time, she had thought little about. But when Gallagher's name appeared on the camp roster and Pat had refused to discuss the unexpected addition, she had begun to wonder if something beside the point guard's play had garnered the coach's interest.

Dawn turned her attention to the conveyor when she heard the loud groan that signaled it had been activated. "Why are you getting so upset?" she asked, happy to see her suitcase was the first to appear.

"Is that it or do you have more?"

"This is it."

"Let's go."

Confused by her lover's attitude, Dawn followed Mandy out the terminal doors and into the parking lot. "Are you going to tell me why you are so upset that Sherry is here?"

Mandy marched toward a bright red Pontiac Grand Prix, using her remote key to unlock the doors. Dawn whistled approvingly. "Nice wheels."

"Get in."

Tossing her suitcase onto the back seat, Dawn settled into the leather passenger seat and waited for Mandy to walk around the car.

"You need to get rid of her," Mandy said as soon as she opened the driver's door.

"What? Who?"

"Pay attention, damn it." With a turn of the ignition, the engine roared to life and Mandy spun out of the parking spot only to have to squeal to a stop at the toll booth seconds later. "Gallagher. You have to make sure she doesn't survive camp." She handed the proper amount of change to the cashier to pay for parking.

"Why?"

"Because I said so." As soon as the wooden gate lifted, Mandy peeled rubber as she screeched toward the highway.

The Cougar locker room looked like any one of the thousands of similar rooms that could be found in any high school, college, or professional arena around the country. The only difference was that the Cougar locker room was a little plusher than most because the team owner liked to show she had the money to spend.

Painted in the team colors, royal blue and gold, rows of lockers occupied the back end of the rectangular room, shielding the entry to the shower area. Instead of the typical hard bench stretched in front of them, each locker was fronted by a straight-back swivel chair. The team owner thought the chairs were more comfortable, but the players hated them, as they made even the simple task of bending over to tie one's shoes awkward. They would have removed them if they weren't bolted to the concrete floor. Between the lockers and the front of the room were several rows of folding chairs, brought in for tryout camp. Players would sit there while listening to Pat and the other coaches, who would make good use of the dry marker boards that covered the wall at the front of the room. The walls to either side were sparsely covered by hand-drawn posters illustrating Pat's thoughts on what made a good player and a good team.

Sherry entered the locker room a little before six, not too surprised to find she was the only one there at that early hour. Walking slowly around the room, she felt like pinching herself to make sure she wasn't still in bed dreaming. No one had been more surprised than she when Coach Calvin had offered the invitation to the Cougar tryout camp. Sherry stopped in front of each of the hand-printed posters thumbtacked to the wall.

Rebound
Rebound
REBOUND

Follow your shot.
No one makes it 100% of the time.

Protect the ball:
We can't win without it.

A champion plays hard every time she picks up a ball.
A championship is won one game at a time.

More games are lost at the charity stripe
than won from the 3-point line.

"That's so true," Sherry murmured as she read the last poster.

"You're here early."

Sherry spun around at the sound of the voice to find the head coach standing in a doorway at the side of the room. "I said I'd be early." Sherry grinned.

"So you did."

Working in her office, Pat had happened to look out the window as the arriving player walked across the parking lot to the rear door of the arena. She had returned to the papers on her desk but after several minutes decided to go to the locker room, where she knew she would find Gallagher. The door between the office area and the locker room was open. Pat leaned against the doorframe and watched the rookie as she wandered around the room.

Gallagher was compact, as most guards were, their bodies seemingly compressed bundles of energy. Her profile listed her as 5'-9", but her compact build made her appear shorter. She wore a pair of shorts and a sweat shirt with the sleeves cut off, making it easy to see that there was no excess weight on her frame. She had short dark brown hair and bright blue eyes that sparkled when she was excited.

Pat smiled when she noticed the well-used pair of hiking boots Gallagher wore. They were definitely not the usual foot gear for a basketball player. "Pick a locker," she instructed. "We'll have lots more players than lockers at the start of camp so it's good to claim one while you can. It's one of the perks of being early. Late arrivals have to use the visitor lockers or make do without one."

Sherry set her bag down in the closest chair that fronted an unused locker. "I want to thank you again for inviting me to camp."

"Like I said, you had some good moves." Pat knew that wasn't the reason she'd offered the spot to Gallagher; she just wished she knew why she had. "You can thank me by getting through camp."

"I plan to give it my best shot."

"Good." Pat smiled. "I've got some paperwork to finish before the others arrive. You need anything?"

"No." Sherry shook her head. "Oh, there is one thing."

"Yes?"

"Is it okay if I shoot some before camp starts?"

"Court is back out that door," Pat pointed to the door Gallagher had entered through, "and to your right. Ball carts should be around there somewhere."

"Thanks."

"No problem. See you later." Pat disappeared back into the office area.

"See you," Sherry whispered into the empty room.

"Cutting it close, Montgomery," Kelley told the player scooting through the arena door just before she prepared to pull it shut and lock it. "Coach is getting ready to talk to the players in the locker room. I suggest you bust your ass and get in there before she starts."

Dawn stood just inside the door looking around. Two corridors led away from the doorway, and she couldn't tell which of the unmarked passageways would lead her to the locker room.

"Not making much of a first impression, Montgomery," Kelley said, already several steps down one of the corridors. "First door on your left," the assistant coach called after the player as she raced past.

Dawn's rapid entrance into the locker room came to an abrupt stop when she spotted Sherry. "What are you doing here?"

"Coach invited me to camp, just like you."

"Is there a problem?" Marcie asked.

"Yeah, she doesn't belong here," Dawn told the assistant coach.

Marcie laughed. "Oh, really?"

"Problem?" Kelley asked when she entered the room and encountered the face-off between Dawn and the other assistant coach.

"The late-arriving Miss Montgomery seems to think she has a say in which players are at camp."

"Hmm." Kelley rubbed her chin thoughtfully. "I don't remember getting a memo about Montgomery having any say on who attends camp. Did you?" she asked Marcie as the other players in the room quieted to listen to the exchange.

"No, don't believe I did."

"I would suggest, Montgomery," Kelley's tone abruptly turned serious, "that you spend what little time you have before Coach comes in here getting ready to play. If she sees you like this," Kelley pointed at the sandals the player was wearing, "your tryout is going to end before it gets started."

"We've got another one to tape," Marcie called to one of the trainers moving between the players.

"I don't need taping," Dawn grunted, sitting in the only available chair, which happened to be directly behind Sherry. "It's only a practice."

"Don't be a fool." Diane Sunndee, a returning starting guard, was standing nearby. "You get hurt in camp, and you can kiss goodbye to any chance of making the team. Mac doesn't give contracts to injured rookies."

Dawn was bent over, removing her sandals. Luckily, she had put on her sweats before leaving Mandy's apartment. Without lifting her head, she knew by the player's footwear exactly who was talking to her. Sitting up, she said, "Hey, Pete. Looks like we'll be playing together this season."

Diane Sunndee had earned the nickname Pete in high school. A natural shooter who could drop the ball into the basket from just about anyplace on the floor, she also had a habit of wearing socks with worn-out elastic. Though her socks began each game pulled up almost to her knees, they would inevitably be pooled around her ankles shortly after play began. A teammate watching an old Pete Maravich game on ESPN began calling Diane "Pete" and the nickname stuck.

Pete shook her head at Dawn. "Girl, are you in for an attitude adjustment." Reaching up to her neat rows of braids, she gathered the ends of the cornrows together and slipped an elastic band around them. "Rookies," she grumbled as she moved to stand near the front of the room.

Dawn leaned forward and whispered in Sherry's ear, "Keep out of my way."

"Montgomery!" Kelley barked. "Quit shooting off your mouth and get taped up. Or leave and quit wasting our time."

"This ain't over," Dawn warned Sherry before she stood to find a trainer.

At five minutes after eight, Pat pushed open the door between the coaches' offices and the locker room and scanned the more than forty women crammed into a space usually used by less than half that number. Some of the returning players stood along the walls on either side of the rows of chairs occupied by the newcomers out to prove they deserved a spot on the Cougar roster.

"Good morning." Pat smiled as she walked to the front of the room to a chorus of "'Morning, Coach." When she reached the center of the marker board, she stopped and turned to look at the collection of players. Most of the new faces turned in her direction betrayed varying degrees of self confidence, while a few showed high levels of apprehension and nervousness. For some reason that escaped her, Pat was glad to see Sherry was in the first group.

"Welcome to the Missoula Cougars tryout camp. As most of you know, the Cougars carry a roster of sixteen active players and four reserves. Currently, we have fifteen of those positions filled." Pat smiled at the few groans she heard. Her eyes darted along the faces of the veteran players, pausing a second or two on each one. "However, as every veteran on the team will tell you," she turned back to face the rows of hopefuls, "there are no sure things on the Cougars. You earn your position each practice. Each game. Each day."

Pat's voice hardened as she spoke. "You can forget everything you learned in high school and college. Pro ball is faster, rougher, and more grueling than anything you're used to. I don't care how big a star you were a few weeks ago. Starting today, you start all over again with a clean slate. I don't have any stars on my team. I don't have any ball hogs, hot-doggers, or show-offs. If that's your style of play, there's the door. Don't waste my time or yours." She paused to make sure her message was getting through.

"For the first week, you'll be put through a series of drills that will allow us to evaluate your strengths and weaknesses. You'll be split up by position so we can see how you compare to one another. If you plan to be here next Monday, I suggest you don't hold anything back. If I, or any of my staff, think you're not giving us everything you've got, you'll be told to leave. There are no second chances. Once you're told to go," she looked straight at Dawn, "you won't be coming back."

"Here are your assignments." Pat pointed to the board behind her, where three columns of names had been neatly printed. "Coach Thomas," Pat waited for Marcie to step up beside her, "will work with those listed as guards. Coach Stockley will work with the post players; I'll be working with all of you, but mainly with the guards and forwards. You'll also be working with Terry Peters, Val Jensen, Pete Sunndee, Tonie Jessep, and Kinsey Donaldson, some of our roster players. Don't think they'll be easy on you." Pat smiled. "Remember, you're trying to take their jobs. And be prepared to get moved around. I need players that can play more than one position." Pat looked at her assistant coaches. "Shall we get started?"

When Kelley nodded, Pat turned back to the waiting players. "Welcome to Cougar basketball, ladies."

"All right, you wannabes," Marcie growled. "Get your asses out on the court, and I don't want to see anyone walking."

As the players leaped up, chairs tumbled backward, crashing to the floor, and some of the players had to pick their way through a jumble of chair legs to get to the door.

Pat grinned as she watched the commotion. She placed a restraining hand on Kelley's arm and waited until all the players had left before addressing her assistant. "Was Montgomery late?" When she'd entered the locker room to address the players, Pat had noticed how unprepared the player, still in the process of having her ankles taped, had seemed.

"She made it in just as I was pulling the door shut."

"She's gonna be trouble." Pat's lips were pursed together as she considered the potential problems the rookie could cause her and the team.

"Chances are she won't make it past this week," Kelley offered as encouragement.

"No." Pat shook her head. "She'll make it through camp. Her ego won't let her fail. Come on. Let's get out there before they start to get restless. But keep a close eye on her, Kelley," Pat said as they walked out of the locker room.

A shrill whistle brought the activity on the basketball court to a halt as the players froze in place.

"Dawn," Kelley walked toward the player, "look around. You've got three defenders hanging all over you; you can't possibly expect to be able to do anything. Look. Marcie and Pete were both open with easy shots. Use your head. Let's run the play again."

It was Friday of the first week of camp, and Kelley and Marcie were running the players through a variety of plays while Pat watched from an upper tier of seats. Three players had already had their names erased off the marker board in the locker room, and Pat was set to cut another half dozen by the end of the day. She was watching the players on the floor intently.

On the court, ten players had been split into offensive and defensive teams. The remaining players watched from the sidelines, waiting for their chance to play. Marcie was playing point guard for the offensive team, and Sherry was guarding her as they ran through the plays from the half-court line. Dawn was playing high post for Marcie's team.

Marcie dribbled up the right side of the court before firing a pass to Dawn.

This time when Dawn spun around to face the basket and the defenders sagged toward her, she flipped a lazy pass in the direction of Val, a forward cutting through the key.

Anticipating the play, Sherry had left Marcie as soon as the ball was passed to Dawn and cut for the key. Her eyes on the pass, Sherry didn't see her teammate step between Val and the ball. Sherry and the other player collided, both tumbling to the floor as the ball flew untouched over their heads to Val, who took one bounce before banking the ball off the backboard into the basket. Again the whistle froze players in place.

Dawn snickered as Sherry and the other player were forced to remain sprawled out on the floor until the coach told them to get up.

"Sherry?" Kelley studied the prone player. "Aren't you a little out of position?"

"Yes, Coach," Sherry agreed, more than a little embarrassed at her current predicament. She tried to see what Pat was doing, but the coach was sitting in shadows and she couldn't make out much more than her shape.

"If you had stayed with your assignment," Kelley continued, "Debbie would have intercepted that pass. Instead, you just gave up 2 easy points."

"Sorry, Coach," Sherry muttered, mad at herself.

"Get up," Kelley told the women. "Dawn, is there something humorous about all of this?" she asked the snickering player.

Dawn just shrugged. Kelley signaled for the ball to be passed to her. As soon as it was in her hands, she rifled a pass at Dawn.

Unprepared for the pass, Dawn threw her hands up to protect herself. The ball smacked into her arms before ricocheting off across the court. "That's what we call a pass." Kelley spoke to the entire group of players. "Not a wounded duck flipped across the court. You better learn how to make them and how to catch them, because nothing less will be accepted. Okay, you teams take a breather. The next two teams are up."

As they exchanged places with the waiting players, Dawn walked up beside Sherry. "Nice fall." She laughed. "Didn't hurt yourself, did you?"

Sherry rubbed the elbow that had taken most of the blow. "No."

"Too bad." Dawn shoved Sherry with her shoulder as she strode past to take a seat on the bench.

Pat watched the exchange, anger building in the pit of her stomach. Reaching for her water bottle, she blew out a long breath. "It's just part of the game," she reminded herself. "Why are you taking it so personally?" A whistle blowing drew her attention back down to the new group of players on the floor before she could come up with an answer.

Sherry entered the locker room after completing her self-imposed free-throw practice. As she had done every day since camp began, Sherry stopped in front of the hand-lettered poster tacked to the wall of the locker room.

More games are lost at the charity stripe
than won from the 3-point line.

Since high school, Sherry had made it a habit to shoot one hundred free throws before and after every practice. The habit had paid off in college with one of the highest free-throw percentages on the team. More than half of the points she had scored at Western Arizona had come from the charity line.

"Aren't you going to look?"

Sherry turned at the sound of the voice. Marcie was picking up discarded towels that had been tossed about the room.

"Afraid to. I made some bonehead mistakes out there today."

"You weren't the only one."

"Coach barely talked to me today."

"It's always hard on Coach when she has to make cuts," Marcie explained. "Go ahead and look. I think you'll be surprised."

Sherry took a couple of hesitant steps to the front of the room, her eyes scanning down the list of guards. There were a few blank spots that hadn't been there that morning, but at the bottom of the list, Sherry Gallagher was still listed. "Damn." She released the breath she was holding. "I don't believe it."

"You got past the easy week." Marcie sat in one of the chairs, stretching her legs out on another one. "It gets a lot tougher from here."

"If this was an easy week," Sherry flipped a chair around to face Marcie and dropped into it, "I hate to imagine what the next few are going to be like." When she received no response, she looked questioningly at Marcie and was surprised to see the assistant coach seemed to be struggling with herself.

Marcie debated saying what she was about to but figured the player had earned it after the effort she had put out the past five days. One thing was for sure, Sherry was about the only player who had given all she had all week. What she lacked in talent, she had made up for with hard work. *Which,* she thought, *probably explains why her name is still on the marker board.*

Marcie decided to say what was on her mind. "I wasn't in favor of you coming to camp, but you proved me wrong. Now I'm not saying you'll make the team, but I am saying you made an impression with the effort you gave this week. Believe me, I've seen lots of players go through this camp, but I haven't seen many who worked as hard as you have." Marcie stood up. "Good luck. You keep working as hard as you did this week and who knows." She left the locker room, walking through the doorway to the coaches' offices.

"Thanks, Coach," Sherry told the retreating woman, a beaming smile spreading across her face.

"I wouldn't count too much on that." Dawn stepped out of the shower room. Her hair was wet, and she had a towel wrapped around her still dripping body.

Sherry had had enough of Dawn's unexpected attitude. All week, Dawn had been riding her, and she decided now was as good a time as any to put an end to it. She leaned back, crossing her arms across her chest. "I don't get it, Dawn." She addressed the player who was now leaning against a row of lockers, the smirk still firmly in place on her face. "We got along fine before, and, as far as I know, I haven't done anything to you since we arrived in camp. So why have you been on my case?"

"Because you're not good enough for this team. You played at a nothing high school and a nothing college. You never even made it to an NCAA tournament, not even the first round. You were barely good enough to play amateur ball, and you're wasting everyone's time being here." As she talked, Dawn dropped the towel. "Maybe now I'll get a decent locker," she mumbled, pulling dry clothes out of her sports bag on the floor.

Ignoring the last remark, Sherry said, "Coach doesn't seem to agree with you. My name is still up there." She gestured casually over her shoulder with her thumb. "Guess I *must* be good enough."

"Like I care what an old has-been has to say. Blew her knee out, my ass. Players have that surgery all the time and play afterward. She probably just choked at the thought of having to prove she could play pro ball."

"You know, Dawn," Sherry stood, shaking her head slowly side-to-side, "it's too bad you don't put the energy on the court that you exert hating people. Maybe if you did, you'd be the player you could be."

"Advice from a wannabe." Dawn laughed. "Just what I need." She shoved the sweats she had worn during practice into her bag and zipped it closed. "See ya Monday, wannabe. Your name won't be there at the end of next week, I promise you that." As she walked by the marker board, she dragged her finger through Sherry's name. Not willing to face a repeat of her lover's tantrum the day before when Mandy learned Sherry appeared to be surviving the first week of camp, Dawn was determined to do whatever was needed to make her words come true.

Sherry forced Dawn and her unexplained animosity out of her mind as she undressed. Moments later she was standing under a stream of hot water, letting the warmth soak into her tired muscles and wondering how she would spend her first weekend in Missoula.

Some time later, Pat walked through the locker room on her way out for the night and saw the damage that had been done to Sherry's name. "Why do I get the feeling that Montgomery had something to do with this?" she said to the empty room. Picking up the eraser in the tray at the bottom of the marker board, she removed the name completely, then rewrote it in her neat lettering.

CHAPTER FOUR

Before getting to Cougar camp, Sherry had spent hours on the Internet researching the recreational opportunities in and around the Missoula Valley. She had happily discovered that there were numerous places to hike, both inside the city limits and close by. Anxious to hit the trails, she had asked her teammates if any were interested in joining her for a Saturday morning hike. Most had simply looked at her as if she had lost her mind for wanting to get up early on their first day off to climb a mountain. A few threw things at her. Only Val had seemed halfway enthusiastic about the idea.

"Look, rookie," Val had told her, "you'd do better to store up that energy for the coming week, because if I know Coach, and I do, you will definitely be needing it."

"I can't just sit here all weekend," Sherry complained to the only person still willing to talk to her. The others were sitting around the locker room doing their best to ignore the conversation. "There's too much I want to see. Besides, who knows how long I may be here?" She hated to think of the possibility she would not make it through the tryout camp. "I don't want to waste a single day."

"Okay." Val tried to understand Sherry's perspective. "You have any idea where you want to go?"

"Rattlesnake National Recreational Area." Sherry almost shouted the answer, so happy was she to find someone potentially interested in going with her.

"Well, first thing you should know," Val laughed, "is we just call it The Rattlesnake. You got a map of the trails? 'Cause it's easy to get turned around up there."

"Yes. I've got this book." Sherry pulled a well-known local hiking book out of her locker.

"It's not the best, but it'll do," Val commented on the rookie's choice. "How about equipment? Boots? Pack?"

Sherry smiled. "Got 'em."

"What about a way to get to the trailhead? It's not far, but you're not going to want to walk there."

"Um." Sherry hesitated, her smile replaced by a frown.

"Gonna need a ride," Val said. "Look, I don't particularly want to get out of bed at the crack of dawn Saturday, so I'll let you use my Jeep. You can drive, can't you?"

"Yes," Sherry said, smiling again.

"Stick shift?"

"Yes."

"All right, I'll leave it with you. You can bring it back on Monday since I don't see me getting too far from my hot tub this weekend. First week of camp is a real killer for me."

"Thanks, Val." Sherry hugged the unsuspecting player. "I really appreciate this."

"Appreciate it by bringing back my baby with a full tank of gas." Val extricated herself from the hug. "She's running on fumes."

"You've got it."

When she reached the site of the old stone chimney, Pat stepped off the trail. She walked the few steps down to the creek and quickly made her way across the trickle of water to the clearing on the opposite side. Slipping her day pack off, she placed it on the ground, then settled on a small boulder. Stretching her legs out in front of her, she loosened the Velcro straps on her knee brace enough for it to slide down her leg to rest at her ankle. "That feels better," she sighed, rubbing the knee to alleviate some of the soreness.

She reached for her pack, lifting it into her lap and pulling out a Baggie of baby carrots, then setting the heavy pack back on the ground. She could have used a smaller pack for her day hiking, but she had learned it was better to be safe when hiking in the mountains around the Missoula Valley. Weather could change instantaneously from a clear sky to a downpour, and she had been caught unprepared by Mother Nature's mood swings more than once. So she carried a complete change of clothing, first aid kit, extra socks, light jacket, baseball cap, and a pair of gaiters, along with water and snacks. Of course, the wildflower and bird books added to the pack's weight, but she liked to be able to figure out what she was looking at if she came across something new.

Leaning back, Pat turned her face skyward. She breathed in a lungful of mountain air and smiled. She liked this spot. The small clearing was shaded by tall ponderosa pine. At the edge of the clearing and alongside Spring Creek, a rock chimney had been built by unknown settlers over a hundred years ago. It was all that remained of a family's homestead in the mountains north of Missoula that were now known as the Rattlesnake National Recreational Area.

Several trails crisscrossed the mountains, but most who came to the area kept to the main trail that followed the Rattlesnake Creek. Pat liked to hike the side trails, where she encountered fewer people and could spend a few hours enjoying the scenery at her own pace. She had just about finished off the carrots when she heard someone coming up the trail.

Sherry tightened the laces of her hiking boots before retrieving her fanny pack from the back seat of the car she had borrowed from her teammate. She adjusted the pack — which held two bottles of water and a few energy bars — around her waist, then picked up the baseball cap resting on the dashboard. After locking the doors, she headed for the trailhead at the end of the parking area. Since it was early morning, only a few cars occupied the gravel parking lot. Sherry curiously noted the variety of license plates they sported. Missoula was a college town, and students came from all over the country to attend the university. She was surprised to see one vehicle with a Missoula Cougars staff sticker on its back bumper, and she wondered who she might run into on her hike.

Sherry started down the wider-than-usual trail that had once served as the wagon road used by homesteaders. Off to her right, she could hear the Rattlesnake Creek tumbling down its boulder-strewn bed on its way to town. To her left, a rock face rose a couple hundred feet straight up from the trail. Millions of years before, the stone had been thrust up from the ground, its hard surface bending and cracking in the process. She hadn't walked far before the trail and creek met and several smaller paths branched off the main trail.

Sherry decided to take the trail that followed Spring Creek deeper into the hills. The path took her through the middle of a large meadow before starting a gentle climb under the protection of a pine forest. She could hear Spring Creek beside the trail, but she had yet to see it through the heavy brush that concealed it from view. As she walked, Sherry spotted evidence of the early homesteaders: an old fence post, a tree with a string of barbed wire buried in its trunk, a rock foundation. She wondered what life must have been like for those who had braved what was then an unknown wilderness with an abundance of the reptiles for which it was named.

Noticing a clearing to the side of the trail and what appeared to be a stone structure on the other side of the creek, Sherry stepped off the trail to investigate.

Pat recognized Sherry instantly. Her stomach did an unexpected flip-flop, and she considered leaving before the player saw her. She knew a seldom-used path that led away from the ruins to another trail on the other side of the gulch. Or she could acknowledge the player, then walk back across the creek, and make a hasty retreat back down the trail. Before she could decide which to do, Sherry was standing in front of her.

Sherry was more than a little surprised to see her coach sitting on a boulder, highlighted by a shaft of sun unblocked by the surrounding trees. Her heart skipped a beat at the sight. "Coach?" she asked, seeking confirmation that the beauty in front of her was indeed the same woman who had nearly run her legs off during the past week.

"Gallagher," Pat greeted, her voice sounding a lot calmer than she was feeling inside. "Beautiful morning for a hike," she added casually.

"Yes...yes, it is," Sherry managed to stutter out. "I'm sorry, I didn't know anyone was here. I'll leave."

"No," Pat said, the word sounding more urgent than she had intended. "I like to sit here. It's such a peaceful spot. Please stay. That is, if you want," she added quickly.

"Thanks. I could use a rest."

"Altitude getting to you?" Pat asked, concerned that the young woman might be falling victim to a common predicament for many newcomers to the valley. When Sherry looked at her quizzically, she explained, "Missoula Valley is around 3500 feet above sea level; it's even higher here in the mountains. Most people who come here don't realize that, so the first few times they go hiking they can overdo things pretty easily."

"Oh." Sherry sat on the ground under one of the trees. "Guess that explains my being so tired after such a short hike. I'm used to going five or six miles or more back home. But I've only gone," she pulled the pedometer she liked to wear off her waistband, "less than two."

"That would explain it." Pat nodded. "You drinking lots of water?"

Sherry held up her fanny pack, showing two empty water bottles to the coach.

"Here." Pat passed over one of her bottles. "Drink it all if you want, I've got more." She had learned over her years of hiking the local trails that it paid to carry plenty of liquid. She was continually amazed to see people carrying little or none, even families with young children.

"Thanks." Sherry gulped down half of the bottle. "Guess I wasn't as prepared as I should have been."

"You shouldn't be out here at all, Gallagher," Pat said, her tone harsher than she intended it to be.

Sherry's eyes grew wide as she waited for the coach to continue.

"That didn't come out the way I meant it," Pat apologized. "You've just put in a pretty demanding week physically, and you should be resting. Believe it or not, the first week is the easiest."

"That's what Marcie told me."

"Well, she's right." Pat wondered why her assistant had been speaking to Sherry. She hoped that Marcie wasn't trying to discourage the player from continuing camp. "Anyway, you should be using the weekend to rest, not climb mountains."

"I don't think I'd consider this climbing a mountain." Sherry grinned, glad that her coach didn't seem all that upset with her. "But I get your point. As soon as I catch my breath, I'm heading back to the trailhead."

"Good. It won't be as bad going down as it was coming up. Just take your time."

"I will."

"Take this." Pat pulled a full bottle of water out of her pack.

"I can't take your water," Sherry protested.

"Take it," Pat insisted. "I've got more. Besides I don't need as much as you; I'm used to hiking these hills."

"Do you hike often?" Sherry asked as she accepted the bottle from her coach.

"As often as I can." Pat bent over and pulled the knee brace back up over her knee. She fastened the straps, securing the brace in place. "Being out here helps me relax. It also helps me put life back into perspective; nothing seems to be quite the crisis when I'm out here. Does wonders for the stress you players cause me." She grinned as she stood.

"I bet," Sherry said, saddened that the other woman was preparing to leave and that their unexpected time together was at an end.

"Well, I've got a few more miles to go before I call it a day." Pat pulled the pack onto her back, adjusting the weight until it was comfortable. She looked sternly at Sherry. "Promise me you'll head straight home."

"I promise. Straight home to a hot shower and bed." Sherry crossed her heart. She was more than sure of the truth of her words; she just hoped she could make it back to the trailhead without passing out from exhaustion.

"Good." Pat smiled. "I expect to see you ready to play Monday."

"I'll be ready, Coach," Sherry assured her.

Pat walked to the creek, making her way back across the shallow stretch of water. When she reached the opposite side, she stopped and turned back. "Gallagher."

"Yes, Coach?"

"Next time take a short hike, one mile at most. Give your body time to adjust to the altitude, and you'll be fine."

"Right. Short hikes. Got it."

"'Bye," Pat said as she made her way back to the trail.

"'Bye," Sherry whispered, her hands wrapped around the bottle of water.

CHAPTER FIVE

Pat was sitting in the top row of seats in the first tier around the basketball court, one foot resting on the back of the seat in front of her and her notebook balanced on her upraised knee as she wrote comments on the players. It was Friday morning of the last week of tryout camp. The time had come for her to make the final cuts, and she was working on creating a list of the players she would release at the end of the day.

"'Morning, Coach."

Pat looked up from her writing. "'Morning, Mac." It wasn't often that the owner of the Cougars came into the arena during tryout camp, so Pat knew she must have something on her mind. She waited patiently for the woman to settle into a seat next to her.

"You're gonna ruin my fancy cushions," Mac said, referring to where the coach's foot rested.

"Don't have much choice," Pat said, her foot remaining where it was. "You've got these seats so close together, anyone over the age of ten must feel as cramped in them as I do."

Mac leaned back in the seat and raised her feet to copy Pat's more comfortable position. "More seats mean more tickets sold, Coach. Besides, that's why I provide you such a lavish office to work out of."

"Can't see the players from in there." Pat's eyes drifted back to the action on the court where Marcie and Kelley were running the players through repetitions of set plays.

Mac followed the action on the floor. "Good group in camp this year," she said appreciatively.

"Yes. It's going to be hard to make today's cuts."

"But you'll do it," Mac said matter-of-factly. She paid her head coach well, and she expected her to make the hard decisions.

"I'll do it." Pat frowned as a player completely missed an easy pass thrown to her.

"Hope she's on your list."

Pat sighed. "She is."

"Want to talk to you about Gallagher," Mac said as the players were shuffled by the assistant coaches and Sherry was brought in to play offense.

"What about her?" Pat tried to sound indifferent even though her stomach unexpectedly dropped to the floor.

"We're heavy in the guard position." Mac told the coach what she already knew. "What do you plan to do with her?"

Pat considered the question, it being a fair one for the team owner to ask. "I'd like to keep her through our first couple of exhibition games." She watched Sherry dribble the ball from the half-court line to the top of the key before passing it off. "I'm not sure if Kinsey is going to make it through the season, and right now Sherry is showing more than Wendy or Amie," she said of two of the returning guards. "And Pete can't carry point by herself."

"All right. You can keep her as long as you're sure she can play at this level."

Instead of answering, Pat watched as Kelley tossed the ball back to Sherry to set up a new play from half court. Sherry dribbled the ball up the right side of the court, midway between the key and the sideline. Pat knew what play was being run and that it called for Sherry to fake a drive into the key, then pull up to drop a pass off to Val cutting along the baseline.

Sherry reached the spot where she was to make her fake. From the corner of her eye she saw Dawn leaving her defensive position at the top of the key to try and cut off her drive. She also saw that Val was having trouble getting through the defenders along the baseline. Sherry took one step straight at Dawn, who, surprised by the unexpected move, froze for a moment to consider her options. That was all Sherry needed. Changing directions mid-step, she cut toward the basket. When the defense began to collapse on her, she pushed off her left foot to slice through them in one long stride. As soon as her right shoe retouched the floor, she bounded skyward to pop the ball over the rim into the basket.

Kelley blew her whistle to freeze the players in place. "Anyone want to explain where the defense was on that play?"

Sherry had been surrounded by all five defensive players and had still managed to make the shot.

Pat smiled, knowing Sherry's display had been purely instinct and not something that most of her other guards could have executed even if they had thought of it. *Great time to pull that off,* she thought to herself.

"She can play," Mac conceded, impressed by the performance.

"I want the same agreement for Montgomery." Pat couldn't wipe the grin off her face, even when she spoke of the troublesome player. She wasn't yet convinced that Dawn could play for the Cougars, but she was willing to give her more time since Mac had wanted the player tried out.

Mac looked at Pat like she hadn't understood the coach's request. "She signed this morning, Pat. That's what I was coming to tell you."

Pat whipped around to stare at the owner. "What are you talking about?"

"She was on the list you sent over," Mac explained, even though she thought it odd Pat would have forgotten which rookies she had approved to be presented with a contract.

"She wasn't on the list, Mac." Pat's voice was low with a tinge of anger. "I didn't even want her in camp, and I sure as hell haven't seen anything to make me think she'll be anything but trouble for us."

"Her name was on the list," Mac repeated, her voice soft in an attempt to calm her irritated coach.

"Oh, I'm sure it was." Pat turned back to face the court. Her eyes, darkening with anger, were fixed on Mandy standing on the opposite side of the court, talking to the newly signed player. Pat had given her assistant a handwritten list earlier in the week to be typed up for the owner. Obviously, one extra name had been added to it. Pat released a long breath to avoid saying what was on the tip of her tongue.

Mac didn't fail to notice at whom the coach's anger was directed.

Martha Ann Christopher had been married and widowed before she celebrated her twentieth birthday. Distraught by the sudden death of her true love, yet determined to make it on her own, she had taken the advice of a friend and invested what little savings she had in the new technology called the Internet. Relying mostly on gut instincts, Mac had bought stock in tech companies and then sold most of those stocks before the crash hit. She had made millions. As her bank account grew, so did the number of relatives with their hands out. She had agreed to take on her niece as a favor to her sister and had placed Mandy in a position within the Cougars organization where she would be unable to cause any trouble. Or so she had thought.

"I'll talk to her, Pat."

"Don't bother," Pat said as she stormed to her feet. "If Dawn has signed, it's too late to change anything. But," she glared down at Mac, who was still seated, "I want it on record that I did not approve of Dawn and that chances are real good I never would have. Any trouble she causes is your problem, Mac. And so is Mandy," she added as she stomped down the steps to the floor, the whistle she had shoved into her mouth blaring loudly. "Sprints, baseline to baseline," she shouted when the players stopped to look at her. "That means everyone." She glared at Dawn when the post player failed to join the rest of the team. "Montgomery, get moving."

Mandy watched Dawn trot to join the rest of the players, then turned and marched across the floor toward Pat. Before she could say anything, Mac stopped her.

"Mandy," Mac called to her niece. "I want to see you in my office. Now!" she barked as her niece's mouth opened to protest.

Pat wasn't paying attention to the exchange; she had already walked to the opposite end of the court to consult with her assistant coaches.

"We're agreed then?" Pat asked Marcie and Kelley.

The three women were sitting at the conference table in Pat's office, discussing the cuts to be announced at the end of that afternoon's practice session. The players had been released for a long lunch break so the coaches could make their final decisions.

"Mac has already offered contracts to Latesha, Polly, and Jade. I'll give her the go-ahead for Ashley."

"Polly turned her down," Kelley announced. After her earlier confrontation with Pat, Mac had decided to pass that bad news on through the assistant coach.

Marcie was amazed that someone would go through tryout camp just to refuse a contract. "Any reason?"

"Homesick, from what Mac said," Kelley reported.

"Damn." Pat drew a line through the player's name on her list. "Guess that moves Sara up." Pat wrote in the name. "That leaves one spot to fill."

"Don't you mean two?" Marcie asked as she reviewed her own list of players.

Pat revealed the unwelcome news. "Montgomery signed this morning."

"What?" both Marcie and Kelley asked at the same time.

"Mac got some bad information." Pat frowned. "She thought Dawn had my approval, and she made an offer. Dawn signed the papers this morning."

"I can just bet how, or who, Mac got that bogus info from," Marcie muttered.

"Doesn't matter now," Pat said with a shake of her head. "She's signed, and we have to deal with the situation whether we like it or not."

"So, who fills the sixth spot?"

"Either Stacy or Sherry," Pat said.

"My vote is for Stacy." Marcie pulled a paper from the clutter spread out in front of her and read the notes she had made on the player they were discussing. "I know you like Sherry, but we have too many guards. Stacy can play both forward and post, and she's made some really good progress during camp."

"Kelley?" Pat asked the other assistant coach for her opinion.

"Hate to say it, because Sherry is the hardest worker of everyone in camp, but Marcie is right. Stacy provides us the depth we need."

"Okay." Pat added the player's name to her list.

"Sorry, Pat." Marcie knew the coach had taken a liking to the play of the guard from Arizona.

Pat shrugged. She wasn't sure why, but the thought of Sherry not being on the court the following Monday morning made her insides churn. "We have one final matter to discuss," she said. "Kinsey saw her doc this morning."

"How bad is it?" Marcie asked. They all knew the aging guard's knees were bad and getting worse.

"He wants to do surgery now. She wants to play one more season."

"What do you think?" Kelley asked.

"I think we owe it to her to let her make the call." Even though she knew she should, Pat couldn't bring herself to cut the veteran guard loose after she had been a loyal and productive member of the Cougars for several seasons. "But I think we need to take steps to be ready to replace her if she can't make it through the season. I've got Mac's okay to keep Sherry for the first couple of exhibition games." Just saying the words made Pat feel better. "That should give us enough time to see what Kinsey is capable of, and if it doesn't look like she'll make it, we can offer her spot to Sherry. Any comments?"

"Sounds like the best we can do, Coach," Kelley agreed.

Marcie nodded. "I second that."

"Okay." Pat added a note at the bottom of her list. "They should be getting back soon," she said of the players. "I want to work them on stamina drills this afternoon. I won't be giving this list to Mac until practice is over, so if you see anything to change your minds, let me know."

Kelley pushed her chair away from the table. "I'm going to grab a quick sandwich before we get started. You guys interested?"

"Yeah, I'll come." Marcie stood.

"Go ahead," Pat told them. "I've got a couple of things I want to clean up before we start."

As Marcie and Kelley opened the door to exit the room, Mandy pushed her way between them. "Pat," she said as she hurried into the room, "you know you told me to add Dawn's name to the list."

Pat growled at the use of her name by her incompetent assistant.

Marcie looked at Kelley. They knew anything could be about to happen, and they had no intention of being around if it did. Pulling the office door shut behind them, they hurried to the outer door that would take them out of the office area completely.

"Mandy, I'm busy," Pat said as she retrieved the papers strewn about the table.

"But you must remember," Mandy continued, as if she hadn't heard.

With the papers gathered up in her hands, Pat pushed away from the table to walk the couple of steps to her desk. "Mandy, I am very aware what names were on the list I gave you. Now if you'll excuse me, I have some things I have to do before practice resumes."

"But, Pat, I just typed what you gave me."

Dropping into the chair behind her desk, Pat refused to respond.

Mandy moved around the desk and stood as close to Pat's chair as possible, then leaned casually against the desk. "Pat," she softened her voice, "I know you're upset with me, but I'm sure I can think of a way to make it up to you." She reached out and lightly rubbed the back of her knuckles against the coach's cheek.

Pat swiped the offending hand away from her face. "Damn it, Mandy," she snapped. "When will you get it through your thick head that I have no intentions of ever sleeping with you?" Pat's voice grew louder with each word. "Now, *get the hell out of my office!*"

Mandy started to say something more, then thought better of it. She smiled at Pat in a way that made the coach feel as though the woman were undressing her to appraise what she might discover underneath. With a flick of her head, Mandy turned to leave as requested. She stopped when she reached the door. "Do you have anything for me to give to my aunt?" she asked, her voice sugary sweet.

"From here on out," Pat said without looking up, "anything I have for Mac, I'll hand to her personally."

"Suit yourself." Mandy shrugged, then left.

Pat jammed her elbows onto her desk and dropped her head into her palms, begging her pounding heart to slow down before it burst out of her chest. "Tell me again," she asked herself, "why I put up with her."

Returning from the long lunch break, Sherry sat in front of her locker. She had been passing the open door between the locker room and the offices when she'd heard Pat's declaration to Mandy. She jammed her elbows into her thighs and dropped her head into her palms, begging her racing heart to slow down. She was sure this day would be her last in camp, and she was just as sure she'd probably never see Pat Calvin again after it ended. So for the life of her, she couldn't figure out why the words the coach had shouted at her assistant had brought such a surge of joy to her heart.

Sherry wasn't surprised to be called to the coach's office after practice, but she was shocked when Pat explained she would be staying with the team past tryout camp.

"I can't promise anything," Pat was saying. "We'll just have to see how things go with Kinsey. If she can play..." Pat couldn't bring herself to finish the sentence.

"I understand, Coach." Sherry was grinning ear-to-ear. At the very least, she'd have the opportunity to be part of the Cougars for two of their exhibition games. At best, she'd be offered a spot on the season roster. As far as she was concerned, it was a win-win situation. And when she factored in the woman sitting on the opposite side of the desk, well, the arrangement just kept getting better.

"That's about it." Pat smiled, feeling better than she had all day. "Unless you have any questions, you can take off for the weekend."

Sherry found that she didn't want the conversation to end. An idea popped into her head, and without thinking, she asked the coach, "I was wondering if you'd like to go for a hike tomorrow? I've been taking short ones, like you suggested, and I think I'm ready for something a little more strenuous."

Pat almost said yes, then better judgment stepped in, and she knew she had to turn down the offer. "I'm sorry, Sherry, but I don't think that would be a very good idea. With me being your coach, well..." She hesitated when she saw the look of disappointment on the player's face. "I mean, it could... You know if someone saw us..."

Sherry was embarrassed that she hadn't thought of what it might look like to someone who saw the coach and a player out on what could be considered a social outing. "Oh, jeez." She blushed as the full impact of her proposal sunk in. "That was really dumb of me. I should have thought before I opened my mouth. Forget I even mentioned it, okay? Really, just act like I never said it."

"Hey." Pat laughed as Sherry rambled on. "It's okay. Really." She smiled to reassure her player. "If things were different, I'd love to go. There are a ton of trails I'd like to show you. Fact is, I don't like hiking alone, but because of my position it's hard to find anyone who wants to go for the hike and not just to say they went with the Cougar coach. Unfortunately, you're a player and I'm the coach..."

"So, bad idea all around," Sherry said, surprised at how sad she felt at the realization she could never enjoy a mountain hike with this woman for whom she had so much respect.

"No. Good idea," Pat said, wishing there were a way to make it happen. "Bad situation."

"I better go." Sherry rose from the chair. "I'll see you Monday, Coach."

"Early," Pat teased.

Sherry nodded. "Early."

"Have a good weekend, Sherry. And take it easy on the hiking; I don't want any twisted ankles to have to explain to Mac."

"I promise." Sherry crossed her heart before bending down to pick her sports bag off the floor. "Have a good weekend." She smiled, turning for the door.

Pat watched Sherry go. She almost went after her to say she'd changed her mind, but common sense kept her in her chair. Spinning around to the office window that overlooked the staff parking lot, Pat watched Sherry walk to the student housing buildings where the rookies had been provided lodging while they attended camp, the university campus being adjacent to the Cougar arena. She suddenly felt an emptiness that she hadn't felt in some time, not since Karen had walked out on their relationship.

As her eyes tracked Sherry, Pat saw a car pull into the lot and speed for the back door of the arena. Dawn jumped into the car, and Mandy sped back out of the lot, squealing tires as she whip-tailed onto the street. It crossed Pat's mind to put a call in to Mac's office; she was sure the owner was still working even if it was early Friday evening. After all, Mandy was a member of the Cougar administration, and with Dawn now a signed member of the team, a social relationship between the two would be as inappropriate as any between herself and Sherry. But at the moment, she didn't much care. Mandy was Mac's problem. And as far as Dawn was concerned, she would coach the player and do everything she could to make her a productive member of the Cougar team — but beyond that, she was Mac's problem, too.

Pat spun back around to her desk. She tidied up, putting loose papers into a drawer and neatening up the items on the top of the desk. The last thing she did was to lock the desk drawers. Then she picked up her bag, snatched up the single sheet of paper lying in the printer tray, and walked to the door. Locking the door behind her, Pat made her way to Mac's office, located on the top level of the arena.

After delivering to the team owner the list of players who had survived tryout camp, Pat wished her a good weekend and walked to her truck. As she walked, she thought. And the more she thought, the more Sherry's invitation appealed to her. There was something about the player that just seemed to bring a smile to her face whenever she thought about her, which she admitted was more often every day. Pat wasn't sure if it was the dimples that framed Sherry's mouth when she smiled or the cute way she grinned when she executed a move that surprised everyone on the court. Maybe it was the way she looked walking into the locker room every morning in shorts, cut-off sweat shirt, and hiking boots or the way she filled out those shorts. Whatever it was, Pat liked it. The only question was — what was she going to do about it?

Sherry was surprised when the phone in the dorm room rang. She was just about to go to bed and wasn't expecting any calls. It could have been for one of her roommates — except that of the four players who had started camp sharing the room, she was the only one still with the team. She padded over to the phone and lifted the receiver to her ear.

"Hello."

"Sherry?"

"Yes. Who's this?"

"Coach Calvin."

"Coach?"

"Listen, I was planning on a hike in the morning." Pat rushed to say what she'd been thinking before she let her better judgment talk her out of it. As she had driven home, Pat thought of a trail that wasn't too far from town but was relatively unused by most day hikers. In fact, the numerous times she'd completed that particular hike, she had rarely crossed paths with other hikers. "Larry Creek Fire Trail. Go south on Highway 93 approximately twenty miles to Bass Creek turnoff. Drive to the campground and take the road to the horse trailer parking area. I'll be there around nine." Before Sherry could respond, the line went dead.

"I'll be there," Sherry said to the dial tone.

CHAPTER SIX

After spending most of the night tossing and turning, Pat finally accepted that she wouldn't be getting any sleep. She rolled out of bed, her tangled sheets evidence of her restlessness. After a quick shower, she dressed, leaving her house long before the sun was up. Tossing her pack on the passenger seat, she drove to the only 24-hour restaurant in town and ordered breakfast.

Having plenty of time before she was to meet Sherry, Pat sipped coffee while staring out the window beside her table. The restaurant spanned the Rattlesnake Creek; the waters tumbled underneath the building as they rushed to join the Clark Fork River a few hundred feet away. She usually found it very soothing to enjoy a meal as the creek flowed by.

But this morning, Pat was anything but soothed by the creek waters. She didn't know why she had made the call the previous evening; it had just seemed like something she had to do. She was in turmoil, wondering if maybe she shouldn't just call Sherry and tell her not to come. She had dug the cell phone out of her jacket pocket so many times that she finally placed it on the table beside her plate.

For the umpteenth time, Pat's inner voice repeated the long list of reasons going on a hike with Sherry was wrong. She was the coach; Sherry was a player. She had a morals clause in her contract: no off-court relationships with players, no matter how casual. Most likely Sherry would be released by the Cougars in a few weeks. Did she really want to start something that could be cut short so soon?

Am I starting something with Sherry? She looked at her reflection in the window and saw a lonely woman staring back at her. When had she begun to look so sad? When had all the joy gone out of her life? Pat knew the answers. Almost five years had passed since Karen had left, taking Pat's broken heart with her. That was a long time to go without feeling anything for someone else. Sherry had somehow changed that.

"Do you need anything else, Coach?"

Pat turned away from her reflection to look at the waitress standing beside the table.

"I'm about to go off shift," the young woman explained.

"No. I'm fine. I'm about to leave myself." She was surprised to discover that she had been sitting long enough for the sun to start peeking over Mount Sentinel.

"Have a good day then, Coach." The waitress smiled brightly, hoping to boost the tip she would receive.

"Thank you." Pat smiled back. One of the drawbacks to being the Cougar coach was that everyone in town thought she had lots of money to throw around. Mac paid her well but not that well.

"Where you off to today, Coach?" the restaurant's manager asked as Pat stepped up to the counter to pay her bill. "Looks to be a good day for fishing or a hike," he suggested, knowing Pat enjoyed doing both.

"Yes." Pat handed the manager her check and a twenty-dollar bill. "It looks to be a good day," she said. Without answering his question, she turned to leave.

"You've got change coming."

"Give it to Donna." Pat named the waitress. *Oh well,* she thought as she calculated the amount of the tip in her head, *might as well keep the myth alive.*

Pat pushed open the restaurant's heavy glass door and stepped out into the morning, taking a deep breath of crisp air. A quick glance at her watch told her she had time to complete a few errands before heading south to meet Sherry. "Shut up," she growled to her inner voice as she unlocked the door to her truck. "I'm going, so just shut up."

The alarm sounded unusually loud in the quiet dorm room, and Sherry forced an eye open just far enough to locate its off button. "Ugh," she groaned, rubbing the sleep from her eyes. "Who hit me over the head last night?" Throwing the blankets off, she scooted to the edge of the bed and slowly swung her legs over the side. It took several moments before she was willing to attempt to stand. "Guess practice took more out of me than I thought," she muttered, swaying slightly as blood started rushing through her now upright body. "The shower is going to feel really good this morning," she told herself, shuffling over to the dresser for a pair of panties and a bra.

An hour later, fully awake and looking forward to her day, Sherry zipped up the pocket of her pack. Not wanting to forget anything, she had double checked its contents — extra clothing, a flashlight, and emergency supplies. After the coach's call, she had looked in her hiking book to find the trail where she would be meeting Pat. It showed the main trail to be a two-and-a-half mile loop gaining 500 feet in elevation. But there was a much longer and steeper trail that branched off of it, and she didn't know which of the trails Pat was expecting to follow. She wasn't too concerned about her ability to complete either trail, but she wanted to be prepared just in case the weather changed or she was out longer than she anticipated.

Sherry swung the pack onto her shoulder with an easy motion she had performed countless times before and started for the door, snatching her keys and jacket off the end of the bed as she walked by. Instead of the usual places in town, she'd decided to eat breakfast at a small family-style diner Val had told her about one day when they were discussing places for the rookie to check out while in Missoula.

With her pack resting on the floor of the back seat of Val's car, Sherry turned the key in the ignition. She chuckled when the needle indicating the amount of fuel in the gas tank barely moved above the E. "I swear, Val, I think the only reason you let me borrow your car is because I fill up the tank," she told her absent teammate as she backed the Jeep out of its parking spot. She wasn't really upset, figuring a tank of gas was a lot cheaper than trying to rent a car or buy one for the short time she would be in town.

Leaving the parking lot, she pointed the Jeep in the direction of a nearby gas station/mini mart. With only one stop, she could fill the empty tank and also pick up some snacks and prepared sandwiches to add to her pack. That would leave only stopping for breakfast before she headed for the trailhead and Pat.

Sherry reached for the radio knob. Soon country music filled the air, and she sang along, a beaming smile on her face.

Pat had one foot on the back bumper of her truck as she tightened the laces on her boots. Her heart raced when she heard the sound of a vehicle approaching, her inner voice shouting last-minute warnings at her.

"Damn it," Pat muttered, walking to the front of the truck to retrieve her pack from the cab. "There's no reason for me not to be here," she told the voice.

What if it's someone else? the voice asked. *Someone you know.*

"What if it is?" Pat answered out loud. "So what? I'm here to go for a hike, something I've done hundreds of times, and there's no reason for me not to be doing it again today."

But today you're not going alone.

"I know." Pat's lip twitched into a grin she was unable and unwilling to stop.

It's wrong, the voice persisted.

"Shut up." Pat slammed the door shut just as a car pulled into the large gravel and dirt parking area.

Sherry spotted Pat's truck before she pulled off the road. She thought of parking beside it, then decided that it would be a better idea to pull into the shady spot under a tall pine tree on the opposite side of the parking area. Turning off the engine, she opened the car door and climbed out. Pausing long enough to wave to Pat, she opened the back door and lifted her pack off the floor. She made sure the car was securely locked before trotting over to where the coach stood leaning against her truck.

Pat smiled at Sherry. "'Morning."

"'Morning." Sherry smiled back. "I was surprised to get your call," she said, wanting to get something clear before their day got started. "Are you sure you want to do this, Coach?"

"Do what?" Pat asked, even though she knew what Sherry was referring to.

"You know." Sherry shrugged. "Us hiking together. I thought you felt it was a bad idea."

Pat hesitated. She had thought that. In fact, she still did. But there was something drawing her to the woman standing so near to her. "I won't lie to you, Sherry," Pat started slowly. "It could mean trouble if someone sees us and draws the wrong conclusions."

Sherry wasn't sure which conclusions would be the wrong ones, but she didn't ask, not really wanting to know the answer.

"But we came in separate vehicles, and we just happened to meet at the trailhead." Pat knew she was setting up a reasonable, if not quite accurate explanation, should one be needed. "We know each other. I doubt if anyone would expect us just to go our separate ways under the circumstances."

Sherry nodded, letting Pat know she understood what she was really saying.

"But if you're having doubts..." Pat offered, hoping that Sherry wasn't. "I'll understand if you want to do just that."

"No," Sherry said, a little too forcefully. "I mean..." She grinned sheepishly when Pat cocked an eyebrow at her. "I want to go with you. I just don't want to cause you any trouble."

"You won't," Pat assured her in a soft voice. "I'd like us to go together," she added, almost shyly.

"Then what are we waiting for?"

When Sherry placed her pack on the ground so she could tighten her boot laces, Pat found herself enjoying the view.

"I read about this trail," Sherry said as she switched feet. "The book says it only gains 500 feet in elevation, so I don't think I'll have much problem," she told Pat while she talked to her shoes. "I've been taking short hikes, like you suggested." She straightened up, pulling her pack up with her and settling it on her back. "I hardly have any trouble breathing now."

"The guidebook description is a little misleading," Pat explained with a wry grin as she led Sherry across the parking area to the trailhead. "It may only gain 500 feet — the book is off by 100 feet by the way — but it sorta goes straight up, then levels off, then comes straight down. That's the trouble with those books, they don't give the real picture."

"Maybe you should write one that does," Sherry suggested, falling into step with Pat.

"Maybe I should." Pat laughed. She'd had the same thought many times. "The trail narrows as soon as we get up there." She pointed up through the trees. "We won't be able to walk side by side then. You want to lead or follow?"

It took Sherry less than a second to make up her mind. "I'll follow." She grinned. *The view will be much better.*

For the first hundred or so yards, the trail was a wide, pine needle-covered dirt path that wove its way through a forest of larch and ponderosa pines. Then the trees became fewer and grew farther apart, replaced by clusters of wild berry bushes and open grassy patches of ground. True to Pat's words, the trail narrowed and steepened for the next half mile. It hung to the side of the slope as it zigzagged uphill. It wasn't so steep that the women had to stop to rest as they climbed, but it was steep enough that talking wasn't easy — so they walked in silence.

Sherry stopped frequently to enjoy the green hillside dotted with wildflowers of every color in the rainbow, and Pat would pause in her own climb, waiting patiently until Sherry was ready to continue. She knew how the player felt and didn't begrudge her the time.

Before her injury, Pat had run the trails, using the exercise as her unique way to train for the rigors of the season. She hated running laps on a track where the scenery never changed. By the time she reached college, she was running the mountain trails as if she had bionic legs, which explained another NCAA record she had set — most minutes played. Few players could run up and down the basketball court for the full length of a game, but Pat could and did, seemingly without breaking a sweat. It wasn't until after her surgery, when she used the trails as a way to rehab her damaged knee, that she had taken the time to appreciate their beauty. Now a trail like this, which could easily be hiked in a couple of hours, might take her all day as she spent her time enjoying the blessings Mother Nature displayed.

A small meadow opened alongside the trail, and Pat halted. Putting a finger to her lips for silence, she pointed to the center of the clearing, where a doe was munching on the dew-covered grass. The deer lifted her head to study the intruders, then, sensing no threat, she went back to her morning meal.

"She's not afraid of us?" Sherry whispered.

"She knows we won't harm her."

"Wow."

"Come on." Pat tilted her head up the trail. "There's a place to sit not too far past that crest. My knee can use a rest," she said, not complaining but stating the truth.

Sherry turned her attention to the coach. She hadn't given Pat's injury any thought; the woman never let any pain she was suffering show. "Are you okay?"

"I'm fine." Pat started up the trail. "Just need to sit for a spell."

Sherry took a final look at the doe before following Pat, noticing for the first time the slightest limp in the coach's stride.

It took them twenty minutes to reach the crest where the trail's slope gentled, the path leading through a meadow much larger than the one where the doe had been. They were above the tops of the trees at the start of the trail, and Sherry was amazed at their unobstructed view of the Bitterroot Valley far below them. As she stopped to look, Pat continued to where a bench had been placed alongside the trail.

The bench was of simple design — a log cut in half, the flat side smoothed and covered in layers of lacquer to seal it. The rounded part of the log rested in two pieces of wood cut to cradle it. The other half of the log formed the bench back, smoothed and polished to match the seat.

Pat slipped off her pack as she neared the bench, dropping it on the ground beside it. As soon as she was seated, she pulled her pant leg up over the brace and began loosening its Velcro straps. She could feel the pain ease as soon as she slid the brace off the knee and down her leg to rest around her ankle.

"Can I help?" Sherry asked, concern clearly evident in the question.

"I'm fine." Pat squinted as she looked up at the woman standing beside her. "Sit," she commanded. "You're standing in front of the sun."

"Sorry." Sherry slipped off her pack and joined Pat on the bench. "I thought the brace was supposed to help."

"It provides support," Pat explained, rubbing the knee in an attempt to ease the aching. "But it also adds to the problem by having to keep so much pressure on the joint all the time. It's kind of a damned-if-you-do, damned-if-you-don't situation. I just need to take the dang thing off once in a while to give the leg a rest."

Sherry sat back, willing to sit as long as Pat needed. "Nice of someone to put this here." She ran her hand over the polished wood surface.

"Yeah, it sure beats sitting on the ground." Pat bent over to her pack. She pulled a water bottle free, lifted it to her mouth, and took a generous drink. "Hungry?" she asked as her stomach rumbled. They were only a fourth of their way along the trail, but she was starving after only picking at her breakfast earlier.

"No." Sherry shook her head. "I had a big breakfast."

"In town?" Pat rummaged around for the energy bars she carried.

"No. Val told me about a little place in Stevensville. I stopped there."

Suddenly Pat was no longer hungry. Her head whipped around, her eyes revealing her panic. "You told Val about today?"

"*No.*" Sherry's head shook violently back and forth. "I would never do that, Pat." She unconsciously used the coach's given name, but neither woman seemed to notice. "We were talking a couple of weeks ago, and she was telling me about different places in the valley that I might be interested in seeing while I'm here."

Pat blew out a breath of relief. "Sorry." She grinned awkwardly. "Guess I'm more concerned than I thought."

"It's okay," Sherry whispered. "I should go back." She made the offer, even though she didn't want to leave.

"Stay." Pat reached out, lightly placing her hand on Sherry's arm. "Please, stay."

Sherry nodded, her hand covering Pat's.

The women stayed like that for several minutes until the cry of a crow flying overhead broke the spell.

As they reached the zenith of the hike and started downward, the forest closed in around them. The trail narrowed, and more rocks and small boulders appeared in the path.

"Hang on a sec," Pat said. Reaching back, she flipped open the clasps holding a pair of ski poles to the side of her pack. She pulled the sections of poles out to the proper length, then fastened them tight.

"I wondered why you carried poles in the summer," Sherry said as she watched Pat.

"I need the extra support on rough ground like this. It's not a bad idea to have a pair handy," she said, slipping her hands into the straps on the pole grips. "They really help take the strain off your legs, especially going up steep hills."

"Now you tell me." Sherry reached down and rubbed her thighs, which had begun to ache after the steep climb at the start of the trail.

Pat laughed as she started down the rocky path. "The good news is, it's all downhill from here. 'Course, sometimes the downhills are worse than the uphills. Which is another good reason to carry these."

"Not funny," Sherry groused as she followed. "Not funny at all."

They hadn't gone far when Sherry noticed a numbered marker alongside the path. She had noticed several before, but Pat had not paid any attention to them. Her curiosity finally got the better of her. "What are those markers for?"

"What markers?" Pat asked as she almost impaled one with a ski pole. "Oh, those markers." She smiled. "Well, technically, this is a self-guided trail that explains the benefits of fire on the forest. But the only way to get one of the pamphlets that explains what the markers are for is to ask the hosts of the campground."

"You've never asked?"

"Nah."

"Why?"

"Just never seemed to get around to it."

"Maybe I'll stop there on my way home today and pick one up. If you're nice, I might even let you read it."

"Gee, thanks."

"Say, Coach?"

"Yes."

"How far back to the trailhead?"

"About a mile, why?"

"Well, I noticed there was an outhouse there. And, I um..."

Pat stopped and turned to look at Sherry. "There are other options, you know."

Sherry looked around. Seeing nothing but trees, bushes, and flowers, she stared at Pat. "What?"

"This is the woods, city girl." Pat chuckled. "Pick a tree."

"You mean just go out here? In the open?" Sherry squeaked.

"Sherry," Pat looked at the player, amused to see the look of bewilderment on her face, "how many people have we seen today? Not counting us."

"Uh, none."

"Right. So go off into the bushes and find yourself a nice spot and just do it. Or go right here if you want. I promise not to look."

"Um, okay." Sherry looked around again. "But, I, um..."

"What?"

"I don't have any tissue."

"Well, to be honest," Pat leaned back, using the ski poles to support her, "unless I'm doing number two, I just kinda air dry. It's better for the environment, less pollution, if you know what I mean."

Sherry eyed her, trying to decide if Pat was being serious or not. "Really."

"Look." Pat lifted one of the ski poles, using it as a pointer. "Go down behind those bushes." She pointed to an area several feet off the trail. "Find yourself a clear spot and dig a small hole with your boot. Then squat and get it over with, but make sure you lean back so you don't pee all over your shorts and boots. It's pretty far back to the trailhead so you might as well take care of it now."

"Um, okay." Sherry stepped off the trail. "You won't look?" she turned back to ask.

"I promise." Pat held up her hand, palm outward. *But I'd like to.* She turned and walked a few feet further down the trail to give Sherry some privacy.

As luck would have it, Pat heard voices coming up the trail as soon as Sherry disappeared behind the bushes. Suddenly, her concern that Sherry might be seen in a compromising position was more important to her than being recognized by whomever was approaching. Before she could go back and warn Sherry, a family rounded a bend in the trail and spotted her. She hoped Sherry would have the common sense to stay put until the hikers passed.

"Hi," a young boy about twelve said as he darted by where Pat had stepped to the side of the trail.

"Hi," Pat answered, but the boy was already several feet up the trail, obviously in a hurry to be the first in the group to reach the top.

"Hello," the boy's mother said as she reached Pat.

"Nice day," the father added as he passed.

Pat smiled and nodded, thankful she didn't recognize any of them and that they didn't seem to know who she was. By the way they were dressed, in new jeans and wearing regular street shoes, she figured they must be tourists staying in the campground. She also noticed they carried no water, something they would regret before they got back to their campsite. She watched them continue up the trail until they disappeared into the trees.

"Are they gone?" Sherry hissed from her hiding spot.

"Yes." Pat didn't have to wait long before Sherry popped up from behind the bushes.

"We haven't seen anyone all day," Sherry grumbled as she made her way back to the trail. "Then I drop my pants, and a circus goes by."

"Hardly a circus," Pat snickered. "It was only three people. It's not like they had elephants and tigers with them. Or clowns. Or acrobats."

"Shut up," Sherry grunted, brushing past Pat and stomping down the trail.

"Sherry?" Pat called after the disgruntled woman. "Sherry, wait."

"What?" Sherry stopped abruptly and spun around. When she saw Pat struggling to catch up with her, she could have kicked herself. "I'm sorry." She started back up the trail to Pat.

"Hey," Pat said as soon as they had joined up again, "are you okay?"

"Yeah." Sherry smiled, ashamed she had made Pat try to navigate the broken ground in a hurry. "I was just a little shook up when I heard them. It would have been pretty embarrassing if they had seen me."

Pat wanted to reach out and touch Sherry to reassure her, but she fought the urge. "Believe it or not," she smiled, "it almost always happens like that. You're out in the woods all day by yourself, but the minute you drop your drawers is when someone will come by. Happened to me one day when I was way out in the boonies."

"It did?"

"Yes." Pat moved down the trail, this time at a more comfortable speed. "I'd been out all day, never saw another living soul. Then I get the urge and find me a nice secluded spot back in the trees and up the side of a hill. I drop my pants and squat and what happens?"

"Someone came down the trail?"

"Worse."

"Worse?"

"A guy came over the crest of the hill, walked down right past where I was peeing. Said hello and kept right on walking."

"You're making that up."

"Scout's honor." Pat looked back over her shoulder at Sherry. "It happened just like that. I was so embarrassed, I just stayed in that position for about a half hour. If a bear hadn't come by, I'd probably still be there."

"A bear? Now I know you're making it up."

"I'm not kidding. A young black bear ambled out of the woods, took one look at my lily white fanny hanging out and took off running. I tell you, after that day," Pat began walking again, "I have no shame. None whatsoever."

Sherry burst into gales of laughter as she imagined Pat squatting in the woods with a hiker and a bear for an audience. By the time she composed herself enough to run after the coach, Pat was well on her way back to the trailhead, whistling happily as she walked.

"No, no, no." Pat stopped play. "That is not how the play is designed to go." She took a few steps to the top of the key. "We have less than a week before our first exhibition game, and you guys look like you've never seen a basketball before. Dawn," she shouted at the player standing less than a foot from her, a bored look on her face, "you are supposed to fake a move up the key. That's a little hard to do if you never move. This team is designed to run, so *move your feet*." Pat walked backward to her viewing position near the sideline. "Sherry, pass the ball, don't lob it. Make it so only one person can catch it and that's the one you're passing to. Let's run it again."

Sherry let the ball drop from under her arm where she'd been holding it. She dribbled as she backpedaled to the circle at half court where a large painting of a snarling mountain lion commanded the area. She continued to dribble in place while the other players set up for the play.

Only five players were on the court; Pat was trying to get the rookies familiar with the Cougar plays. With the exhibition games rapidly approaching, she had been working the team hard during practice. The upside to that was she was able to watch Sherry's skills develop as she became more comfortable on the court. The downside was that Sherry had been so tired after the exhausting practices that she had passed on joining Pat for any more hikes.

When the other players were set, Sherry bounced the ball between her legs, then trotted up the court, angling to the right sideline. When she stepped even with the free-throw line, she took a half step in Dawn's direction and fired a bullet that smacked loudly against the post player's palms.

"That hurt." Marcie winced, then grinned as Dawn grimaced.

Pat held in her own grin.

Dawn turned for the basket and took a step into the key before bounce passing the ball to Latesha, who was running into position at the bottom of the key for a lay-up. When the ball dropped through the net, Dawn turned triumphantly toward her coach.

Pat smiled, but not because the basket had been made. *Now's as good as time as any to burst her bubble.* "Starters on the floor," she called to the players sitting along the sidelines watching the action. "The rest of you stay where you are, and give Dawn the ball."

Latesha, having caught the ball after her basket, tossed a lazy pass back to Dawn that dropped a few feet in front of the waiting player.

Pat smiled humorlessly. *Oh goodie, this is really turning out to be a fun group.* "Play defense," she told the five new players. When they were in position, she turned to Dawn. "I want you to make that *exact* same pass to Latesha. Think you can do that?"

Dawn smirked. "Sure, Coach."

"Okay, do it."

Dawn looked to bounce pass the ball, but instead of a clear passing lane to her teammate, all she saw was a wall of waving arms and a web of legs.

"Well?" Pat asked. "Make the pass."

"There's no way I can get the ball through them," Dawn complained.

"That's right. That's the whole point of you *faking* a move to the basket and drawing the defense to you. Like this." Pat slapped the ball out of Dawn's hands, turned her back to the basket for a second, then spun around and stepped into the key, causing the defensive players to sag in on her. As soon as she had the defense on the move, she made a quick step to the right for a clear passing lane to Latesha and snapped the ball at the rookie forward. The ball slapped hard against Latesha's hands and fell harmlessly out of bounds.

Shocked at the rookie's failure to control the pass, Pat stared at her. "Okay, listen up. I don't know where some of you learned how to pass, but if you can't do it right, you won't be playing for this team. And you better be able to handle them when they come, because I won't accept anything less. Marcie," she called her assistant coach over, "take the rookies to the other end of the court. I want them to know how to deliver a pass and how to catch a pass by the end of the day."

"Yes, Coach." Marcie nodded. "All right, let's go," she said, trotting down the court, not bothering to see if anyone was following. She figured the rookies should know who they were.

"Now," Pat turned to face her senior players, "let's run through these plays like we know how. Kinsey, take the point."

For the rest of the afternoon session, Pat split her attention between the veteran players at her end of the court and the rookies at the other. By the end of the day, she had seen a significant improvement in passing skills from all but Dawn.

Pat blew her whistle to get everyone's attention. "Hit the showers," she told the players. "I want to see all of you in the weight room at eight tomorrow morning."

To a chorus of groans, Pat walked to the sideline where she'd placed her notepad earlier. Flipping through the pages she had for each player, she jotted down notes and observations from that day's practice. When Dawn walked by her on the way to the locker room, she stopped the player. "Dawn, can I see you a moment?"

Dawn shrugged her shoulders. "Yeah, whatever." The look she received from her coach told her not to push the attitude any further.

Pat waited until the floor cleared of players. "Look," she said to the disinterested player, "I don't have time to waste with you. This isn't college where you have a scholarship and a free ride. I'm not going to coddle or pamper or beg to get you to do what you're supposed to do." That was one advantage of coaching a pro team: The players were paid to play, and they were expected to do just that. "Either you start to put out the effort and become a part of this team, or I talk to Mac about cutting you loose so I can get another player in here before the season starts. And if she won't do that, you better get yourself a nice comfy pillow 'cause your butt will never get off the bench all season. Do I make myself clear?" Without waiting for an answer, she turned around, picked up her bag, and strode off the court, hoping her limp wasn't too noticeable to the player staring slack-jawed after her.

Dawn glared at Pat's back until she entered the corridor and vanished from sight. She didn't like being talked to like that by a has-been, but she needed to stay with the Cougars the full season to get what she wanted. She'd do what she had to do to keep her position on the roster, but no more.

"I thought you were going to take care of Sherry today," Mandy said, walking up beside the obviously irritated player.

Dawn twisted around to look at the woman who could make her time in Missoula bearable. If only she could take care of the matter her lover kept pressing her to do. "The opportunity didn't come up."

"I'm tired of your excuses. I got you on the team when you needed it; now it's time for you to take care of what I need."

"I get the message. I'll take care of it."

"When?"

"First chance I get. Now, let's get out of here. Are you done for the day?"

"I can be. Got something on your mind?" Mandy ran a finger up Dawn's arm, scraping her fingernail along its length.

"Let me grab my bag." Dawn trotted across the floor to the locker room.

Mandy lagged behind, knowing no matter how fast she ran she could not catch the long-legged player.

"There goes trouble," Marcie muttered.

"Yeah," Kelley agreed, having seen, but not been able to hear the exchange between the player and the owner's niece. "Let's hope they don't drag anyone else into it."

CHAPTER SEVEN

Pat was running a full-court scrimmage between mixed teams of rookies and returning players. She had only two days left to determine which combinations of players worked well and which didn't before the team traveled to its first exhibition game. It was an aspect of the game she took more seriously than most coaches. As a player she knew that if you were comfortable with the players you shared the court with, you usually played better. Too often the opposing team was able to run off a couple of quick baskets if a new combination of players couldn't get into rhythm immediately. Pat didn't like substituting players willy-nilly. She wanted the five on the court to be comfortable with each other and jell immediately.

"Sherry," Pat was yelling as the rookie dribbled down the length of the court, "Pete's got the angle, give her the ball."

Sherry knew the other guard had been leading her down the court on the opposite sideline. Out of the corner of her eye, she had caught Pete beginning her cut toward the basket just as the coach yelled at her. She snapped a pass to the other guard, then cut across the floor to take the position Pete was vacating.

Pete charged for the key, pulling up sharply when she reached it. Spinning around, she flipped the ball out to Val, unguarded in the corner just beyond the 3-point line. Without taking a step, Val popped into the air as soon as the ball was in her hands, shooting for the basket. All the players converged under the basket, jockeying for position to gather in the rebound should the ball bounce off the rim.

Sherry stayed at the back of the pack, prepared to set up the play again if the ball bounced her direction. The ball hit the rim, ricocheting off the backboard into a high arc toward the top of the key. Sherry was in the best position for gathering in the rebound, but as she started her leap upward, Dawn crashed into her. Before she could recover, the ball had been nabbed by Pete, who took a couple of quick steps away from the others, squared up with the basket, and popped in a 15-foot jump shot.

Pat's whistle blew, stopping the action.

Rubbing her shoulder, Sherry walked to the side of the court where her water bottle sat on an empty seat in the first row of bleachers.

Marcie trotted up beside her. "You okay?" Dawn was quite a bit bigger than the guard and quite capable of doing damage if she wanted.

"Yeah." Sherry continued to knead the knot in the muscle that had formed where Dawn's elbow had jabbed into it. "Just need a drink, then I'll be ready to go."

"Okay, hurry back in," Marcie said as she signaled the coach that the player was all right.

Pat turned her attention back to the other players as soon as she saw Marcie's signal. "Dawn, you and Sherry are on the same team. Do you think it's smart to be fighting over a rebound like that?" she asked, even though she was sure Dawn had purposely rammed Sherry.

"I was just going for the ball, Coach," the post player objected.

After her talk with Pat a few days before, she had been doing everything asked of her in practice. And doing it well, impressing both the skeptical coaching staff and the other players. At the same time, she had been looking for the right opportunity to do damage to the guard her lover wanted off the team.

"It's important that you always know where your teammates are." Pat addressed the entire team. "This time it didn't hurt us; Pete picked up the ball and scored. But it could just as easily been Wendy or Jade." She named the two players on the defensive team who had been nearest the loose ball. "And they could have taken it the other way. Sherry." She acknowledged the guard rejoining the group and noticed she was no longer rubbing her shoulder. She didn't have time to wonder if it was because it wasn't bothering the player anymore or she was trying to hide an injury from her coach. "You get the trainers to take a look at that shoulder after practice." She waited until the guard nodded her agreement. "Okay, let's run that play again. Only this time, Sherry, I want to see more speed when you're bringing the ball up court. Remember, the Cougars are one of the fastest teams in the league, and we have to prove that every single time we have the ball. The faster we bring it up court, the less time our opponents have to set up their defense. Okay?"

"Gotcha, Coach." Her comment was echoed by many of the other players.

"Okay, let's go again. This time, make sure you know who you're fighting over the ball with."

As the players trotted into position, Marcie moved to stand beside Pat. "You know Dawn plowed into her on purpose."

"I know."

"Aren't you going to say anything to her?"

"Yes, but not now. Besides, Sherry is going to have to learn to take hard knocks and keep playing. She'll get a lot worse in the games."

"If she gets injured, she'll be gone."

"I know. Faster, Sherry, faster," Pat shouted as the players move across the center-court line. "That's it. Have Dawn come to my office after practice," Pat told Marcie, her eyes never leaving the action on the floor. "Better. Much better," she called out to the players. "Good shot, Val." She praised the forward who made the 3-point shot this time. "Okay, let's switch up. Dawn, Pete out. Ashley, Kinsey in."

Mandy pushed open the door to the office without knocking. Pat looked up from the papers she was reading. "I've told you before not to do that," she told her administrative assistant, not bothering to mask her displeasure.

"Dawn is here. She said Marcie told her you wanted to talk to her. Is there a problem?"

"Did I miss the memo about you joining my coaching staff?" Pat asked sarcastically.

"Mac will want to know if there's a problem with one of her players," Mandy said, resting her hip on the edge of Pat's desk, her skirt hiked up and showing off most of her thigh. "Is there a problem?" she asked again, her fingertips trailing suggestively down bare skin.

"Not with any of the players." Pat pursed her lips together, disgusted by the woman's obvious display. "Did you check on the reservations for Denver?"

"Yes. Everything is confirmed. Perhaps this time you'll let me take you to dinner when we're there," Mandy purred, shifting her leg so that Pat, if so inclined, could see she wasn't wearing any panties.

"Get off my desk," Pat glared at the woman, "and get out of my office."

Mandy stood but slowly. "You're making a mistake, Pat." She sighed, adjusting her skirt back into place.

"Will you ever give up?" Pat slumped against her chair back. "How many ways do you have to be told no before you get it?"

Mandy grinned smugly. "You don't know what you're missing."

"It'll be a mystery I take to my grave." Pat shook her head in disgust. "Get out, and tell Dawn to come in."

"If that's what you want." Mandy sashayed for the door.

"And make sure you put those confirmations in my box before you leave."

With a wave of her manicured hand, Mandy walked out of the office. A few moments later, Dawn entered.

"You wanted to see me?"

"Yeah." Pat was still thinking of Mandy's behavior and what she should do about it. "Have a seat." While she waited for Dawn to sit, she reached down to rub her aching knee.

"Well?" Dawn asked when the coach remained silent for several minutes.

"Um, yeah." Pat straightened in her chair. Maybe some time with an ice pack would help her knee. "Listen, I wanted to say how much I've appreciated the change in your attitude. You've really been working hard and showing some good moves out there. You've got the makings of a good player, Dawn."

"But?" Dawn asked, detecting a trace of disapproval in the coach's voice.

Pat's tone hardened. "But if you ever pull another stunt like you did today, I'll personally throw your butt out of this arena. With or without Mac's approval."

"Wait a minute," Dawn protested, standing to stare down at the coach. "That was a clean play. It's not my fault if Sherry's too slow to get out of the way."

Pat struggled to keep her anger from her voice when she responded. In her mind's eye, she saw Sherry absorb the blow of the larger woman and almost crash to the floor as a result. "It was a dirty shot, Dawn. You know it, and I know it. Don't make the mistake of doing it again. It's hard enough getting through the season with the injuries our opponents will inflict. I don't need to lose any players because you can't control your jealousy."

"Jealousy? You think I'm jealous of that wannabe?"

"Sit down, Dawn," Pat instructed, tired of looking up. "I think you felt you were the star when you played for Karen's team, and you just can't get over the fact that I offered Sherry a spot at camp the same time I offered one to you. I've looked into your background." She relaxed when Dawn settled back into the chair. "You two played at different high schools in different states. You played at different colleges in different leagues. Fact is, I can't find anything that suggests you and Sherry knew each other or were even aware of each other's existence until you showed up to play for Karen. And I've talked to her about it. She said you had no problems with Sherry then, either. So all this started the night I offered you both a spot in camp. So yeah, I think you're jealous.

I think you feel Sherry has somehow taken some of the spotlight away from you, and you can't stand it."

"You're wrong," Dawn muttered, not able to admit the truth behind her actions against Sherry.

"Am I?" The coach looked steadily at her player. When Dawn dropped her eyes, Pat wondered if there was more to the matter than she thought. "If I am wrong, prove it. Lay off Sherry." *Because if you don't, I'll personally use your head the next time I want to try a slam dunk.*

"Is that it?" Dawn asked, still looking at the floor.

Pat sighed. "Yeah, that's it."

Dawn literally jumped out of the chair and rushed to the door, yanking it open.

Pat watched as Dawn stopped at the desk in the outer office. From where she sat, she couldn't see Mandy, but she knew that had to be who Dawn was talking to. She could hear desk drawers being shut, and the lamp on the desk went dark. Then Mandy joined Dawn.

"'Night, Pat," the assistant called out as she and Dawn walked arm in arm out of the office area.

"Trouble with a capital T," Pat muttered, turning off her desk lamp.

Sherry finished her private free-throw practice and headed for the locker room. The shoulder was tight, and she was sure she'd find a noticeable bruise when she pulled off her jersey. Luckily, Dawn had slammed into her left arm, leaving her shooting arm undamaged. She wasn't surprised to find the locker room empty of players.

"Coach said to take a look at you." A dark-skinned woman sat in one of the chairs facing the dry marker board. "Said to wait until you were done out there," she told the player.

"I think it's okay," Sherry lied, the shoulder aching as she rotated it to verify her statement.

The woman smiled. "Well, I get paid to make those decisions, so let me do my job."

"All right." Sherry smiled back. "I'm Sherry," she said, embarrassed that she had spoken to the woman on several occasions but didn't know her name.

"Elizabeth," the trainer replied. "I've taped your ankles a time or two," she reminded the player, a slight chiding in her tone.

"I know." Sherry's cheeks colored. "I'm sorry, that really was rude of me. I just never thought to ask your name."

"Most don't." Elizabeth shrugged. "Let's go into the treatment area; the light is better in there."

Chagrined over her bad manners, Sherry silently followed the woman to the back of the locker room. Two doors shared the wall at that end of the room — one led to the showers, the other to the room where the training staff had their supplies and equipment.

"Over on that table should work." Elizabeth pointed to a table mostly used to tape players' ankles before practices. "Take off your shirt."

Pat was sitting in an empty whirlpool tub, her legs stretched out in front of her and a large ice bag wrapped to her bad knee with an elastic bandage. She rested in the dark, having turned off the lights in that corner of the large room that served the needs of the Cougar medical staff. She heard Elizabeth come in and guessed Sherry must be the player she was talking to.

When the trainer instructed Sherry to remove her shirt, Pat felt her stomach flip, and her heart missed a beat. She knew with only a slight turn of her head she'd be able to see the player, but she forced her eyes to stay where they were — focused on the end of the tub. It wasn't that she hadn't seen most of the players in various stages of undress; after all, she frequently was in the locker room when the players were changing clothes. But for some reason, she had never felt comfortable when it was Sherry, and she would avert her eyes or move away whenever the player was in the process of dressing.

"Let's take a look." Elizabeth frowned at the large bruise revealed when Sherry's shirt was removed. "What she hit you with, a two by four?"

"Her elbow," Sherry answered.

Pat felt anger building in her stomach and spreading throughout her body. The difference in height between the post player and the guard would make it easy for Dawn to drive her elbow into Sherry without it looking too obvious. Though she had had a clear view of the blow, she had missed that the post player had led with her elbow.

"Can you lift your arm?"

Sherry lifted her arm above her head, stopping when the shoulder protested. She grimaced. "It's tightened up a little."

"More than a little." Elizabeth grinned as the player tried not to let the pain show on her face. "It doesn't feel like any more than a bad bruise," she said as her fingers probed the tender tissue. "Let's put an ice pack on it, and you can take it easy for a bit before you go home."

"It's not that bad." Sherry was afraid the trainer would report the shoulder had been injured enough to keep her from playing. "You can't tell Coach it's that bad."

"Won't have to." Elizabeth grinned. "She's over there." She gestured with her thumb to the dark corner of the room.

"Damn," Sherry muttered, looking into the shadows.

"Find someplace comfortable. I'll get another ice pack."

"Um..." Sherry hesitated. "Can I put my shirt back on?"

"We're all ladies in here," Elizabeth said with a laugh. "But if you're shy, sure."

Sherry wasn't exactly shy. And normally she wouldn't have given a second thought to sitting with her shirt off while she waited for the trainer to return. But for some reason the thought of Pat seeing her like that made her... *What does it make me? Warm and fuzzy all over,* came the unexpected answer. *Oh, yeah.* She mentally slapped herself. *The shirt is definitely going back on.* She grabbed the garment off the table and slipped it over her head.

Elizabeth chuckled as Sherry redressed. Sherry wasn't the first woman to react to the coach's magnetism. She, herself, had fallen victim to it when she first started working for the Cougars. "I want to take a look at you before practice tomorrow. And that means before you go out for your hundred free throws. You don't pick up a ball tomorrow until you see me. Understand?"

"Yes." Sherry watched as the ice pack was attached to her shoulder in a way similar to the one on the coach's knee. "Thanks, Elizabeth."

"Like I said, it's what I get paid to do." The trainer smiled. "And my friends call me Lizzie."

Sherry smiled back. "Thank you, Lizzie."

"You need anything, Coach?" Lizzie called across the room.

"No."

"Then I'll head home."

"Have a good night, Lizzie. Thanks."

"Make sure she keeps that ice pack on a while."

"Will do."

"'Night, Coach."

"'Night."

Without thinking, Sherry slipped off the examination table and walked across the room to where Pat was resting. She eased herself down into a chair next to the tub. "Looks uncomfortable," she said as she took in the coach's position in the empty tub.

"It is. But it's not as bad as laying on one of those cold tables."

"If you say so." Sherry adjusted the ice pack on her shoulder.

"It was a cheap shot." Pat nodded at the shoulder. "Mind telling me what you two have against each other?"

"Wish I knew," Sherry said, grateful that the shoulder was already responding to the ice. "We never had a problem until she showed up in camp."

"That's what I thought." Pat reached down and unwrapped the bandage holding the ice pack to her leg. "So how is it, really?" She smiled to let the player know she wasn't digging for information to keep her from playing.

"Sore, but this is making it feel better."

"Good." Pat leaned back against the end of the tub, flexing her now unencumbered knee. She smiled again. "Missed you on the trail this past weekend."

"I, uh..." Sherry felt a blush rising up her cheeks. "I'm sorry. I just didn't feel like moving too far from my couch. You run a nasty practice session, Coach." She grinned, trying to cover her uneasiness.

"No need to be sorry. I'm happy you're smart enough to know when not to push things."

"I'll be ready next time," Sherry said, a little quicker than she had intended. But she didn't want the coach to think she was no longer interested in their private hikes.

"Relax." Pat smiled. "It'll be a while before we have time. Denver this weekend and Seattle next will keep us too busy for much of anything."

"I'm looking forward to the games."

Pat thought for a moment before responding. "Look, Sherry, I hope you don't get too disappointed if you don't play. I really need to use these games to test Kinsey's knees. You probably won't see much action."

Sherry was disappointed. She knew the only reason she was still on the team was in case the aging guard was unable to make it to the start of the regular season. Pat had been honest with her about that. But she had been working hard in practice, and she had hoped that might get her some playing time in the two exhibition games. "I understand." She tried to sound upbeat, but by the look on the coach's face, she knew she had failed.

"I'm sorry, Sherry." Pat knew what the player was feeling. She felt the same way every time the Cougars took the floor and she had to face the fact that she would only be on the sidelines. She rubbed the injured knee that kept her from playing the game she so loved. "I really wish things were different."

"It's okay, Coach." Sherry pursed her lips together in a forced smile. "Kinsey deserves the shot." She meant it. She knew a lot of the Cougars' success in prior seasons was due to the play of the guard. It was only fair she be given every opportunity to play one last season if her body would allow it.

Placing her hands on the edge of the tub, Pat pushed upright. "Don't give up just yet," she said, stepping out of the tub. "I'll be in my office. Let me know when you're ready to go so I can lock up."

Sherry didn't answer; she simply sat and watched the gorgeous woman walk away.

CHAPTER EIGHT

"What the hell is this?" Pat threw the itinerary sheet onto her assistant's desk. "Do you realize the plane reservations you made leave us with less than two hours to get from the airport to the arena and ready for tip-off?"

She was more upset with herself than her assistant. She should have expected Mandy to do something like that, but she hadn't taken the time to check the reservations when the confirmations were put in her inbox. Regardless of which one of them bore the primary responsibility, Mandy was going to suffer the coach's wrath. After all, the assistant's job was to handle the scheduling of the team's travel.

"I did the best I could, Pat." Mandy looked calmly at the paper, trying to keep the smile off her face. "If you didn't like the reservations, you should have let me know when I made them. It's too late to change them now."

Confronted with her assistant's blithe insubordination, Pat could feel her rage growing. "Do you have any idea what this means for us, Mandy? We won't have time for pre-game warm-ups. And the players will have to dress on the bus since there isn't going to be time once we get to the arena." At the smug look on her assistant's face, she said loudly, "Do you even care how this screw-up affects the team?" She struggled to bring the volume of her voice lower so it wouldn't be overheard in the locker room next door, where the players were preparing for the last practice before they left town.

"I'm sorry, Pat." Mandy smiled, but her eyes challenged the coach. "If you don't like the way I schedule, maybe you should take more time telling me exactly what you need. Perhaps," the assistant leered at the furious coach, "tonight, dinner for just the two of us. There's going to be a full moon."

Pat leaned forward, placing her hands palm down on Mandy's desk. She glared into the woman's eyes, a sneer growing on her lips. "It's never, *ever* going to happen, Mandy. So get *your* head out of *my* ass and do the job Mac is paying you to do."

"Mac doesn't seem to have any problem with the way I do my job."

"She will when she hears about this." Pat eased herself off the desk, her sneer replaced by a grin. "One thing you haven't figured out yet is Mac expects to win, and she doesn't take kindly to anything *or* any*one* getting in the way of that."

"Whatever." Mandy shrugged, unconcerned about her aunt's reaction to the situation since she doubted Pat would even mention it to the team owner. The coach hadn't run to Mac before; there was no reason to believe she would now.

Pat stormed into the locker room. Marcie, running through some plays on the marker board with the point guards, judged her head coach's mood immediately. "Okay, get out on the floor," she told the players. "We'll continue this out there."

The players looked at Pat and, immediately deciding being out of the room was best for them, jumped to their feet and ran out of the room.

Sherry hung back. She could tell that Pat was upset about something and wondered if there was anything she could do to help. She took a half step toward Pat but stopped when the coach shot her a warning look.

Despite the look of concern on her player's face, Pat knew it wasn't the time for Sherry to approach her. With a slight shake of her head, she forced a smile onto her face to reassure the player.

Sherry took the signal for what it was and turned to trot out of the room.

Marcie hadn't missed the exchange between coach and player, but let it pass without comment. "Problems?" she asked Pat.

"Yeah. Mandy booked us on a four o'clock flight."

"I thought the game started at eight."

"It does."

"Damn, Pat." Marcie's voice rose. "That doesn't give us time—"

"To do much more than walk into the arena and start the game. I know."

"What are you going to do about it?" Marcie didn't understand why the coach hadn't yet talked to Mac about the crap her niece was pulling. Anyone else would have and long before now.

"Not much I can do about it. We travel tomorrow; there isn't time to change flights." Missoula had a limited number of flights in and out of town each day and most left full, so it was next to impossible to change plans so close to the day of departure. "Is everyone out on the floor?"

"Yes."

"Okay." Pat moved toward the door to the corridor. "Let's break the news to them."

"Any word on Kinsey?" Marcie asked as she followed the coach.

"Nothing new. Her doc wants her to quit; she wants to play."

"Guess we should know more after these next two games."

Pat's lips twitched into a smile. She hoped Kinsey could play, she really did. But the prospect of a certain rookie guard getting some playing time was also quite appealing.

"When do you plan to do as I asked?" Mandy asked Dawn. They were dressing after sharing a late morning shower.

"What?" Dawn was sitting on the edge of the bed, naked from the waist up, pulling on her socks.

"Sherry. Remember? You were supposed to get rid of her. Today's our first game, and that bitch is still on the team."

"So?"

"So? I told you I wanted her gone."

"Yeah, you did." Dawn leaned over to tie her shoes. "But you never said why."

"That doesn't matter. When do you plan to do it?"

"When I get around to it."

Mandy walked over and stood in front of her lover. "And that would be when?"

"Damn." Dawn flopped back on the bed. "Why the hell does it matter?"

"It just does." Mandy crawled onto the bed to lie on her side next to Dawn, bracing herself on an elbow. "You promised," she said in a silky voice. "I kept my promise, now you have to keep yours."

"I'm not sure I can." Dawn slipped a hand behind Mandy's head, pulling her down until her mouth was just inches from where her hand was drawing lazy patterns around

Dawn's breasts. Her lover didn't disappoint her; Mandy sucked an aroused nipple into her mouth. "I have plans, Mandy. And they can't happen if I'm sitting on the bench. Coach already said she'd bench me if I tried anything else with Sherry."

Mandy tried to lift her head to protest, but Dawn was too strong and held her in place. Sharp teeth bit down on sensitive flesh.

"Ow!" Dawn cried out. She shoved Mandy away from her and sat up, rubbing her breast. "Why the hell did you do that?"

"Who do you think you're playing with? I got you on the team, and all I've asked in return is for you to get rid of that bitch."

"Why?"

"It doesn't matter why. Just take care of it."

"I can't."

Mandy glared at Dawn. "What are these plans of yours? And why are they more important than me?"

"You have your secrets, I have mine." Dawn stood. "But I have to be able to play if they're going to happen. And pissing off Coach by taking out Sherry will only get me benched or kicked off the team. I can't afford that. So if you want Sherry off the team, do it yourself. Damn, this hurts," she said, still rubbing her breast. "It's going to be real fun playing tonight with my tit bruised. You dumb bitch." She stormed into the bathroom, slamming the door behind her.

"Shit!" Mandy grabbed a pillow and flung it across the room.

Mac strolled into Pat's office and took a seat in one of the two chairs in front of the desk. "Correct me if I'm wrong, but we do have a game this evening, do we not?"

"Yes," Pat answered, leaning back in her chair. Letting out a long breath, she waited for the inevitable questions.

Sensing a problem, Mac tensed. "Might I ask why you're sitting here, then?"

Pat indicated her paper-strewn desk. "Got some things to go over before the players arrive."

Mac frowned; it was obvious her coach wasn't going to lay things out for her. She was willing to play along for a while, but a very short while. "I suppose there's a reason why the team isn't here yet."

Pat looked at the clock on the office wall; it was a quarter past ten. If the team had had reservations on the noon flight, like she'd expected, they would be preparing to board the bus to the airport now.

"Bus won't be here to pick up the team until two-thirty. No point in them sitting around until then."

"Two-thirty?" Mac asked, the muscles in her neck beginning to twitch. When Pat nodded, the twitch became an ache. "The game starts at eight. Why the hell is the bus picking you up at two-thirty?"

"Because..." Pat stiffened. She wanted to tell Mac just how upset she was with being saddled with the owner's niece who'd had only one thing on her mind since she'd first walked into the Cougars' offices. And that one thing was something Pat was sick and tired of having to guard against. But she knew this wasn't the time. "Mandy booked us on the four o'clock flight," she said as calmly as she could under the circumstances.

"She what! Why? That doesn't make sense," Mac sputtered as she calculated the timetable in her head. "Hell, Pat, that barely leaves you any warm-up time before the game."

"That's right." Pat looked at the team owner. "Nor does it leave time for the team dressing, getting taped, or going over pre-game adjustments. We'll have to do all that on the plane. It's a nasty situation, any way you look at it."

"Mandy knows how important it is for the team to arrive well before a game. Why would she do this?"

"I suggest you ask her."

"You told her what you wanted, right?"

Pat reached for her desk file drawer, pulled it open, and removed a piece of paper from one of hanging folders. She flipped the paper across her desk. "Those are the instructions I gave her."

Mac picked the paper up and read it. "Damn, what's the matter with her?"

Pat again thought about telling the owner the motivation behind her niece's behavior but thought better of it. It was something Mac could discover on her own. There was no reason for her to get any more involved in it than Mandy had already made her.

The women heard someone enter the outer office. Moments later, Pat's assistant flounced through the doorway into the coach's office.

Great timing, Mandy, Pat thought.

"Pat," Mandy said, her voice sugary sweet, "you didn't make coffee this morning, you naughty girl. You know I can't start my day without a good cup of coffee."

Pat didn't respond. Instead she looked at Mac, clearly expecting the woman to handle the situation.

"Good morning, Mandy." Mac swiveled the chair around to face her niece, who was arriving more than two hours later than her work schedule required.

"Mac?" Mandy was surprised by the sudden appearance of her aunt. "Pat, you should have warned me the big, bad boss was here." She laughed uneasily, trying to make light of her aunt unexpectedly overhearing her inappropriate flirting with the coach.

Pat couldn't keep the grin off her face as Mandy glared at her.

"Mandy," Mac was seemingly oblivious to the exchange between the two women, "I understand there was a mix-up in the plane reservations."

"Oh, yes," Mandy answered quickly, happy her aunt hadn't pounced on her comments to the coach. "I misunderstood Pat's *needs.*" She purred the word. "I'm sorry the flight is so late, but by the time Pat told me about it, it was just too late to change things."

"I see," Mac said noncommittally. "Well, I'm sure you have things to do, Coach." Mac stood up. "So why don't we continue this conversation in my office, Mandy?"

Mandy looked shocked. "I don't know what else we could possibly have to talk about, Auntie. I told you, Pat gave me the wrong information."

"Yes, I heard you. Now let's go to my office and leave the coach to her job of getting my Cougars ready for their first win." Mac turned to Pat. "Good luck, Coach. I wish I could be there tonight, but it looks like I've got some business to attend to here."

"But," Mandy protested, "I booked you a ticket. You go to all the games."

"I try to," Mac said, turning to leave the office. "Come on, Mandy."

"Auntie," Mandy hurried after her aunt, "I have things to do myself before the bus comes."

"Oh, I think you'll have plenty of time to take care of them, since you won't be going either."

"I won't be going?" Mandy's voice rose into a high-pitched whine. "But, Auntie..."

Pat snickered as she watched Mandy change from a confident sexual predator into a spoiled little girl as she followed her aunt out of the office, still arguing her case.

Sherry, as usual, was the first player to arrive at the arena. She stood staring at the neatly folded uniform that had been placed on the chair in front of her locker. Picking up the gold jersey, she held it in her hands, enjoying the smooth feel of the nylon fabric against her skin. Turning the jersey over, she smiled at the name GALLAGHER stitched in brilliant royal blue lettering across the back. Royal blue trimming bordered the drop neck and armholes, and a royal blue side panel ran from the armholes down the side of the jersey. The shorts were also gold, with a continuation of the side panel of royal blue down the outside of both legs and a snarling cougar on the front of the left leg.

Sherry wasted no time in changing into the uniform she had, up to that very moment, only dreamed of wearing. Then, too nervous to sit and wait for the rest of the team to arrive, she trotted out to the court to practice free throws. She was surprised to see the coach sitting a few rows up in the stands near the mouth of the corridor, her eyes closed and her head slowly weaving from side to side. As she stood watching, Pat seemed to sense her presence and opened her eyes.

"Hi." Sherry smiled uncomfortably, not sure what she might have interrupted.

Pat smiled back. "Hi, yourself. Free throws?"

"Um, yeah." Sherry moved a few steps closer. "Since we won't have time for any practice when we get there, I thought I'd do it here."

"Wish a few more of the players took free throws as seriously as you," Pat grumbled. At least half the players on the roster averaged less than 70 percent completion from the charity line, and as far as Pat was concerned, that was about 20 percentage points too low. As much as she tried to convince them they needed more practice, they would do only what was demanded by their coach and no more.

"Um." Sherry wasn't sure how she should respond to the coach's comment. "Mind if I ask what you were doing?" Sherry asked hesitantly.

Pat shrugged. "You'll think it's silly."

"No, I won't."

"I miss playing," Pat explained, her tone low, revealing her pain at the loss of something she truly loved. "But I miss it the most on game days. I used to get so jazzed before a game." As she spoke, a far away look entered Pat's eyes as she relived a past she would never experience again. "I'd come to the arena hours before anyone else and sit in the stands and just imagine what the game would be like. I'd think about the players I'd be facing and visualize how they might respond in certain situations, and I'd come up with ways I could counter them. I'd play the whole game in my head..." Her voice trailed off. "Stupid, huh?"

"No." Sherry shook her head. "Is that what you were doing? Visualizing it as if you would be playing tonight?"

"Yeah." Pat bit her bottom lip. "I really miss playing," she said, her voice on the verge of cracking. She had never talked to anyone about this, and she wasn't sure why it felt so good to be telling Sherry her secret. "I guess it's my way of staying in the game. I'm not ready to let it go."

The look on Pat's face was so heartrending that it was almost too painful for Sherry to see. She wanted to rush to Pat's side and wrap her arms around her, but she knew she couldn't. Shouldn't. "Are you okay?" she asked, her voice scarcely above a whisper.

"Yeah." Pat pursed her lips together in a sad smile. "Like I said, game day is the worst."

"Can I do anything?" She wanted to ask Pat why she no longer played the game. After all, Dawn was right when she said many players had suffered the same type of injury and had returned to the court after surgery. She wondered what it was that kept the woman from playing the game that she obviously missed so much.

"Go on, do your practice shots." Pat stood. "I'd better go make sure everyone else is showing up. First game usually means at least one person is late for the bus, and today we don't have any time to spare." She slowly descended the few steps to the arena floor as Sherry walked back to the middle of the court. "Uh, Sherry," she called.

"Yeah, Coach?"

"Thanks."

"You're welcome," Sherry said, but when she turned around to look, the coach had already disappeared into the corridor.

Mandy stood in front of the wall of glass in Mac's office waiting for her aunt to finish a phone call that had interrupted their own conversation. She saw Pat come out of the corridor and walk into the stands where she took a seat several rows up from the arena floor. As she watched, the coach seemed to go into some kind of trance. Mandy wondered what she was doing but really didn't care. She was about to turn away from the window when she saw Sherry emerge from the corridor.

Now very interested in what was happening below her, she was frustrated at being unable to hear the women's conversation or make out their facial expressions. But their body language seem to indicate that whatever they were talking about, it was more than just a casual discussion between coach and player.

Mandy frowned. Why didn't Pat ever respond to her in that friendly manner? Mandy smiled. Maybe there was something going on between the coach and player? Perhaps there was another way to get rid of Sherry. She would have to dig further into the women's relationship. If Dawn refused take care of Sherry on the court, maybe she could get rid of the guard herself another way.

Mandy turned around when she heard her aunt end the call. If she could get this reprimand wrapped up in the next few minutes, she'd still be able to catch the bus to the airport. And then she could talk to Dawn about Sherry. But Mac spoke before Mandy had a chance.

"Sit down, Mandy," Mac instructed. She continued without waiting for the girl to comply. "Do you understand your position with the Cougars organization?" When her niece didn't respond, she said, "Well?"

Mandy was confused, not at all expecting this line of questioning. "Um, yes," Mandy answered.

"Then you understand that you are to handle certain arrangements so that Pat can do what I pay her to do, and that's to coach. I don't pay my coaches to make airline reservations, Mandy." Mac's tone was all business. As far as she was concerned she was talking to an employee, niece or not. "I pay you to do that."

"But, Auntie," Mandy whined, failing to read the businesslike attitude.

"Don't '*but, Auntie*' me." Mac's tone was harsh. "Do you realize that your incompetence could very well cost us the game tonight? The team will be lucky to get to the arena before tip-off. Do you know what will happen if they don't? We forfeit, that's what. We start the season with a big fat one in the losing column." Her anger and her voice were rising as she spoke. "I don't accept numbers in the losing column, Mandy. Losing teams don't sell tickets. Losing teams don't become champions. Losing teams are *not* what the Cougars are. Damn it, Mandy, if we lose tonight because of you, you can kiss your cushy little job goodbye. Niece or no niece, if we lose, I'm going to boot your ass outta here so fast you won't know what hit you. You got that?"

Mandy could only nod; she had never seen her aunt so mad. Maybe playing games with the team's travel arrangements hadn't been such a good idea. But how else was she to get the very desirable coach to pay her some attention?

"Pat gave you a list of games and her travel requirements. Did you take care of them?"

"Yes, but—"

"All of them?"

"Yes."

"I want to see what arrangements you made."

Mandy smiled. She'd have to go down to her office to get the information; she'd be able to talk to Dawn. She bounced to her feet. "I'll go down and print it off."

"Why?"

"Why what? I thought you said you wanted to see—"

"Mandy." Mac looked at her niece, trying to figure out what she was thinking. "I assume you have the information on file in your computer."

"Um, yes."

"All our computers are networked. You can bring the file up on my computer; you don't have to go to your office."

SHIT, Mandy screamed in her head. *I forgot all about that.* Now she really had to get back to her office and fast. If Mac ever read her email files, she'd be dead. Dawn wasn't the only player she'd had relations with. And then there were all the emails she'd sent to Pat suggesting things she'd like to do with her in bed. She winced. *SHIT, SHIT, SHIT.*

Mac was a little concerned about her niece's sudden pallor. "Is something wrong, Mandy?"

"I'm fine," Mandy stammered. "I just thought of something I need to do." She moved around Mac's desk to her computer. After a series of keystrokes, the file of travel reservations appeared on Mac's screen.

Mac took a few minutes to compare Mandy's file with Pat's instructions while her niece paced nervously about the office.

"This is not acceptable, Mandy. Almost none of these meet Pat's requests."

"Um, it's the best I could do."

"No, it isn't." Mac glared. "I want you to take this list," she pushed the paper with the coach's notes across her desk, "and go down to your office and reschedule every one of these to Pat's specifications. Then send me a copy so I can look at it."

"Okay." Mandy glanced at her watch. *Still time to catch the bus.* "I'll take care of it just as soon as we get back from Denver."

"No, you'll take care of it now. I want the new itineraries on my desk before you leave today."

"But—"

"Mandy, I'm not kidding." Mac was more than a little concerned that her niece didn't seem to understand the seriousness of the situation. "You are to take care of this today. I'm not going to lose games because you screwed up the travel plans. Now either you do this, and do it right, or I'll hire someone who can." *And my sister can pawn her worthless brat off on someone else in the family.* She kept that thought to herself.

"All right, I'm going." Mandy glowered. "But I don't think it's fair I don't get to go to Denver with the team."

"There'll be other games, Mandy," Mac assured the disgruntled girl. "This is more important right now."

Mandy walked to the office door without another word. Once out of Mac's sight, she quickened her steps. Maybe if she hurried, she could catch Dawn in the locker room. There was no way she'd be able to talk to her lover if she'd already boarded the bus.

When Mandy didn't board the bus, Dawn asked Marcie about the administrative assistant and was told that she wouldn't be making the trip.

"Why not?" Dawn asked, annoyed.

Marcie looked at the player quizzically. It really shouldn't concern any player if Mandy traveled with the team or not. But she was aware there was some kind of relationship between the owner's niece and this particular player. She wondered how much Dawn was willing to disclose. "Any particular reason you need to know?"

"Forget it." Dawn tossed her bag on a seat and slumped down beside it. "Just asking a question. You don't need to make a federal case out of it." She glanced to the front of the bus, saw Pat watching her, and quickly looked away. *Bet she's got something to do with it,* she told herself. *Damn, looks like it's going to be a long night in Denver.* Dawn groaned inwardly. *And I was so looking forward to that room with the hot tub you said you were booking for us. You better have a darn good reason for this, Mandy.*

The Cougars watched anxiously as the bus approached a side entrance at the Denver Pioneer Memorial Arena less than a half hour before the scheduled tip-off. A representative of the Pioneer organization was pacing on the sidewalk next to the building.

Pat was already standing at the top of the steps, waiting impatiently for the driver to pull to a stop. As soon as the doors swung open, she hurried down the steps. "Sorry," she apologized.

"I take it the flight was late," the Pioneer official said, stepping back out of the way of the rush of players scrambling off the bus.

"Flight was on time." Pat watched the players exit the bus and gather near the door to the building. "Traffic was bad."

"Usually is this time of night," the official said. "Door's open," he told Pat and the players. "Locker room is second door on the right."

One of the players pulled open the outside door, and the team swarmed inside. "Thanks." Pat nodded to the Pioneer's greeter as she hurried after her players.

"Tip-off is in eighteen minutes," the man called after her.

"We're ready," Pat called back, hoping it was true.

She was glad she'd had the players wear their uniforms and warm-ups on the plane. Lizzie and her staff had been able to get most of the players taped on the bus ride from the airport, so the team was ready to play as soon as they clambered off the bus.

"All right, drop your bags, and let's get out on the floor," Marcie instructed as soon as the team entered the locker room. "Grab some balls, and get in as much practice as you can."

Pat didn't even bother to enter the locker room, walking right past it to the end of the corridor and the court. As soon as she heard the pre-game commotion of the spectators and the pounding music being piped through the PA system, she could feel her palms sweating and her heart racing. It wasn't long before some in the crowd recognized her, and a wall of cheers began to swell, surging around the arena. She might be the coach of the opposing team, but she was still a well-respected and universally loved player of the game. A smile formed on her face, and she took the time to enjoy the moment.

Kelley stepped up beside Pat. "We're ready, Coach."

Pat turned to see the Cougars huddled at the end of the tunnel, waiting for her signal to take the court. "Then let's get out there," she told her players.

The players let out a roar as they raced for the opposite end of the floor and the basket they would claim as their own for the first half of the game. A few of them snatched balls off the ball racks they ran past, and the severely shortened pre-game drills began.

Sherry ran onto the court with the rest of the team, but when she cleared the corridor, her steps slowed until she came to a stop a few steps in front of her coach. She stared up at the row upon row of occupied seats circling the court. "Whoa." She gawked, having never seen so many people in one place before. Her college team had been well supported but had never had more than three thousand fans attend any one game. As her eyes scanned the wall of faces, she guessed there were probable at least five times that number in attendance.

Pat went to Sherry and nudged her forward. "Scary, isn't it?"

"Downright frightening," Sherry murmured, continuing to stare as she walked. "I'm not sure I can do this." The noise inside the building was deafening. "There's so many of them."

Pat grinned at the look on her player's face — amazement, fear, shock, and awe, all rolled up into one. She remembered the first time she'd walked out to play in the NCAA tournament and had felt the same emotions and doubts Sherry was feeling now. "Don't worry about them," Pat told the nervous player, having to shout a little to be heard. "You won't be playing against the people up in the seats. Just worry about what's happening on the court. That's all you care about."

Sherry turned away from the fans to look at her coach. "But the noise..."

"You focus on the game and only the game; you won't even hear them. Come on." She went over to where Marcie and Kelley were rounding up the team.

Rolling Pat's advice over in her head, Sherry trotted over to join the team. At first she didn't think it could be possible to block out the crowd, but remembering that Pat had played in front of crowds this large for most of her college career and that the coach had played for the national title in front of crowds many times this size, she started to believe. *If you did it, Coach,* she said to herself as she joined the huddle, *then I guess it can be done.*

The PA system came alive with the voice of the game announcer starting the buildup to the player introductions. As was normal before most games, the home players were introduced to thunderous applause while the visitors received mostly boos and jeers intermixed with a smattering of supportive cheers from their fans who were in attendance.

Pat stood on the sideline, waiting for the coaches to be introduced so she could shake the hand of the Pioneer coach. Then the game would be on. She heard her name and met the other coach in front of the scorer's table.

"Glad you could make it." The Pioneer coach laughed as he offered his hand. "I was beginning to think you were just going to hand me my first victory of the season."

Pat smiled at her friend. "Wishful thinking."

Roland Sweever accepted the Pioneer head coaching position the same year Pat started her career with the Cougars. They had met and gotten acquainted at the numerous off-season league functions all coaches were expected to attend. It hadn't taken long for them to realize they shared an offbeat sense of humor. Before long they had developed a friendship, and the Pioneer coach was one of the few people in the game Pat felt comfortable seeking advice from.

Pat firmly grasped the outstretched hand, squeezing it firmly. "Good luck tonight, Rolle," she said, using the man's hated nickname.

Sneering good-naturedly, Sweever yanked his hand free. "You should have stayed on the plane, Pat. But since you're here, we're going to wipe the floor with you."

"Nah." Pat grinned. "It doesn't look that dirty." Not waiting to hear his reply, she returned to her team. Pat glanced up at the scoreboard hanging above mid-court; she didn't have much time. "Listen up," she yelled, clapping her hands to get her players' attention. "They're going to expect us to come out slow. We got here late, had no time for practice or warm-ups, and they expect us to be sluggish. But we're not going to give them that satisfaction." She grinned wickedly. "We're going to come out running. Kinsey, Pete, I want you pushing the ball up court. Terry, Val, Tonie, you'll have to muscle for position under the basket, but you've got size on them, use it. I want to see everybody running and making crisp passes. And rebounding, lots of it. We've got lots of talent on the bench, so if I think you're tired or dogging it, I'm pulling you. Got it?" She looked each of her starting players in the eye. "And if you need a break, say so."

The referee came over and warned, "Coach, we need your players on the court."

"Okay, let's get out there," Pat told her starters, who immediately ran to take their positions for the tip-off. Too energized to sit, Pat walked down the sideline in front of the rest of the team to the end of the bench where she would watch the tip-off. She noticed all the reserve players except Dawn were standing as they waited for the game to begin, most bouncing in place to release some tension. Dawn was slumped on the bench, hardly paying any attention at all to the activity on the court. Pat walked past the sullen player without comment and then turned to watch the game.

Terry waited in the mid-court circle while Val, Pete, and Tonie jockeyed for position around it. Kinsey faded back to midway between the circle and the key in front of the Pioneer basket.

The ball was tossed high in the air. Terry leaped the highest, tapping the ball back over her head to Kinsey. Kinsey was already moving when the ball reached her. Without breaking stride, she knocked the ball to the floor and dribbled up court. Pete broke for the right side of the court while Val, Tonie, and Terry took up positions on the left.

Terry stopped at the top of the key with her back to the basket, legs planted and arms spread wide as she screened her defender from the developing play. Tonie went deep into the key, drawing two defenders with her, then cut to the right side of the court, crossing paths with Val who was moving across the key with another defender in tow.

The three Pioneer players, confused as to which of the Cougars to continue guarding, got jammed up in the key.

Kinsey snapped a pass to Val as soon as she came open. Val took a step toward the sideline looking to flip the ball to Pete, who was moving in to take advantage of the screen Val was setting. Seeing that two of the Pioneer players had released from the key and were charging toward Val, Pete planted her feet and popped into the air, catching Val's pass on her way up. Her jump shot dropped through the net with barely a whisper.

Cougars 2 Pioneers 0

Pat allowed herself a smile. The play had taken less than fifteen seconds, and the confusion in the Pioneer defense confirmed that they weren't prepared for the Cougars' quick start. She watched as Tonie, Val, and Terry ran to the opposite end of the court to set up their defense. Pete stayed to guard the inbounds pass, and Kinsey hovered around mid-court to help press the Pioneer guards.

Pete almost stole the inbound ball when the Pioneer player was lazy with the pass. As she played tight defense on the guard moving the ball up court, Kinsey moved in to add more pressure. The guard, uncomfortable with the double team, tried to pass to her trailing teammate, but Kinsey anticipated the move and slapped the pass out of the air. Pete chased down the loose ball and rifled a pass to Kinsey, who was racing for the basket.

Kinsey easily out distanced the two Pioneer players, who were caught flatfooted by the rapid turn of events. With the ball back in her hands, Kinsey flipped up a lay-up as she ran under the basket.

Cougars 4 Pioneers 0

"Yes," Pat hissed under her breath.

"Time out!" Coach Sweever screamed at an official, who whistled a stoppage of the play.

Pat greeted the players as they trotted to the sideline where they were met by their celebrating teammates. "Nice work. That's a great start, but we've still got a lot of game left. Pete, Kinsey, I want you to keep up the pressure. Now that they've seen it, they're going to come out expecting it. Let's not disappoint them. They're going to try and pass it up court to avoid our press. So, Val, keep your eyes open. If you think you can snag a pass, go for it."

Val nodded. "Right, Coach."

A loud buzzer announced the end of the time out.

"Keep it up, ladies," Pat encouraged as they returned to the court. When she walked down the bench to reclaim her spot near the corner of the court, she noted that Dawn had never left her seat during the team huddle. She pursed her lips together, glaring at the player.

Dawn didn't seem to notice her coach's displeasure. She stretched her arms over her head, her mouth opening wide in a yawn.

Pat stood in front of the troublesome player. "Game boring you, Dawn?"

Dawn shrugged, not at all caring whether the coach liked her attitude or not. "Most do, 'less I'm playing." The trip had been a disaster from the start. First, Mandy didn't make the trip. Then, all the activity on the plane as Pat went over game plans meant she couldn't sleep like she'd planned, and the long night before spent with Mandy was starting to catch up with her. Then the long bus ride from the airport. And to top it all off, she was sitting on the bench instead of playing.

Pat bent down to look Dawn in the eyes. "Your time on the bench is to be spent observing. It is a time for you to learn what's expected of you when, and *if,* you ever get into a game. I strongly suggest you bag the attitude and get with the program. And quickly." She glared at the player, her jaw so tight she thought it might break just by moving it to speak.

Dawn glared back at her coach.

"You have something on your mind you want to say?" Pat challenged.

Dawn thought about it but backed down. "No."

"Good." Pat leaned in closer. "This is your last warning, Montgomery. Next time, I'm throwing you off the team." She straightened up and turned to see what was happening on the court.

Frowning, Dawn stared at Pat's back, ignoring the action on the floor.

"Why do you do that?" Latesha asked when Pat moved away moments later. She was sitting next to Dawn and had heard the exchange between the player and coach.

"Do what?" Dawn snapped at the black woman.

"Act like you don't want to be here." Latesha had played college ball for Old Dominion and had worked hard to impress the pro scouts. Receiving her invitation to Cougar tryout camp was a dream come true, and she was puzzled as to why Dawn appeared so indifferent to being on the team. "You've acted like you've had a stick up your ass since you showed up for camp. I don't get it. You've got a chance to play for one of the best teams in the league, and you're pissing off Coach like you want her to cut you. Why?"

"Maybe you like sitting on the bench, but I should be out there." Dawn indicated the court with a toss of her head.

"You've got to *earn* being out there." Latesha laughed derisively. "And you're a long way from that." A whistle blew on the court, and she stood to meet the players returning for the break. "A real long way," she said before joining the rest of the team.

Dawn slowly got to her feet and shuffled to the back of the group huddled around Pat. She glanced up at the scoreboard; her teammates held a slight lead.

Cougars 11 Pioneers 8

"You're looking really good out there," Pat was telling the starters. "Let's keep the pressure on. Tonie, I need to see more from you on the boards, okay?"

The player nodded. "Got it, Coach."

"Good. Let's go." Pat sent the starters back out onto the court.

The first team was on the floor the remainder of the first half, and when the buzzer announced the end of play for the period, the scoreboard showed them with a comfortable lead.

Cougars 47 Pioneers 32

"All right, settle down," Pat instructed. "I don't want to spend any more time in here than necessary. We need to get back out there and get in some of the practice we missed before the game. Especially from the free-throw line." She looked down at a sheet of statistics Kelley had handed her. "Six for 14 isn't going to cut it. We can't waste those opportunities, ladies." She frowned. "Okay, any injuries or problems I need to know about?" She didn't bother to look over to the side of the locker room where Lizzie was using elastic bandages to wrap bags of ice around Kinsey's knees. When no one said anything, the coach continued.

"Listen, things have been going well for us," Pat told her players. "But you can bet they're going to come out ready to play, so we can't get lazy. We're going to keep pressing. They haven't come up with a way to handle that yet, and until they do, we keep it up. I want more movement around the basket, no standing." She looked at Terry, who had been trapped more than once by the Pioneer defenders because she had stopped moving.

Terry nodded, acknowledging the coach's reprimand and underlying warning.

"We'll start the second half with the same five on the floor, but I'm going to start rotating the starters out." She looked at the reserves. "Rookies, when I send you in, don't try anything fancy. I just want you to get the feel of being out there. Your job is to hold the lead. If things start to get ugly, the starters go back in, understand?" Receiving nods from all, including Dawn, she continued. "Sherry, get with Pete and find out what to expect from their guards."

Dawn's head snapped up at the mention of Sherry's name, but she said nothing, content to simply sneer in Sherry's direction.

"Anything to add?" Pat asked her assistant coaches.

"Yes." Kelley spoke up. "Tonie, you're still getting boxed out under the basket. Before you go out there, I want to see you, Ashley, and Stacy," she told the post players. "Let's come up with a way to prevent that."

"Good." Pat nodded. "All right, get out and get some practice. Stay loose."

Pat waited until the players had run out of the locker room before walking over to sit next to Kinsey.

The guard did her best to hide her pain, but her coach caught the grimace before she could extinguish it.

"I'm not going to ask, Kinsey," Pat said, rubbing her own aching knee. "I know you hurt."

"I'll be ready to play, Coach."

Pat nodded. "Season is long, K. It's only going to get worse."

"You telling me to quit?" Kinsey asked, her eyes reflecting the anguish she was suffering over the prospect.

"No."

Kinsey waited for the coach to say more, but Pat remained silent. Finally she couldn't stand the silence any longer. "How long do I have, Coach?"

"The Seattle game," Pat told her. "I'll need to make a decision before our first season game."

"I can play, Coach." Kinsey almost cried when she said the words, she wanted so much for them to be true.

"Then do it." Pat reached out and rested her hand on top of Kinsey's arm. "If you can, the position is yours." She gently squeezed the guard's shoulder.

"Thanks, Coach."

"You earned it, K." Pat stood. "Get out there in time for the second half. I want you at point."

"You got it, Coach." Kinsey grinned. The coach's support meant a lot to her, and she didn't want to do anything to make Pat regret giving her a chance.

As the starters took the floor at the start of the second half, Sherry returned to her place on the bench. Just the thought of getting into the game was making her so anxious, she was having trouble sitting still. She sat on the edge of the bench, her legs twitching with nervous energy.

Standing at the end of the bench, Pat watched Sherry, wondering if the guard would shake her teeth loose. She walked back and sat next to her restless player. "You want to slow down some." She smiled at Sherry. "You're bouncing so much, I'm starting to get seasick."

"Sorry, Coach." Sherry flushed, forcing her legs to remain still. "I'm just a little nervous, I guess."

"I know." Pat softened her tone. "But try to keep that energy for when you're out there; that's when you're going to need it."

"I'll try."

"Good. I'm going to send you in with Pete. I want you on point."

Sherry was surprised that the more experienced player wouldn't be handling the key position. "Are you sure, Coach?"

"I'm sure. You can do this, Sherry." Pat settled a calming hand on the guard's knee.

Sherry's sharp intake of breath wasn't caused by the thought of taking over the responsibility of the point guard position; it was the feel of the warm hand against her bare skin that caused her reaction.

Pat slowly removed her hand, wondering why she had put it there in the first place and why she didn't want to remove it now that she had. "Um." She knew she wanted to say something but had forgotten what.

"I'll, uh..." Sherry placed her hand on the patch of skin Pat's hand had warmed. "I'll be ready, Coach. Um, whenever... Yeah, whenever you are."

"Yeah. Whenever I am. Yeah, ready," Pat mumbled as she stood watching the game with unseeing eyes.

A buzzer announced a break in play and broke Pat's spell.

"Sherry, get in there, and watch out for No. 17. She's quicker than she looks."

Sherry ran to the scorer's table. "Coach said for me to play point," she told Pete, trotting out on the court next to her.

Pete grinned easily. "It's yours." As long as she was playing, she didn't care what position she took. "And Sherry..."

"Yes?"

"Relax." Pete smiled. "You'll do fine. Coach wouldn't put you in if she thought different."

"Thanks. I hope you're right, on both counts." Sherry glanced up at the scoreboard.

Cougars 55 Pioneers 40

"Just hold them, huh?"

"Just hold them," Pete assured her.

"Cougar ball, end line," called one of the trio of officials.

Pete trotted to the spot the official was indicating and waited for him to put the ball into play.

Sherry bounced in place as she waited for play to resume. When the official tossed Pete the ball, Sherry sprang into action. She sprinted for the end of the court, running in a wide arc that took her directly in front of Pete. Her defender was caught off guard by her quick movement, and she was able to pluck Pete's pass out of the air uncontested. By the time her defender caught up with her, she was almost to mid-court. Running the same play Kinsey had set up at the start of the game, Sherry dribbled across the line as Pete ran past her on the right.

The Pioneers were ready this time, and when Latesha and Tonie ran their crossing pattern through the key, their defenders smoothly made the necessary switch in their defensive coverage.

Sherry saw that the play wasn't going to work: Latesha was covered, and another defender had come out to pick up Pete. She had to do something. With the Pioneer players sagging off to the right side in anticipation of the Cougars' play, Terry stood at the top of the key relatively unguarded. Sherry snapped a pass to Terry. Realizing their mistake, the Pioneer players adjusted to stop the post player from taking an easy stroll down the lane. Sherry ran around the back of Terry and down the left side of the key, drawing even more of the defense to that side. "Pete," she barked at Terry as soon as the other guard's defender dropped off.

Terry took one step toward the basket before flipping a no-look pass out to the open guard, who quickly popped into the air for a short jump shot.

Sherry smiled as the ball dropped through the net. *That felt good. Maybe holding them won't be so hard after all.*

Cougars 57 Pioneers 40

An instant later, if Sherry could have taken back her exultant thought, she would have. The player Pat had warned her about grabbed the ball before it hit the floor after the score and flipped it to a teammate waiting out of bounds beyond the end line. A split second later, the ball was flying through the air in the direction of mid-court, where it dropped back into the hands of Pioneer player No. 17.

Sherry raced after the ball and player, but before she could catch her the ball dropped through the net at the other end of the court.

Cougars 57 Pioneers 43

"Welcome to the big leagues, rookie," No. 17 said as she backpedaled past Sherry.

Sherry looked for Pat, sure that her coach would be wanting to say something to her. She was surprised to see Pat standing calmly on the sidelines, her lips slightly upturned in the beginnings of an "I told you so" smile. Sherry grinned, mouthing the word "oops" as she shrugged her shoulders at her coach.

Sherry played another few minutes before Pat sent Wendy, another reserve guard, in to replace her. Kinsey was sent in at the same time to replace Pete.

Pete grinned as she trotted toward the bench with the rookie. "Told ya, you'd do okay."

"Except for that open 3-pointer I gave up." Sherry shook her head.

"Lucky shot." Pete laughed. "Normally, she can't hit anything outside twelve feet."

"Great night for her to get lucky," Sherry grumbled.

"Hey, you didn't let it get to you," Pete told her. "She didn't get past you again, and that's what's important."

Pat smiled at the returning players. "You did good out there, Sherry. You, too, Pete."

"Gee, thanks, Coach," Pete retorted, grabbing a cup of water and emptying it.

Cougars 83 Pioneers 74

With less than three minutes left in the game, Pat pulled an obviously limping Kinsey out of the game and sent Sherry in. She also sent Dawn in to replace Tonie.

"'Bout time," Dawn griped when she got to the scorer's table. "Don't get in my way out there, rookie," she told Sherry, bumping into her when they were waved onto the court by the referee.

Sherry let Dawn run past without responding to her comment or the physical contact. She had too much to worry about without taking on her own teammate: No. 17 was waiting at the other end of the court. She trotted to within a few feet of the player, shifting easily from one foot to the other while she waited for play to resume. She wasn't really looking forward to the next few minutes of play. The Pioneer player never stopped moving. Even though she'd manage to contain her pretty well before, she knew it was only a matter of time before No. 17 broke free. She pressed her lips together, determined not to let that happen.

The whistle blew, and play was on. The teams traded baskets, with neither being able to make much of a change in the number of points that separated them on the scoreboard. The Pioneers had control of the ball, but a badly directed pass sent the ball out of bounds and turned possession over to the Cougars.

With play stopped, Pat wondered if she should take Sherry out; the rookie was beginning to look tired. She glanced up at the clock — less than forty seconds remained to play — and decided to leave her in.

Pete took the ball from the official and flipped it to Sherry, who started up court, closely guarded by Pioneer 17. The play Pat had signaled her to run called for Dawn to set a screen at the top of the key. Sherry dribbled straight for her teammate, Pioneer 17 dogging her every step. She caught the movement of Pete running up the opposite side of the court, her defender playing well off of her. Pulling up short, she surprised Pioneer 17, who ran past her. Free of her defender, she snapped the ball to Pete.

Pete slowed her dribble to allow Dawn time to set the screen, something the center seemed to be having difficulty doing.

Seeing Dawn struggling to rid herself of her defender, Val moved into the key, taking her own defender with her and drawing another out of position. With the key jammed with Pioneer players and Dawn still jockeying for position, Val cut through the crowd, coming out at the top of the key, momentarily undefended. She planted her feet, back to the basket.

Pete fired the ball to Sherry, who was moving in fast to take advantage of Val's screen.

Sherry grabbed the pass, dribbling another couple of steps toward Val before pulling up for a 3-point attempt. Just as she prepared to release the ball, Pioneer 17 left her own feet.

In attempting to block the long shot, Pioneer 17 flew through the air. Her momentum carried her into Sherry, knocking the ball from her hands and the rookie to the floor.

Sherry landed hard. Whistles blew, stopping play as the Pioneer player was called for the foul.

"What the hell was that!" Pat shouted at the officials. She was several steps out on the court before Marcie and Kelley corralled her. "Let me go," Pat growled, as her assistant coaches struggled to pull her back to the bench. "That was an intentional foul!" she yelled at the officials over Marcie's shoulder.

"Pat, what's the matter with you?" Marcie yelled, standing her ground between the irate coach and the officials. "Back off before you get called for a technical."

"She's right, Coach." Kelley was having trouble holding the larger woman back. "Look, Sherry's okay. She's back up."

Pat looked over Marcie's shoulder to see Sherry walking to the free-throw stripe, apparently uninjured. The rookie was looking back over her shoulder at her coach with a look of dismay.

Sherry wondered why Pat seemed so upset by the contact. Even though she'd been knocked to the floor, it wasn't that bad a hit, and she hadn't been injured. The blow she'd taken from Dawn in practice had caused more damage. Her forehead was creased with concern as she watched Marcie and Kelley force Pat back to the bench.

"You okay?" Marcie asked, more than a little worried over Pat's unusual behavior.

"Yeah, I'm okay," Pat said, slowly moving backward.

"You need to get off the court, Coach," an official said as he approached the women.

Pat hastened her backward motion. "I'm off," she said when she felt the edge of the bench on the back of her legs.

The official stood watching a few seconds, deciding what to do, then turned back to the game without making any call against Pat.

The Pioneer fans wasted no time in strongly voicing their opinion about the non-call.

Pat dropped onto the bench as the ball was handed to Sherry for her first free-throw attempt. Marcie and Kelley moved down to the opposite end of the bench and sat down.

"What the hell was that about?" Marcie asked as Sherry made her first shot.

"Don't ask me," Kelley answered. "I've never seen her react that way before."

"It wasn't even that bad a hit."

"I know," Kelley said as the second free throw dropped through.

"Weird."

"Very."

"Wendy, in for Sherry." Pat readied the player sitting next to her without taking her eyes off Sherry as she prepared for her final free throw. Even with only a handful of seconds left to play, she wanted the rookie out of the game. Wendy hustled to the scorer's table.

The third free throw dropped true, and Sherry trotted to the bench, taking the spot Wendy had vacated.

Pat waited until play resumed before asking, "You okay?"

"Yes," Sherry assured her coach, very aware of the woman's reaction to the play. "She didn't hit me that hard. I'm fine. What about you?" The words were out before Sherry realized she was going to say them.

Pat looked at the rookie, considering whether she should answer the question or not. "I'm good." She grinned, embarrassed by her uncharacteristic outburst. "A little crazy, but good."

"Good." Sherry smiled.

The buzzer announced the end of the game.

Cougars 97 Pioneers 89

Pat followed the team off the court, measuring her steps to give the players time to celebrate when they reached the locker room. She also wanted a few moments to get control of her own emotions. Why had seeing Sherry take the hard blow caused her to react the way she had? Since the very first time she'd seen Sherry, she'd been doing things out of character, starting with giving her the invitation to tryout camp. Why? What was happening to her? As she tried to make sense out of it, Coach Sweever fell into step beside her.

"You know, that wasn't intended to be a cheap shot."

"Yeah, I know."

"I, uh..." Sweever hesitated. He wasn't sure if Pat meant what she said or not. "I don't think I've ever seen you react that way, Pat. I just wanted you to know — Crystal may play hard, but she's not a dirty player," he said in defense of his player.

Pat stopped, facing her friend. "Look, Roland. I..." She ran her fingers roughly through her hair. "I don't know what happened to me. I've never done that before and... Well, I just don't know why I did it tonight. Look, I'm sorry. I know it wasn't intentional."

"Okay, Pat." Sweever breathed out a sigh of relief. "As long as we're okay."

"We're fine." Pat nodded. "I've got to get to my team."

"Sure. Good game, Pat." Sweever watched his distracted friend walk away.

After a night in a hotel, the team rose early in order to catch their scheduled bus ride to the Denver airport. Then, because of the reservations arranged by Mandy, they were forced to sit and wait in the terminal for their flight to Missoula in the afternoon. Pat was furious, but there was nothing she could do but suffer along with the players. By the time the bus arrived in the parking lot at Cougar Arena, day was turning to night, and everyone was grateful that Pat had given them the next day off.

Pat waited for everyone to depart the bus before she stepped down to the pavement. Most of the players walked directly to their cars to head home for some much-needed rest. A few, including Sherry, were walking to the side door of the Cougar Arena. Pat felt her lips twitching into a smile as she watched the player enter the building.

Squealing tires broke the evening stillness. Pat glanced toward the end of the parking lot where Mandy's car was whip-tailing toward an exit.

"No doubt Dawn is with her," Marcie commented as she watched the car. She had been helping Lizzie and Kelley pull equipment bags out of the storage compartments under the bus.

Lizzie frowned as the car sped through an intersection just as the light changed to red. "The way Mandy drives, Dawn will be lucky to survive the season if she keeps hanging out with that one."

"I'm surprised Mac hasn't clipped her wings yet," Kelley said. "She's nothing but trouble."

"If Mac doesn't do something soon..." Marcie hefted a heavy bag onto her shoulder. Seeing the coach walking toward them, she didn't finish her thought.

"Let's get this stuff inside." Pat picked up a bag. Even though she agreed with what they were saying, she didn't like Mac being talked about in that way. "We have a team to coach," she told the women as she walked away. "Let Mac take care of the other stuff."

Marcie thought about saying something but was stopped by Kelley's hand on her arm and shake of her head.

"She's the coach, Marcie," Kelley said, bending down to lift a pair of bags off the ground. "She'll deal with Mandy and Dawn when the time comes. Until then, let's just do what she says."

"Let's hope she doesn't wait too long," Marcie grumbled, following Kelley.

Pat walked down the corridor and continued past her office, choosing instead to carry the bag she'd picked up outside into the training room where it belonged. As she walked through the locker room, she spied Sherry sitting in front of her locker changing into a pair of hiking boots.

"Little late for a hike, don't you think?" Pat said.

Sherry laughed. "Yeah, it probably is. But besides my basketball shoes, these are the only other kind I own."

"Must make it awkward on a date."

Sherry looked up at Pat, wondering what put that thought into the coach's mind.

Seeing the expression on her player's face, Pat felt her cheeks redden as she realized what she had said. "Sorry," she mumbled. "I need to get this bag put away."

Pat hurried into the training room, leaving Sherry staring after her, an intrigued smile on her face. She was tying her boot laces when Marcie, Kelley, and Lizzie walked through on their way to the training room.

Mac entered the locker room and looked around, hoping to spot her coach. "Good game, ladies," she said to Latesha and Amie, who were heading outside.

Latesha smiled. "Thanks, Mac."

"Coach around?" Mac asked.

"I think she went into the training room," Pete answered, hurrying to catch up with the others.

"Thanks." Mac walked toward the back of the room, pausing when she saw Sherry. "Good game."

"Thanks."

Mac chuckled when Sherry started to stand. "Stay. I don't expect my players to stand whenever I enter a room. Although, I've heard that a couple of the owners do." She grinned. "You looked pretty good out there last night." She had watched the game on one of the sports channels.

"Really?" Sherry blushed. "I was so nervous, I felt like a three-legged dancer."

"You didn't look it." Mac leaned against the row of lockers. "About that last play, you get hurt?"

"No." Sherry shook her head. "Just got knocked on my ass."

"Was it dirty?"

"No, it was a clean play." Pat walked out of the training room. She had heard Mac's voice and guessed the owner would be looking for her. And she was pretty sure why. The Cougar owner did not approve of a coach who threw unjustified tantrums during a game. "I overreacted."

"Any particular reason?" Mac asked. It was the first time she had seen Pat come unglued, and she wanted to know why. Her tone wasn't angry, but curious.

Sherry looked at Pat, more than a little curious herself to hear the coach's response.

Pat ran her fingers through her short hair, blowing out a long breath. "It was the end of a long day, Mac. I don't know why I reacted like I did. I blew it." She pursed her lips together in an apologetic grimace. "Can we just leave it at that?" she asked, hoping the owner would let the matter drop.

"All right." Mac pushed herself away from the lockers. She wasn't quite ready to let it go entirely, but she wasn't willing to question her coach in front of a player, either. "Practice tomorrow?"

"I gave the team tomorrow off," Pat said, relieved that Mac wasn't pursuing her atypical behavior in Denver. "It was a long trip for an overnight stay," she said, her voice hardening when she thought of all the time the team had had to waste because of the owner's niece. "They can use the rest. We'll have an afternoon practice day after tomorrow. Then we'll get back in the swing of things the next day."

"Seattle is only five days away," Mac needlessly reminded her coach.

"We'll be ready."

"Good. New travel itineraries are on your desk. Make sure you take a look at them," Mac told her coach. "Let Mandy know if you want any changes."

"All right." As Mac left the locker room, Pat frowned. She'd have to review those before she left for the night. So much for her plans to grab something for dinner on the way home and go to bed early.

Sherry laughed, shutting her locker door and spinning the dial on her lock. "Guess that's why you get paid the big bucks."

"Huh?"

"Always something to do," Sherry said. Seeing that the coach still wasn't following, she added, "Checking the itineraries."

"Oh, yeah." Pat grinned. "I signed on to coach basketball, and I spend half my time doing everything but."

"Sounds like you could use a good assistant," Sherry teased. It was no secret on the team that Mandy had not been Pat's choice for the position.

"I could. Got anyone in mind?"

"Not at the moment, but I'll keep my ears open."

"Gee, thanks."

"You need anything from us tonight, Pat?" Kelley asked, coming out of the training room.

"Nah, go home and get some rest. Take tomorrow off, then we'll meet Tuesday morning and go over things before practice."

"Sounds good. You got any plans for tomorrow?" the assistant coach asked.

"My legs need a good stretching after all the sitting I've done in the last 48 hours. Thought I'd go for a little hike." She looked out of the corner of her eye to see if Sherry was paying attention. Her heart skipped a beat when she saw the player trying not to look like she was listening.

Marcie came out of the training room with Lizzie. "Where to this time?"

"Haven't done the Lee Creek trail in a while, so I'll probably head up there in the morning." She was looking at Marcie and the others, but she was talking to Sherry. "You could join me," she offered, crossing her fingers that this wouldn't be the time they decided to take her up on it.

"Go on a hike with you?" Lizzie laughed. "The last time I did that you practically ran up the mountain, brace and all. No thank you. I don't have a week to recover right now."

"Wimp," Pat teased.

"Don't know why you call what you do hiking. You should be honest and just say you plan to charge up a mountain, then turn around and charge back down. Hiking implies getting some enjoyment out of the experience. With you, it's just seeing how fast you can get from point A to point B."

Sherry thought about contradicting the trainer's comment. She always enjoyed her hikes with the coach. Then she remembered she couldn't tell anyone that.

Pat chuckled. "Wuss."

"Humpf," Lizzie huffed. "Come on, let's go get something to eat," she told Marcie and Kelley. "Leave this masochist to her 'hiking'. Doubt anyone in this town is fool enough to go with her."

Pat smiled to herself. She was pretty sure there was at least one person who would show up at the trailhead in the morning.

"If you go," Kelley said as Lizzie was pulling her toward the corridor, "be careful." She had also hiked with the coach on a few occasions and knew how Pat pushed herself on the trails. She worried about her being alone if her knee gave out.

"I will." She waited until she heard the door at the end of the corridor slam shut before turning to face Sherry. "Seems we're last out again."

"Seems so."

"Any plans for tomorrow?"

"I was thinking of taking a hike."

Pat nodded. "Go up Highway 12 out of Lolo. Look for the Lee Creek campground." She knew Sherry was still getting used to where places were located. "Start up the trail. I'll meet you where it opens up coming out of the trees."

"Okay."

"Good night."

"Good night, Coach."

CHAPTER NINE

Sherry pulled off the highway at Lee Creek campground and turned in to the small parking area located just before the entrance to the campsites. She was surprised to see the lot vacant and checked her hiking guide again to make sure she was in the right place. Satisfied she hadn't made a mistake, she pushed open the car door and got out. There was an interpretative sign at the side of the parking area, and she walked over to read it.

The sign said that the trail beyond was part of the original Nee-Me-Poo Trail, the Indian trail that Lewis and Clark had followed on their trips to and from the Pacific Ocean. "Interesting," she murmured. Returning to the car for her pack, she made a mental note to ask Pat if she'd ever hiked it. Maybe they could do so another day.

Sherry shrugged her pack onto her back and locked the car before crossing the parking area. The trailhead for the trail where she was to meet Pat started a short distance up the forest service road that bisected the campground. At the junction of the parking area and the forest road, she saw a box of pamphlets describing the trail and pulled one out to read as she walked. She was interested to discover that the trail Pat had chosen was actually an interpretative trail, offering living examples of the effects of natural and man-made events on the forest. The trail wound its way through sections of forest that had been burned, logged, or blown over by gale-force winds. The hiker would be able to observe how birds building their homes affected trees and how the process of trees decaying rejuvenated the forest.

She tucked the pamphlet into her pocket when she reached the trailhead, which was no more than a narrow, pine needle-covered path leading up the side of the sharp slope behind the campground. At first, the trail provided only a view of the campsites and campers, but as Sherry climbed up the steep grade, the campground was left far below, and she found herself surrounded by pine trees of every shape and size. Looking around at the lush green forest she was passing through, she found it hard to believe she would see the devastation described in the pamphlet.

It took several minutes for Sherry to make the climb up the grade that marked the start of the trail. She was breathing heavily when the trees suddenly fell away, leaving her standing in a small clearing that was dominated by a huge mound of granite that had been forced up from the center of the earth eons ago.

Sitting on top of the mountain of rock was Pat, arms stretched behind her and propping her body up as she leaned back with her face tilted up to the morning sun.

Sherry gasped at the sight. *She's absolutely beautiful.*

Pat heard the sudden intake of breath and sat up, swiveling her head around in search of the source. One could never be too careful when out in the woods; at any time, a deer, elk, or even a bear might cross the path. When she saw Sherry standing a short distance away, she smiled. "Good morning," she said, pushing herself up to standing. "I was beginning to think you'd changed your mind." She brushed her hands together to rid them of granules of rock.

Sherry moved closer to the boulder. "No, it just took me a little while to make it up this first stretch. I had to stop and rest a few times." She grinned sheepishly.

"Still getting used to the altitude?" Pat asked, climbing down from the boulder.

"Seems so. I didn't see your pickup down there."

"Parked a ways up the forest road. Didn't think it would be too good an idea to have both our cars parked there. This trail doesn't get much use, other than by the campers, but the other trail gets plenty. The lot will probably be full in an hour or two."

"I was going to ask you about the other trail."

"Don't let the sign fool you." Pat chuckled. "The section of original trail is about a hundred feet long, then it disappears into a jumble of logging roads and more recent trails. Almost impossible to follow just where Lewis and Clark were supposed to have walked."

"Still, it would be interesting to walk that hundred feet."

"It is. You should do it just to have the experience. If you go early enough in the day, you won't have to do it with a thousand tourists."

"Is that why you picked this trail? Fewer people?"

"No." Pat stopped in front of Sherry. "I like it." *And I like you, and I want to show it to you.* She heard the thoughts coming and somehow managed to keep from saying them. She wasn't as successful in stopping her arm from lifting to settle a hand on Sherry's arm.

"Hope it's not all like that first section." Sherry twisted around to look back at the path that had brought her to this point, the movement averting the coach's touch. "Don't want you calling me a wuss because I have to rest all the time." She recalled the conversation the day before and the coach's use of the word with Lizzie. She turned back around, hoping Pat wouldn't still be standing so close. It wasn't that she didn't want the woman to touch her; it was more that she was confused over her feelings for Pat. Or maybe not.

"It's not." Pat stepped back a few steps, creating a safety zone of extra space between Sherry and herself. "From here it switches off between ups, downs, and flat sections. But if you need to rest, I won't think you're a wuss." She smiled, her voice softening into almost a purr. "I promise."

"Thanks." Sherry bit her lip.

Pat thought she looked adorable. She bent low at the waist and swept her arm toward the trail. "Shall we?"

"Sure." Sherry giggled. "You lead."

"Why me?" Pat asked as she started up the trail.

"Because it's early, and we're probably the first people to walk along here today."

"So?"

"So you get to break through all the spider webs." It hadn't taken Sherry long to figure out that hiking in the mountains came with its own unique annoyances, and she really hated walking through the invisible strands the spiders draped across the trails in hopes of trapping a fly or other bug in the sticky threads.

"Gee, thanks," Pat grumbled.

"You're welcome." Sherry skipped a couple of steps, happy beyond words to be where she was and with the woman walking a few steps in front of her. She'd worry about the whys and wherefores another time.

"It's beautiful here," Sherry said, gazing into the ravine below her seated vantage point.

They had followed the trail for a couple of miles, stopping often to explore interesting sights they came upon. They had finally reached a junction where the trail split, offering them several choices for continuing: reverse their steps and follow the trail back to their vehicles; take the trail splitting off to the left and follow it to the hot springs several miles away; or take the trail to the right and work their way back down to the forest road where Pat had left her pickup. They'd decided on the fourth option — to take the trail that continued in the direction they had been hiking. It wasn't yet noon, and neither woman was ready to part company with the other.

The trail took them up over the crest of a ridge, dropping down on the opposite side into a U-shaped ravine. The trunk of a fallen tree provided the perfect place to sit and enjoy the view and their lunch.

"Look." Pat pointed to a stand of trees at the bottom of the ravine where a doe and fawn were cautiously approaching a pool of water.

"It's so cute," Sherry gushed, watching the baby animal explore its surroundings.

Pat turned to look at the entranced woman, a grin spreading across her face.

"What?" Sherry swiped at her mouth. "Do I have peanut butter stuck to me or something?"

"No."

"Then why are you looking at me like that?"

Pat almost told her. Almost. "No reason." She turned away.

Sherry studied the woman beside her. She was attractive, very attractive. And she was fun to be with — away from the team. She wanted to reach out and touch her, and she felt her heart beat double time as she merely thought about it. Maybe it was as good a time as any to face the obvious. "Pat."

Pat turned around; her breath caught at the look on Sherry's face. It was a look she had seen on her own several times since they'd met. "We can't," she whispered.

"Why?" Sherry asked, although she already knew the answer.

Pat didn't say anything; she just sat and looked at the woman who invaded her thoughts more and more frequently every day. Slowly she raised a hand, laying it tenderly against Sherry's cheek. Her thumb gently traced the lips she so longed to kiss.

Sighing, Sherry leaned into the touch. "I—" She was stopped by a finger pressed against her lips.

"Don't," Pat whispered, pulling her hand away. "Please."

Sherry waited for more.

"I'm your coach, Sherry." Pat's soft voice broke the awkward silence. "I can't have an affair with a player."

"Is that what you want?" Sherry asked just as softly.

"I...I don't know what I want," Pat said honestly. "I won't lie and say I'm not attracted to you."

"But?"

"There isn't a 'but'," Pat said sadly. "I would like to take this further, Sherry, but—"

"Ah, so there is a 'but'." Sherry grinned, attempting to ease the tension building between them.

"Yeah, I guess there is. It's in my contract — no relationships with players beyond the game. I'm breaking my contract just being here."

"So why are you?"

"I don't know." Pat reached for her water bottle and took a long swallow of the cooling liquid. "Heck, I haven't known why I've done anything when it comes to you since I saw you playing for Karen. I don't know why I asked you to camp. I don't know why I asked Mac to keep you on the team after camp. I don't know why I went bonzo in Denver."

"I kinda hoped you wanted me for the Cougars because you thought I was good player," Sherry said, her feelings slightly bruised by the coach's comments.

"You are a good player," Pat told her. "You would have no trouble finding a place on any roster in the league."

"But?"

"But I didn't need any more guards."

Pat scrubbed her fingers through her hair, a habit Sherry was noticing the coach had whenever she was nervous. Was Pat as anxious now as she was?

"What I'm saying is..." More scrubbing of her scalp. "Hell, I don't know what I'm saying. Look, Sherry, I'll admit there's something between us. Something I'd very much like to see where it would lead, but I can't. Not in our present circumstances. I'm sorry."

"Can we still do this? Be friends?" Sherry thought her heart would stop beating if Pat said no.

"Oh, gods, yes." Pat grinned. "I'm not sure I could function otherwise."

"It'll mean breaking the rules," Sherry reminded her.

"If we keep doing it the way we have been, we should be okay. We come in different vehicles, so it's not like we're together, together. And we can always go our separate ways if we meet anybody on the trails." What she was describing sounded so dirty, like she was sneaking around in back alleys to have an illicit affair with a married woman. That's not how she felt, and she looked at Sherry with regret, hoping she understood. When Sherry nodded, she continued.

"As long as this is all we do, it should be okay," Pat said, trying to convince herself more than Sherry. It was wrong and she knew it, but she was ready to accept the consequences. She thought. She hoped.

"All right." Even though she wanted more, Sherry understood Pat's position. At least her head did. Her heart was screaming, *Kiss me, you idiot!*

"We'd better start back," Pat said. She knew that if she didn't get up and start moving right then, she was going to do something stupid — like kiss the lips that looked so inviting. She stood, pulling her pack on, and waited for Sherry to do the same.

With each woman absorbed in her own thoughts, they retraced their steps back to the trail junction in silence. Pat waved a quick goodbye before taking the cutoff that would lead to her pickup.

Sherry watched Pat until her movements were completely hidden by the trees, then she backtracked to the trailhead. When she came to the large boulder where she had first seen Pat that morning, she climbed to the top and sat in the same spot Pat had been sitting. It was almost sundown when she finally climbed down and returned to the car to drive back to town.

CHAPTER TEN

Seattle Seafarers Arena: Missoula 37 Seattle 23

Sherry dribbled up court, looking for Val to make her move across the bottom half of the key while Terry and Pete switched positions at the top half, jamming their defensive players between them. She saw Val run her defensive player toward Dawn, who was to set a pick to free the forward.

Instead of being screened from the play, the defensive player slid past when Dawn was slow at moving into her new position, and the defender rushed to guard Val, preventing her from having any chance to get the ball.

Sherry cross-stepped a few feet to her left, switching the ball from right hand to left as she dribbled.

Terry, seeing the play had been broken, ran back through the key and set a screen for Sherry.

Sherry took a step toward the screen, pulling up for an easy 15-foot jumper. Just as she left the ground, she picked up the motion of Pete slipping down the other side of the key behind the defense, and instead of shooting, she attempted to pass the ball through the crowded key to Pete. A Seattle player swatted at the ill-advised pass, knocking it out of the air and into a teammate's grasp.

Sherry realized her mistake as soon as the ball left her hands. She backpedaled, trying to get into position to prevent a fast break by Seattle.

The Seattle player dribbled to mid-court, flanked by two teammates, setting up a three-on-one break. Sherry continued to backpedal, trying to read the eyes of the player controlling the ball. The Seattle player flipped the ball to her teammate on her right, who flipped it right back. Sherry continued to focus on the middle player. She slowed, spreading her arms wide in hopes of stopping any run at the basket the player might try.

The Seattle player smirked at the lone guard, popping into the air to attempt a long 3-pointer. Raising her arms, she momentarily held the ball over her head as she took aim. When her arms moved forward, her wrists flipped perfectly to send the ball straight for the basket.

Pete, chasing the play, saw the Seattle player leave her feet. Anticipating the shot she altered her course, running diagonally at the shooter. Dashing alongside the Seattle player, she threw her left hand up just in time to catch a piece of the ball and send it bouncing harmlessly out of bounds.

"Time!" Pat screamed at the officials.

A whistle blew, stopping play. The referee looked at Pat to find out how much time she wanted.

"Thirty seconds," Pat called out above the crowd noise, tapping her shoulders with her fingers, the signal for a short timeout. She didn't wait for the players to run over to her before she started telling them what was on her mind. "Sherry," she stepped out a few feet further onto the court to greet the player, "don't you ever pass up an open shot again."

Sherry nodded guiltily. She knew the coach was right. It had been a rookie mistake, and she wasn't very pleased with herself for making it.

"Look." Pat reached out, placing her hand gently on Sherry's shoulder. "You're a shooter." She leaned in so she wouldn't have to yell. "Trust your shot, okay?"

"Okay, Coach."

"Good." Pat turned to face the other players. "Dawn, you've got to start hitting your marks. The last three plays have fallen apart because you were out of position." She waited for Dawn to respond and wasn't impressed when she didn't. "Tonie," she shouted to the starting post player. "Go in for Dawn."

"But, Coach—"

"I expect a response when I talk to you," Pat told Dawn. Her voice sounded calm, but her veteran players knew she was on the verge of loosing her anger on the difficult rookie. "You want to play, you'd better learn that. Tonie," the coach pulled the other player into the huddle when she came back from the scorer's table, "they're playing a switch down low. I want you to release to the opposite side of the key when you see it. Sherry, Pete, be alert. That should open Tonie up for some easy baskets underneath."

Both guards nodded their understanding as the buzzer sounding the end of the timeout blasted through the arena.

"All right." Pat glanced up at the scoreboard hanging above the court. "We have a comfortable lead; let's try to hang on to it until halftime. No more rookie mistakes," she growled, winking at Sherry to let the player know she still had her coach's confidence.

The five players ran back onto the court as the rest of the team returned to the bench. Dawn snatched a cup of water and a towel off the stack at the end of their bench before slumping into an available seat. "Bitch," she spat under her breath.

Wendy was sitting next to her, her eyes following the action on the court. "What?" she asked.

"I should be playing, not that bitch."

"Damn." Wendy turned her head to look at the rookie. "Do you have mud between your ears or what? You're getting to play, or haven't you noticed?"

"So why am I sitting here?" Dawn sulked.

"Because you won't follow Coach's rules, that's why. You get yourself taken out most of the time because you refuse to do things her way."

"Maybe her way isn't the right way," Dawn grumbled, the argument sounding weak, even to her ears.

"You're an idiot." Wendy turned back to the action. "She's the coach, so her way is always right."

Dawn looked down the length of the bench to see Pat watching her. "Shit," she muttered.

Halftime – Missoula 43 Seattle 32

"Things are going pretty well, ladies. Tonie, good job at low post, I don't think they were expecting that change." Pat was standing on a bench in the locker room in order to be seen and heard by the players. "But we can't give them any more runs like they had at the end of the half. We need better action on the boards. They're out-rebounding us two to one. That's something we have to reverse in the second half. And, damn it, try to make some of your free throws. Except for Sherry, we've missed..." she looked down at a sheet of paper in her hand, "we've *missed* 64 percent. Come on, ladies, that's 17 points."

Most of the players looked anywhere but in the direction of their coach. They knew they were in for some long sessions of free-throw practice when they got back to Missoula.

"Anything I need to know about?" Pat asked, searching the faces of her players for any signs of someone trying to hide an injury. "Lizzie?"

"All good here, Coach," the trainer responded from the back of the room where she was re-taping Val's ankles.

"Okay, get out there and get in some practice before the second half. From the free-throw line!" Pat yelled after her players. "Sherry, hang on a minute," she said, stopping the guard from exiting the room.

Sherry nodded, stepping out of the way of the other players. "Sure, Coach. Problem?"

"No." Pat stepped down off the bench and sat on it, motioning for Sherry to do the same. "I just wanted you to know — you'll be sitting out the second half."

"Oh?" Sherry was disappointed. She thought she'd been playing well.

"You're doing a real good job out there." Pat smiled to assure the player she meant it. "But I have to play Kinsey."

Pat had been troubled when the veteran guard had asked to be taken out of the game after playing less than half of the first period. When she'd spoken to Kinsey on her way into the locker room, the player had said her fatigue was due to not sleeping well the night before but that she was ready to return to the floor. Pat wasn't convinced. She knew Mac was in the stands watching the game, and she also knew Mac was looking for an answer on whether or not Kinsey could go the season. It was a question she was having trouble with herself. Pat knew she had to test the guard one last time before she and Mac could make a final decision.

"Kinsey is going to play the full half," Pat told Sherry. She really didn't owe the player an explanation, but it felt good to give voice to her thoughts. Besides, it allowed her a few more minutes with the young woman who was starting to haunt her dreams. "Wendy and Amie will rotate with Pete."

"Okay, Coach." Sherry wasn't sure why Pat was telling her the game plan, but she didn't care, glad to be able to sit there and look at the coach's face. Her beautiful brown eyes. Her perfectly formed chin. The luscious lips. *Uh, oh.* Sherry jerked herself upright and out of her thoughts before they led someplace she wasn't prepared to go. At least, not yet. "Is it okay if I still take some practice shots?" she asked, standing.

"Uh, sure." Pat ran her fingers through her hair. "Go on."

Marcie joined the coach, sitting in the spot Sherry had vacated. "Here are the official stats on the first half." She held out a sheet of paper. "Sherry had a heck of a half: 15 points, 8 assists, 2 steals. Those are good numbers." When Pat didn't say anything, she waved the paper in front of the coach's face.

"Huh?" Pat shook herself out of the haze that had enveloped her.

"You okay?"

"Yeah. What were you saying?"

"Sherry's stats for the first half are pretty impressive."

"Oh." Pat looked at the paper Marcie shoved into her hand. "I'm sitting her out the second half."

"Testing Kinsey?"

"Yes. Mac wants an answer when we get back home."

"She looked sluggish the first half."

"I know."

"I hate to say it, Pat," Marcie opened her notebook, "but with the way Sherry is playing, Kinsey is losing her hold on point guard. Fact is, she never put up the numbers the rookie has."

"I know." Pat didn't have to look at the hard numbers to know Sherry was showing signs of becoming a premier player.

"Time to get out there, Coach," Kelley said as she checked her watch.

"Kinsey stays in until she asks to come out," Pat told her assistant coaches. "This is her last chance."

"Does she know that?" Marcie asked.

"Yes."

Two days had passed since the team's return to Missoula after winning their second exhibition game. Pat arrived in her office early in the morning and was sitting behind her desk making notes on several papers spread out before her. She was sorting through different lineups, seeking the perfect combination to take the Cougars all the way to the championship. She didn't look up when someone tapped on the office door.

"Come in, K," Pat called to the unseen player. She had asked the veteran to come to her office before the rest of the team started arriving for practice.

Kinsey smiled halfheartedly when she pushed the door open. "'Morning, Coach."

"Come on in and sit down," Pat said, even less enthusiastic about their meeting than her player seemed.

"Let's not drag this out, Coach," Kinsey said before the door was shut behind her.

"Come over and sit down," Pat repeated. "We have some hard decisions to make, so we might as well be comfortable."

"I can play, Coach." Kinsey stood in front of Pat's desk. "I've got a release from my doctor." The player pulled a folded envelope out of her pocket, flattening it on the desk in front of Pat.

"Will you please sit down?" Kinsey dropped into the chair. "This isn't easy for me, Kinsey." Pat leaned back in her chair. "But I think we both know, regardless of what that says," leaning forward, she tapped the envelope, "you can't last the season."

Pat had been disappointed when Kinsey asked to be taken out of the second half of the Seattle game after playing only six minutes. She returned to play a few more minutes, but it was apparent the guard's knees were causing her great pain.

"I may not be able to play the minutes I used to..." Kinsey wasn't willing to let go of her position with the Cougars without a fight, "but I can still play. I'm willing to take a backup role," she said, her voice sharp with desperation.

"I don't have room on the roster for another backup," Pat said sadly. "Look, K, if there was any way for me to keep you on the team, I would. Even if it meant you sat the bench the whole season. But you and I both know that isn't going to happen. I have one position to fill, and I need a point guard that can play more than six minutes a half."

Kinsey sat back in the chair, blowing out a long stream of air. "Damn, Coach."

"Yeah."

"Guess I should be better prepared for this day." Kinsey frowned. "I've known it was coming for a while."

"It's not easy giving up the game." Pat knew all too well how that felt.

"How'd you do it?"

"I cussed a lot. I screamed, hollered, threw things. Blamed everything and everybody I could think of. Then I cried," she said quietly. "And then I got on with my life."

"Don't think too many teams are looking for a washed-up point guard for a coaching job," Kinsey said cynically, referring to Pat's good fortune after her career-ending injury.

"I'm not going to lie and say that getting the offer from Mac didn't help." Pat looked at the player. "But I would have found something to do even if Mac hadn't called me. The point is, Kinsey, no matter how much it hurts now, there is more to life than basketball." As she said the words, Pat wondered how much more of her life would pass before she actually believed them. "And you'll find something."

"Okay." Kinsey's tone hardened. "It's obvious you plan to cut me. Just give me the details, and let's get it over with."

Pat studied her player. Would she react any more gracefully if she were placed in the same situation? She doubted it. Not looking forward to saying what she had to, Pat steeled herself into her no-nonsense coach mode. "I've talked to Mac, and she's agreed to let you choose how you want the announcement made. You can announce your plans to retire, or she'll issue a statement saying your contract is being dropped. Either way, you've played your last game for the Cougars."

"Not much of a choice. Least you'd think I'd get is a chance to play one more game at home. Have something to remember my time here by," Kinsey said, envisioning the farewell she'd receive from the hometown fans.

"I gave you all the time I could, K. We have to have our roster finalized by the end of the week. You know the league rules as well as anybody."

"When do you need to know?"

"Before you leave this meeting."

"I'm signed for the full season, Coach. What does Mac plan to do about that?"

"That's between you and her. I don't have anything to do with the contracts or their conditions. You can go talk to her when you're finished here; she's up in her office."

"All right." Kinsey stood slowly. "It's not the way I want to go out, but I guess neither one of us has much control over it. You can tell Mac I'm retiring."

"I really am sorry, Kinsey." Pat stood and walked around her desk. Considering hugging the woman, she stopped herself at the last minute, stretching a hand out instead. "You were a hell of a point guard. It's too bad we never had a chance to play together."

"That would have been fun." Kinsey took the offered hand, squeezing it gently. "You're a good coach, Pat." The now ex-player used the coach's name for the first time. "You win that championship." She forced a smile to her lips even though tears were streaming down her face.

"If we do, you'll be there as a member of the team. That's a promise."

Kinsey choked up, afraid to believe she would actually be given the opportunity to claim a part of that particular victory. But if it were to prove true, it might just be enough to help her get past the ending of her playing career.

"You earned it," Pat said, not knowing that she was holding out the gold at the end of the rainbow to the ex-player. "We never would have made it as far as we did last year without you leading the team on the floor." Pat retrieved a box of tissues and handed it to Kinsey.

"Thanks." Kinsey wiped at the tears on her face. "Guess I should go see Mac."

Pat smiled. "Stop by the locker room and wash your face."

"Good idea." Kinsey handed back the box of tissues. "I probably look a mess."

"It's to be expected. I'll give her a call and let her know you're on the way."

"Thanks."

"One more thing, Kinsey," Pat said as the woman reached the door.

Kinsey turned around. "Yes?"

"About the team." Pat hesitated, uncomfortable at having to ask the question. "How do you want them to find out?" Practice would be starting soon, and it would not go unnoticed that the veteran player was missing.

"I can't face that now, Pat. Just tell them the truth, and I'll come by in a few days to say my goodbyes."

"Okay." Pat watched Kinsey leave, the slump of her shoulders exhibiting the player's feelings. "Damn," she muttered, yanking a couple of tissues out of the box and blowing her nose.

"Yes, she's retiring," Pat told Mac. She had called the owner's office as soon as Kinsey left their meeting. She wasn't surprised when Mac answered the call herself; it was still too early for her secretary to be at work. "She'll be up there in a couple of minutes."

"Any problems?" Mac asked, wanting to be prepared when the soon-to-be-ex-Cougar arrived at her door.

"It was hard." Pat sniffled. "But I think she knew it was coming."

"It's never easy, Pat. But it's business, just remember that."

Pat understood what the owner was telling her, but Mac had never played the game, and she didn't really understand what it meant to step off the court for the last time. "Give her a fair deal, Mac," she told the owner. "She's earned it twice over."

"Don't worry." Mac chuckled. "I may be the 'cold-hearted bitch' that owns this team, but I do know what a player like Kinsey means to the game."

"Didn't know you knew your nickname," Pat said, startled by the owner's use of the descriptive term some of the players had for her.

"Not much goes on in this building that I don't know, Pat. Remember that."

"Guess I'll have to." Pat hoped that Mac hadn't meant it as the warning it sounded like. "Do you want me to send Sherry up?" The rookie's temporary contract was set to expire at the end of the week. With Kinsey being cut, Sherry could be signed for the full season.

"I'll let you know when. Let me take care of Kinsey first."

"Okay." Pat hung up the phone when the line went dead; Mac wasn't one to say goodbye when she was finished talking. Needing to get out of the tight confinement of her office, she headed out to the arena floor. Before she reached the end of the corridor, she knew by the distinct pattern of a ball bouncing on the hardwood floor that Sherry was practicing free throws.

Sherry saw Pat walk out of the shadows of the corridor and sit a few rows up from the arena floor. It wasn't unusual for the coach to sit in the bleachers during her practice, but she normally had her notebooks with her. Sherry could see that Pat's hands were empty, and she wondered if something was wrong. Cutting her practice short, she moved over to the side of the court closest to Pat, bouncing the ball as she walked. "Hi," she said when she could go no further without climbing up into the rows of seats.

"Hi." Pat rested her feet on the back of the seat in front of her. Bending at the waist, she rested her arms on her knees and her chin on her crossed arms. "Being coach sucks," she pouted.

Sherry laughed. Pat looked so miserable, yet so adorable, she wanted to wrap the woman in her arms and tell her everything would be all right. "Want to share?"

"Can't."

"You okay?"

"Yeah."

The women looked at each other for several minutes, both wanting to go to the other but neither able to breach the unspoken barrier holding them apart.

"You done with practice?" Pat asked, breaking the awkward silence.

"Still have fourteen." Sherry was meticulous about keeping count of every free throw.

"You better go finish. The rest will be showing up any minute."

"Okay."

Pat stood up. After watching Sherry for a few more minutes, she walked down to the court. "Mac is going to want to talk to you later," she told Sherry as she walked back to the corridor. "I'll let you know when."

"Anything I should be worried about?" Sherry asked. Pat was almost to the corridor, and she wasn't sure the coach had heard her question. "Coach?" she called out, almost afraid to hear the answer.

"Good news for you," Pat called back over her shoulder. "Crappy news for Kinsey," she muttered. *Great news for me,* she thought, a contemplative smile spreading across her face. "But being coach still sucks," she groaned.

Kelley blew the whistle hanging around her neck to stop the practice. "Hold up."

"Bet you're proud of yourself, getting Kinsey cut from the team," Dawn sneered at Sherry, brushing against the smaller player.

Sherry, shaking her head in frustration at the endless stream of insults coming from her teammate, moved a few feet away from the post player who had been trying to bait her ever since Pat had announced Kinsey's retirement earlier in the week. She was glad Friday had finally arrived, and she'd have some time over the weekend to be away from Dawn and her irritating comments.

"Dawn." Kelley walked into the midst of the players on the court. "Are you in the right position for this play?"

Dawn forgot about Sherry for the moment. There'd be plenty of time to hassle her later. "I think so," she told the assistant coach.

"Think so?" Kelley blew out an exasperated breath. Trying to coach Dawn was a real study in patience. She wondered anew how Pat had maintained hers for so long. "Don't think, look!" she barked at the player. "Where are you supposed to be?"

Dawn casually looked from side to side, noticing for the first time that by going after Sherry she had taken herself several feet out of position. "Sorry, Coach," she mumbled, shuffling over to where she should be.

"Let's run it again," Kelley said, stepping back out of the way.

Sherry trotted to the mid-court line. When the rest of the players were set, she dribbled for the key.

Pat was having the team practice a new play she was hoping would help open up their offense. Dawn, at low post, and Terry, playing high post, were on the left side of the key, each standing four feet off the hash line. Val and Pete took up identical positions on the right side. This spread out the Cougars who were acting as defensive players, making it difficult for any one player to be double-teamed.

Sherry dribbled to the apex of the 3-point arc painted on the floor. Pete cut across the top of the key, catching a snap pass from Sherry, who followed her pass by running straight down the middle of the lane. The defense sagged into the key to protect against the high-scoring guard getting the ball back.

Pete dropped the ball off to Terry, then spun around the high post and cut for the corner of the court and the screen Dawn was supposed to set.

If the defense reacted the way Pat expected them to, the post player should have five options for scoring available to her. If open, she could take the shot herself. Standing at the top corner of the key, she was well within her range. Or she could rifle a pass to Pete, who should have a shot behind Dawn's screen. If the defense followed Pete, then Val should have a shot or Dawn should be in position for an easy turn-around jumper. If none of those options were there, she could always pass the ball back to Sherry, who would be coming toward her for a shot from the top of the key. But for the play to work, it required split-second timing and everyone had to be in position and ready, since Terry was instructed to pass to whichever of her teammates was open.

Terry spun around to face the basket, the ball held out of the reach of the player guarding her. Dawn was having trouble holding her screen, so Pete was out. Sherry's defensive player had stayed with her, no shot there. She snapped the ball to Val, who was momentarily unguarded.

Val popped in the air, the ball leaving her hands for the basket. *Swish.*

"Run it again," Pat said.

Sherry retraced her steps to mid-court and started the play again.

Pat had them run the play several times, each time noticing that regardless of where the defensive players were when she reached the top of the arc, Sherry passed the ball to Terry, passing up some relatively open shots. Before the team could set up for another repetition, she called Pete over to her.

Pete listened to what Pat told her, nodded, then ran back out on the court. As the players ran through the play again, she made a note of how open Sherry had been when she gave possession of the ball to Terry.

"Five-minute break," Pat called out when the ball dropped through the basket. "Marcie, Kelley, let's talk." She really had nothing to say to her assistant coaches, but she wanted Pete to have time to talk with Sherry.

As Sherry trotted for the sideline and her bottle of water, Pete appeared beside her. "Why didn't you shoot it?"

"I'm supposed to pass it to Terry," Sherry said, grabbing her water bottle and taking a long swallow. "That's the way the play is designed."

"I know, but Coach doesn't expect us to run it exactly like she drew it. She lets us play, if you know what I mean. If you have a better shot or play, you take it."

Sherry looked at the veteran guard, a look of intrigue and confusion on her face. She'd had no such freedom in college. In fact, she'd been yanked out of more than a few games because she hadn't followed a play exactly as her coach had diagrammed it. The thought of being able to follow her own initiative if she thought she saw a way to put the ball in the basket was something she was happy to consider. "Really?"

"Yeah, really." Pete grinned. She could almost see the wheels turning inside Sherry's head as she visualized all the ways she could put into action what she was being told. "Only thing Coach cares about is if you score. If you do, no problem. So, go with your instincts, Sherry."

"All right. I'll try."

"Good. Besides, it'll help keep the other teams guessing. Remember, the point guard sets the tone for the game. If they can't figure out what you're going to do, they can't cheat on defense. It makes it easier on the rest of us."

"Right." Sherry took another long drink. She'd often thought about how much better a player she could have been in college if she'd had a coach who had thought that way. Being restricted in her movements on the court had not only held back her development as a player but had also kept her natural talent well hidden.

"Don't think." Pete grinned. "In your case, I don't think it helps your play."

Sherry frowned. "Gee, thanks."

"No, that's not what I meant. You've got good instincts out there. Great, really. Just go with them."

"Okay, ladies." Kelley called the players back onto the court. "Sherry, set it up again."

This time when Sherry dribbled for the top of the arc, she didn't hesitate like the past times, waiting to drop a pass off to Terry. Halfway between mid-court and Terry, she saw the key was wide open as the defensive players followed their assignments. She performed a quick half-step to kick into high gear. In less than two strides, she went from jogging up court to boring down the center of the key at full speed, leaving her defensive player gaping open-mouthed at her. Completely uncontested, Sherry approached the basket, laying the ball off the backboard for an easy 2 points.

Pat smiled. *I knew she would do that,* she told herself. But she wasn't upset. It was exactly what she hoped would happen after Pete talked to the rookie.

"Look out, league, we've got a dynamo at point," Marcie said quietly to the coach.

"Ain't that the truth," Pat responded happily. "Okay, gather up," she called to the players. "Nice play, Sherry." She grinned as the point guard trotted up to her. "That's a good lesson for everyone. You can't assume what is going to happen when you're out there. You've got to pay attention and be ready to adjust at any second. Wendy," she said to the guard who had been Sherry's defensive player, "you should have been prepared for Sherry to make that move. There's no way she should have caught you flatfooted."

"I'll be ready next time, Coach," Wendy mumbled. She was still shocked at how fast the rookie's move had been. Having played in the league for the past three years, she could not think of any other guard who possessed the same quickness.

"Make sure you are." Pat chuckled, trying to ease the veteran's embarrassment. "Listen up." She addressed the whole team. "Tomorrow night we play our first home game. From that game on, we don't have any time to let down. Yes, we have two wins under our belts, but they don't mean anything. The only wins that matter are the ones we start counting tomorrow. We have a mission this year, ladies, and that mission is to win the championship. I promised Kinsey she'd be there to hold that golden basketball, and I don't break my promises."

Sherry was surprised at Pat's revelation, as were several other players. Many would not have expected Pat to show such empathy toward the player they thought had been forced into retirement.

"Like I said, we have a mission. Mac wants it. I want it. Marcie and Kelley want it. The only question is whether you want it." She paused to let the players think about what she was saying. "I believe that the team standing here, right now, is the team that can, and should, win the championship. But I can't make that happen. Only you can. *Do you want it?*"

"*Yes!*" came the shouted response of several voices.

"Good." Pat smiled. "But we have some problems, ladies. Problems we have to deal with now or we'll destroy our chances. First, we have to start thinking and playing as a team. We don't have stars on this team. Every single one of you is here because I thought you brought to the Cougars some element of the game we needed." She looked into the eyes of every player, laughing a little to herself when she saw the surprise in Sherry's eyes and the obvious doubt in Dawn's. *Okay, you two weren't on my wish list, but you're here,* she thought. *In one case, I'm very glad of that. In the other...well, we'll just have to wait and see.*

"So quit thinking about who's getting playing time that should be yours, and start thinking about what you can do to nail down the victory when you're in the game. I want the petty differences to end now." She glared at Dawn. "Next, we'll never get to the championship with our current free-throw percentage. Starting today, every practice will end with each of you shooting one hundred free throws. And don't think you can just stand at the stripe and toss the ball in the general direction of the basket. Every shot you take will be recorded. And if you don't show continual improvement, I'll make it two hundred every day."

Several players groaned at the possibility. Not only did they not like to practice free throws, but it took a long time to shoot one hundred. They didn't even want to contemplate the time it would take to shoot two hundred.

"Glad to see you're paying attention," Pat told the players. "Kelley, Marcie, and I will be out here watching you shoot. If we see something that we think needs to be changed, we're going to tell you. I don't care if it's the way you've been shooting since grade school. Or it's the way Daddy taught you. Or the way your college coach wanted them shot," she said, knowing that most players were somewhat superstitious when it came to shooting free throws and very reluctant to change their patterns. "I do care if you're missing more than you're making. So if one of us comes to you with a suggestion, *listen to what we're saying.* Got it?"

"*Got it, Coach?*"

"Good. Sherry, Val, Wendy, and Pete, you can skip it. You're all shooting above 80 percent. Something to aspire to, ladies," Pat told the other players. "Marcie, split 'em up," Pat instructed her assistant, "and let's get started."

"Hey, Pete," Sherry called out to the other guard as she trotted down the corridor to the locker room.

Pete turned around but continued walking backward. "What's up, rookie?"

"I was wondering if you might have some other tips for me." Sherry slowed to a walk when she caught up with the veteran player.

"Lots." Pete grinned. "I was hoping you'd ask. Come on." She reversed directions, heading back down the corridor to the arena floor. "Let's go back out here where we've got some room to work."

"Great." Sherry smiled, running after Pete.

"Not very good," Pat grumbled, looking at the tally sheets Marcie and Kelley were handing her. "Damn, four for a hundred." She glanced to the top of the sheet to read the player's name. "She's on double practice immediately."

"I told her you'd probably say that. She says she didn't shoot many free throws in college, and her coach didn't push it," Kelley explained.

"Her coach now is going to push it. Four lousy percent," Pat muttered, writing a note on a page in her notebook. "Tell Jade to start coming in before practice to take the other hundred. I'll work with her then."

"Okay."

The coaches were sitting at what would be the scorer's table during a game but was now just an empty surface to spread their papers on. The arena was empty except for Pete and Sherry working together at one end of the floor. The rest of the players had been released for the day.

"Anything else?" Pat asked.

"Don't think so." Marcie was watching the two players out on the court. "She's a fast learner," she said of the rookie guard, who seemed to be having no trouble repeating the moves the veteran was showing her. "Wonder why we never heard about her before."

"Good question," Pat murmured, not bothering to look up from her note writing.

"Played in a small conference, never made it to an NCAA tournament." Kelley reviewed the bio they had on Sherry. "Put up decent numbers, but nothing outstanding." She shrugged. "Just another average college player."

"That we almost missed recruiting because we thought that way." Pat looked at her assistant coach. "I keep telling you — numbers don't show the whole picture. Maybe now you'll believe me." She gathered up her papers and shoved them into her bag. How close had she come to never meeting Sherry? If it hadn't been for Mandy talking Mac into taking a look at Dawn, she might never have met the woman she was having so much trouble not thinking about. *Guess I owe Mandy for that,* she thought. *Yeah, like I'd ever tell her.* "Unless you have something else, I'm going to my office to finish this." She pushed herself up from the table and walked away.

"What was that all about?" Kelley asked as the coach stormed off.

"That's a very good question." Hearing Pete laugh, Marcie turned her attention to the two remaining players. "Hey, guys, call it a night, will ya?" she shouted across the floor. "You have a game to rest up for tomorrow. Remember?"

"Yeah, Coach." Pete waved. She turned to Sherry. "She's right. We should be going home."

"All right. Thanks for the help."

"I'm glad to be of service. I just wish some of the other rookies would ask."

"I'll mention it to them," Sherry offered as they trotted down the corridor.

"I wouldn't waste my breath if I were you. Most rookies come into the league thinking they know everything. That's why most of them never last more than a year or two."

"Well, I plan to be playing for a long time." Sherry pushed open the door to the locker room, snatching two towels off the pile kept just inside the door. She tossed one to Pete and used the other to wipe her face dry.

"And you will." Pete wrapped the towel around her neck, soaking up the sweat. "Damn, I didn't realize it was so late," she said, looking at the clock on the wall. "I'm supposed to be going to a business dinner with my husband tonight. He's gonna kill me. Look, I've got to run," she said, already rushing for her locker. "I've just got time to get home, showered, and dressed before we have to leave."

"I didn't know you were married," Sherry said, stepping behind the rushed player to reach her own locker.

"Six years," Pete told her, pulling her car keys out of her locker. Slamming the locker door, she snatched her bag off the floor and ran for the door. "Later."

Sherry laughed, watching her go. Her smile slowly faded into a frown. *Wonder if I'll ever have someone to run home to like that?* she said to herself, bending over to untie her shoes.

"Any plans for Sunday?"

Sherry looked up to see Pat standing a few feet away.

"Um." Sherry straightened back up. "Not that I know of."

"Home games kinda get me pumped up. I like to go out in the woods afterward to get re-grounded, so to speak."

Sherry smiled and nodded. She knew she didn't have to say anything for the coach to know what she meant.

Pat looked toward the door when she heard voices in the corridor. "Stop by my office on your way out, I'll give you directions."

Before Kelley and Marcie walked into the locker room, Pat had already disappeared through the side doorway into the office area.

"You wanted to see me, Coach?" Sherry said as she walked into Pat's office. Kelley was sitting in the next office with the door open.

"Hang on a sec, Mac," Pat said into the phone.

"Sorry," Sherry whispered. She hadn't looked to see if Pat was busy before she entered her office.

"No problem. Here's that play I was telling you about." She pushed a piece of paper across her desk.

"Oh." Sherry wasn't expecting that cover, but considering the coach was on the phone with the team owner and there was an assistant coach sitting not twenty feet away, she thought it was probably a safe way for Pat to handle the situation. "Thanks." She picked up the paper and shoved it into a pocket in her jeans. "I'll see you tomorrow." She turned for the door.

"Come ready to play, Sherry," Pat called after the player before returning to her call.

CHAPTER ELEVEN

Pat stood at the front of the locker room, watching the players prepare for their first home game. A low roar told her the PA announcer was pumping up the fans for the team's arrival on the court. She looked at the clock.

"All right, ladies." Pat clasped her hands together in front of her chest while the players settled, ready for the coach's pre-game pep talk. "This is it. Our first home game. Our first victory on the road to that." She pointed behind her to an oversized photograph of the championship trophy that had been taped to the marker board. "That's our goal. That's our mission. Tonight, we take the first step in achieving it. The Raiders are a good team," she said of the Boston team they would be playing, "but you're better. They're fast...but you're faster. They're hungry...but you're hungrier. Because you want that." She pointed again at the picture. "*Do you want it?*"

"*Yes!*"

"Then let's go out and get it."

The players jumped to their feet, running for the front of the room. They stopped at the closed door, looking anxiously to their coach for the signal to leave.

"Ready, Coach?" Marcie asked. Pat nodded.

Yanking the door open, the players rushed out into the corridor. Before they were halfway to the court, Pat heard the cheers building. The walls of the locker room shuddered as the arena exploded with the noise of foot-stomping, screaming fans.

Pat sighed. Running onto the court before a home crowd had always sent a chill up her spine. It was one of the most exhilarating feelings a player could experience and one of the hardest to explain to someone who had never been fortunate enough to experience it.

"Let's go," Pat said, leading her coaching staff out the door.

As soon as the coach was spotted coming out on the floor, the cheers changed to chants of "KODAK, KODAK, KODAK." It was the nickname Pat had received after becoming the first Kodak All American from Missoula. She had made the town proud that year, and they continued to shower her with admiration.

Pat smiled, walking alongside the court to the Cougar bench. The team of officials walked over to greet the coach.

"'Evening, Paula." Pat shook the hand of the referee, a former player she'd done battle with more than once.

"Good to see you again, Pat. I see you still have the crowd on your side."

"Anything to help get those close calls," Pat teased.

"Right." Paula grinned. "I don't think you've met my colleagues tonight. Sam Bennett," she said as a dark-skinned man stepped forward to shake Pat's hand. "And Deb Hartley."

"Nice to meet you," Pat greeted.

"Have a good game," Paula said, then the trio headed over to the Boston bench to repeat the introductions.

Pat turned to her assistants as soon as the officials walked away. "Anything?" she asked, knowing Marcie and Kelley would have spent the past several minutes watching the Raiders' pre-game drills.

"Nothing new that I can see," Kelley said.

"Good. Get the team over here, and let's get this show on the road."

The first half of the game passed relatively quickly when the trio of officials chose to let the teams play without interrupting too often with foul calls. The buzzer ending the half sent the Cougars into the locker room with a 6-point lead.

Midway through the second half, Pat stood next to the bench watching Sherry set up a play. Sherry moved left, her guard matching her step for step. Pete faded back, providing the point guard a release pass if she needed it. Tonie was manhandling her guard under the basket, jamming up the key with their large bodies. Jade and Val were switching back and forth through the key to confuse the defense.

Sherry took a look at Pete but decided she didn't have a clear passing lane to get the ball to her teammate. She dribbled closer to the key.

Tonie made a quick move to the side, sending her defender, who seconds before had been pressed shoulder-to-shoulder with her, stumbling behind her as she was caught off-guard by the unexpected move.

Seeing Tonie free, Sherry snapped the ball to her. Tonie caught the pass, turned for the basket, and banked the ball off the backboard for 2 points.

"Time," the Raider coach called. Looking up at the scoreboard, he saw that the 6-point halftime deficit had ballooned to almost 30, and he had no idea how to stop it from growing larger. His team was being outplayed, and he simply didn't have the talent to match their opponents.

"Terry, Dawn, Wendy, Amie, Latesha, you're in," Pat told the players on the bench.

"Little early to be taking out the first team, isn't it?" Marcie asked.

"If they can't hold the lead, we'll put the others back in," Pat answered. "It's going to be a long season. I need everyone ready, and you can't get that way sitting on the bench."

Marcie nodded. She didn't necessarily agree, but Pat was the coach.

"Okay, let's just keep doing what we've been doing," Pat told the five players who would be taking over after the timeout. "Nothing fancy. Hold your positions and work together out there. Wendy, Amie, let's give them something new to think about. Press the inbound pass to mid-court, then drop off."

"Okay, Coach," Wendy said, with Amie nodding agreement.

"Dawn, they've been pretty physical under the basket. If you start to get tired, let me know." Pat had been rotating Stacy and Tonie most of the game because of the roughness of the play.

Dawn nodded, but there was no way she'd ask to be taken out of the game. Not after sitting on the bench thus far. She'd heard Marcie's comment about the "first team", and she was about to prove she belonged on it.

The buzzer sounded and the players ran onto the court. The teams exchanged baskets for the next several minutes, with the differential in the score changing very little. A media timeout brought play to a stop with less than three minutes to play.

"Anybody need a breather?" Pat asked when the team huddled in front of their bench.

"I could use one, Coach," Amie said. Keeping up a half-court press had been hard on the player, who had seen little playing time.

"Sherry, you're in. Anybody else? Dawn, what about you?"

"I'm fine," Dawn growled, irate that the coach had singled her out.

"Okay, good." Pat knew her post player had to be tired, but if she wanted to stay in, she'd let her. Dawn had actually been playing well, and she wanted to see more from the troublesome player. "Let's just keep up what we've been doing. Wendy, back off the press and let Sherry handle it. She's got fresher legs."

Wendy nodded, happy for the relief.

With less than a minute to play, Sherry was dribbling up court, looking to set up the final play of the game. Pat signaled for her to run the play they had been practicing the day before, and she held up three fingers to pass the information to her teammates. She could see Latesha and Terry struggling to gain position on their defensive players when Wendy started her cut. She snapped the pass to Wendy, who dropped the ball off to Terry. Terry spun around without having a firm grasp on the ball, and her defender slapped the ball loose.

Sherry saw the ball bounce free and took off after it, her opponent racing to get to it first. Most of the players converged on the ball, but Dawn held her position. Sherry reached the ball first, snatching it off the floor. Sensing she didn't have much time, she scanned the floor for an open teammate. Seeing Dawn standing alone under the basket, she spun to the right and faked a pass to Wendy a few feet away. When the defense went for the fake, she swung the ball behind her back, flipping it to Dawn.

Dawn caught the pass, turned, and popped the ball into the basket just as the buzzer sounded the end of the game. Smirking, she trotted over to the bench to accept her accolades for making the game-ending basket.

Pete rushed up to Sherry and hugged the rookie. "Great pass. I didn't think you'd be able to get the ball to Dawn."

"Nice pass, rookie." Wendy slapped Sherry on the back as she ran past on her way to the water at the end of the bench.

"That's the way to hustle," Marcie told Sherry. "Good play."

"I made the basket," Dawn grumbled when no one said anything to her.

"Ha." Latesha laughed. "An easy 2-foot lay-up. Hope you didn't strain anything while you were standing there waiting for the ball." She hadn't been the only one to notice Dawn had made no effort to retrieve the loose ball.

"Nice game, ladies," Pat told her players before leading them off the court to the cheers of the fans.

Sherry glanced again at the directions Pat had written on a sheet of paper. She was to drive up Highway 12, turning off the highway onto a forest service road just before the Lee Creek campground turnoff. She had a pretty good idea where the turnoff was because Lee Creek had been where she'd met Pat the last time they'd gone hiking. She smiled, remembering how she'd found Pat sunning herself on top of the huge granite boulder.

This set of instructions was a little vague at the end. Sherry was to drive up the dirt road until she saw Pat's pickup.

Driving a straight stretch of the mostly winding road, Sherry looked out the side window at a large meadow that bordered the road to her left. She spotted several deer grazing on the meadow grass under the cloudy gray sky. She was glad she'd added a heavy sweatshirt and pair of nylon pants to her pack before leaving home that morning. Although it wasn't predicted, she wouldn't be surprised to see a few snowflakes before the day was out.

Up ahead, Sherry could see the road curved to the left, and she slowed in order to safely maneuver around a sharp turn that was immediately followed by three more snaking turns. Coming out of the last turn, Sherry saw the Lolo Hot Springs Resort spread out on both sides of the highway and knew the road she was looking for wasn't much further ahead. Just past the hot springs, a forest service road led off to the right, and the road she was to meet Pat on led off to the left immediately after.

Turning off the highway, Sherry brought the car to almost a complete stop. Pat had warned her of the deep potholes and loose cattle guard at the beginning of the road. She drove slowly over the obstacles, then maintained that speed as she continued along the road. The dirt road narrowed in several places, and being unsure what was around each bend, she decided not to take any chances. Besides, the road paralleled a creek, and she was enjoying the scenery. Spotting a moose standing on the opposite side of the creek with its head under the surface of the water, Sherry pulled off on a wide spot to watch the large animal, which was no more than twenty feet away.

The moose raised its head, water running off its thick hide back into the creek. As it chewed the tasty treats it found growing under the water, it studied Sherry with big, brown eyes. Never having seen a moose this close, Sherry was a little concerned whether she was safe and was relieved when the animal made no movement in her direction. After several minutes, the moose dropped its head back under water, and Sherry left it to its early morning meal.

She didn't have to drive much further before spotting Pat's pickup parked off the road. She pulled up behind the vehicle, expecting the coach to be close by. When Pat didn't appear, she looked around, but other than her pickup, she saw no evidence of the other woman. She got out of the car.

"Pat?" Sherry called. She heard movement on the opposite side of the road as someone, or something, moved down the overgrown slope. "Pat?" she called again, hoping it was the coach and not another moose.

"I'm here," Pat called back, stepping out from the cover of the thick undergrowth. "Sorry, I had to...uh...well, you know, I had to..." She motioned over her shoulder with her thumb, her cheeks glowing pink.

Sherry smiled, realizing the activity she had caught Pat in the process of completing. "Guess there aren't too many public restrooms around here, huh?" she teased.

"Well, actually, that depends on what you would classify as a public restroom." Pat smiled, walking across the road to where Sherry was waiting. "Hi."

"Hi, yourself. So what would you call a public restroom?" Sherry asked as Pat walked past the car and her pickup to squat down at the edge of the creek.

Using a handful of the fine, water-polished gravel, Pat washed her hands. She stood, shaking the water off her hands. "I like to refer to Montana as the land of a million bathrooms." She swept a hand around, indicating the surrounding trees. "Take your pick, if you're of a mind to."

"Thanks, but I'm fine right now."

"Still afraid to pee in the woods?" Pat lifted her pack out of the back of her pickup, then walked up to the passenger side of the car, looking over the top of it at Sherry. The grin on her face echoed her challenge.

"No. I just don't have to go right now. When I do, I'll pick my very own tree."

"That's good. 'Cause a woman who can't pee in the woods is no good to me."

"Is that a fact?" Sherry asked, wondering if Pat realized what she had said.

"That's a fact." Pat laughed, pulling the back door of the car open and tossing her pack inside. "We'll leave my truck here. You drive." When Sherry climbed back into the car, Pat said, "Turn left at the fork up there. At the top of the grade, the road splits again. Take the right fork."

Sherry grinned as she drove, following Pat's instructions.

"What's so funny?"

"Nothing."

"Must be something," Pat muttered. "You look like you just got some really good news."

"Well," Sherry smiled, "I think I did."

"Huh?"

Sherry drove over the crest of a small grade and turned right as Pat had instructed. As soon as she turned, she saw the access to the road was blocked by a locked gate. "Road's closed," she said.

"I know. That's why we're here. Park any place."

She drove right up to the gate to park.

"Drop back a bit," Pat told her. "Last thing you want to do is block one of these gates. It's a good way to have your car pushed over the side if the forest service needs to get through while you're gone."

"Oh, good to know." Sherry let the car roll backward for several feet until she could pull to the extreme side of the road. Before she shut off the engine, she made sure there was plenty of room for other vehicles to get by easily.

"This is good," Pat told her as she got out and retrieved her pack from the back seat.

"So where are we hiking?" Sherry asked, grabbing her pack.

Pat pointed up the gated-off road. "Up there."

"Nice wide trail," Sherry teased.

"Yeah, but some of these are the best kind: not too likely to meet anybody else, for one thing; easy hiking, for another. And these old logging roads get you up on top of the ridges where you can see forever." Pat eased her way around the end of the gate, being careful not to slip down the rocky slope beside the road.

"Where's this one go?" Sherry asked, following Pat's lead.

"Goes in this direction for about a half mile, then switches back and goes the opposite direction about the same distance, climbing the whole way. When it levels out, you're way up there." She pointed straight up from where they were walking. "It keeps going for some distance, so we can go as far as we want and turn around whenever we're ready. There's a nice spot about three miles in to stop for lunch and some real nice views along the way, too."

"Sounds good." Sherry smiled, falling into step with her coach.

The women were on their way back down to the car after having walked about four miles up the road and eating lunch next to a small spring.

"I can't believe how far you can see from up here." Sherry was standing on the edge of the road, gazing out at ridge after forested ridge that seemed to go on forever.

"Yeah, amazing isn't it. And not a single manmade thing in sight, unless you count the logging roads."

"It really is beautiful." Standing a respectable distance away, Sherry turned to face Pat. "I'm glad you brought me here."

"My pleasure." Pat smiled. "I'm glad you enjoy it as much as I do. Not too many do." Her voice faded as she remembered the times she had brought other women to this very spot, one of her favorites. Those dates hadn't been as appreciative as Sherry. Pat's head snapped up. *Whoa, who said anything about this being a date? But isn't that what it is? Really, if you look at it honestly, wouldn't you consider it a date?* Afraid Sherry might be able to read her thoughts, she glanced in the player's direction, letting out a sigh of relief when she saw Sherry was engaged in digging into her pack for something.

Having noticed that Pat was preoccupied with her thoughts, Sherry decided it would be a good time to pull the sweatshirt out of the pack and put it on. On top of the ridge there was little protection from the wind, which had been getting noticeably cooler as the day went on.

"Cold?" Pat asked, glad for something to think about other than the date issue.

"A little." Sherry pulled the sweatshirt over her head. "The wind is chilly."

"Won't be able to do this much longer," Pat told her. "At least, not in shorts. There'll be snow falling up this high in another week or two."

"Bummer." Sherry settled her pack back on her shoulders. "I like the days we spend together."

"Just as well." Pat turned away abruptly and started walking down the road.

Sherry was confused by Pat's sudden change in demeanor. Moments before, the coach had been laughing and joking, and now, seemingly without reason, she was serious, her tone solemn and formal. "Pat?" She trotted to catch up with her companion. "Is everything okay?"

Pat stopped, waiting for Sherry to reach her. "Listen, with the season underway, I won't have time to do this anymore. I've got to concentrate on the game, and so should you." The words tumbled out more brusquely than she had intended.

"Okay," Sherry said, her insides quaking at the meaning behind the coach's words. "Did I do something wrong?" she asked quietly.

Seeing the look of hurt on Sherry's face, Pat almost reached out to embrace the woman. Almost. Instead, she blew out a long, calming breath and started again. "I'm sorry, Sherry. Really, I am. That sounded so..."

"Harsh?" Sherry choked out.

"Yeah. I'm not sure what's going on between us, but I can't let it go any further. Not now, not under these circumstances. I'm your coach. I have clauses in my contract against this very thing. I think that it's best if we just concentrate on basketball the rest of the season. It's better for both of us. I wish it could be different, I really do, but right now it can't be. I'm sorry."

"Me, too," Sherry murmured. She knew Pat was right. It could mean both their jobs if they began a relationship and someone found out. But she also knew she was falling in love with her coach, and that wasn't going to change. "Maybe," she whispered, her soft words almost lost in the growing wind, "when the season is over..."

"I can't think that way, Sherry. I can't. Please don't make this any harder than it already is. Please."

Sherry felt the tears forming, and she wrapped her arms around herself, wishing that it were Pat's arms circling her instead of her own.

Seeing how miserable Sherry looked, Pat could hold back no longer. She closed the distance between them, wrapping her arms around Sherry and holding her tight. "I'm so sorry," she murmured.

CHAPTER TWELVE

Pat was alone in her office. Tip-off for the Cougars' second home game was scheduled to take place in approximately two hours, and she was reviewing her notes on their opponents, the Raleigh Patriots. They were a young team with a first-year coach leading them, and Pat was hoping to get past them with few, if any, problems before the Cougars faced their first series of games on the road.

Kelley poked her head through the doorway. "The players are ready, Coach. You want to talk to them now or after warm-ups?"

"Have them take their warm-ups, then bring them in a few minutes early. We need to go over some changes for tonight," Pat said without looking up from her work.

"Problems?" Kelley asked.

"Their post player, Gibbs, still bothers me some." Pat raised her head to look at her assistant coach. "She's played in the league a lot of years, and I'm concerned Tonie and Dawn may not be able to handle her."

"Thought that's why we spent the last two days practicing ways to control her." Kelley stepped into the office so they could talk more comfortably. "The team looked pretty good in practice. Why are you worried about it now?"

"Practice isn't a real game situation, and I'm concerned, that's all. Last year, Gibbs dominated play under the basket. I just don't want her doing it again tonight."

"She also played for Eugene last year. They came close to making it into the finals. Gibbs doesn't have the same caliber of players around her this year."

"So you don't think she'll cause us problems?"

"I think she's big and strong, and she'll still dominate her area on the floor. Eventually."

"Eventually?"

"She's playing with a young team, and for a while she's going to have her hands full making sure she doesn't plow over her own teammates as they try to sort out their positions. I doubt she's going to feel comfortable out there for several games. So to answer your question," Kelley shrugged, "yes, I think she'll cause us some problems, but I don't think she'll do it tonight. So quit worrying."

"I'm the head coach." Pat smiled thoughtfully. "I get paid to worry. I hope you're right, but don't forget, Dawn is a young player, too."

"You could sit her out tonight."

"I could, but I don't want to. She's been working hard in practice, and I don't want her to use sitting out as an excuse to go back to her old ways."

"Then what?"

"Good question." Pat scrubbed the side of her head. "Go on. Get them out on the floor for warm-ups. Maybe I'll have an answer by the time you bring them back in."

Kelley left the office, walking across the outer office and into the locker room. "Let's go, ladies," she shouted above the chatter. "Get out on the floor for warm-ups." She waited until all the players had jogged out of the locker room before following them.

Marcie fell into step beside the other assistant coach. "Coach okay?"

"Seems so. Why?"

"She's been kind of quiet the past few days."

"So I've noticed."

"You ask her about it?"

"No."

"You going to?"

"No."

"Yeah, me neither."

Halftime — Patriots 47 Cougars 43

"We have to do better on the boards, ladies," Pat told her team. "Gibbs is killing us out there." Regrettably, she had been right about the Patriots' low post player, who had spent the first half controlling play under the Raleigh basket.

"Sorry, Coach." Tonie frowned. "I've tried everything with her, and I can't move her. She must have spent the entire off season in the weight room."

"Okay, we're going to have to try double teaming Gibbs. Give her more to worry about than just one player at a time. Terry, I'm pulling you out. Dawn and Tonie will play low. Val, you move out high." She paused to give the players time to acknowledge their new assignments. "Tonie, Dawn, you need to box her out on rebounds. Make her come over or through you; maybe we can get her in foul trouble." Both post players nodded.

"Terry, Ashley, you'll be rotating in. I want to tire her out, force her to start making mistakes. Sherry, push the ball up court, make Gibbs run to catch up with the play. And keep the ball outside, for gosh sakes. Forcing it under the basket is doing absolutely nothing for us. You, Val, and Pete can all hit from outside; start proving it. Okay, the good news is they're only shooting 37 percent. So if we can stop their second, third, and fourth chances, we can turn the score around. We need to concentrate on rebounding. Control the ball. We're still in this game, ladies, and I, for one, have no intention of losing our first game tonight." Pat went over and stood beside the picture of the championship trophy, which now had Kinsey's team picture hanging next to it. "Remember what we're playing for." Pat looked at her players. "What do we *want?*" Pat shouted.

"*Championship!*" the players shouted back.

"Then let's *go get it!*"

Second Half — Patriots 67 Cougars 65

"Time!" Pat yelled at the officials when Dawn was called for a foul. She glanced up at the scoreboard: 6:10 to play. Pat huddled the players around her. "What's going on out there?" She looked at Dawn and Tonie. "You're supposed to box her out, not the other way around."

"I'm trying," Dawn snapped.

"Try harder." Pat glared at the player. Dawn had been trying, but the coach didn't need the attitude right now. "Sherry, you need to come in close when they take a shot." She normally had Sherry hang back around the top of the key in order to be in position to start fast breaks if the ball should take a long bounce off the rim. "Try to jam things up underneath."

Sherry nodded, toweling the sweat off her face.

"Okay, just keep up the pressure," Pat encouraged. "We should have the lead by the next timeout."

As the players trotted back out onto the court, Marcie stepped up beside Pat. "That's four on Dawn. Shouldn't you take her out for a while?"

Pat frowned. Players were allowed six fouls, but a lot could happen in six minutes. Did she want to chance Dawn fouling out? She looked to her bench.

Terry, Ashley, and Stacy were sitting there, waiting to be sent back into the game whenever their coach needed them.

"Let's leave her in for now," Pat said as play resumed.

Twenty-six seconds remaining on the game clock — Patriots 79 Cougars 80

Sherry kept close watch on the player she was guarding as the Patriots worked the ball around the 3-point arc. The Raleigh players were passing the ball almost as soon as it reached their hands, attempting to get it to a teammate with an open shot.

The seconds were ticking down. Dawn was guarding Gibbs, trying to keep her body between the post player and the ball.

Ten seconds

Gibbs planted her legs, pressing her body against Dawn's side. When she felt Dawn press back, she spun away, leaving Dawn stumbling backward as she was caught unbalanced by the quick move.

Nine seconds

Seeing Gibbs break free and in the perfect position for an easy basket, a Raleigh player rifled the ball in her direction.

Eight seconds

Sherry saw Dawn fall out of position. Leaving her player unguarded, she ran to help out.

Seven seconds

Reaching for the pass, Gibbs glanced over her shoulder to make sure Dawn hadn't recovered.

Six seconds

Dawn regained her footing and scrambled to retake her position.

Five seconds

Catching the ball, Gibbs turned to square up to the basket.

Four seconds

Dawn pulled up when she realized any attempt to block the post player's shot would probably result in a foul being called and Gibbs being given two free shots.

Three seconds

The post player raised her arms to take the uncontested shot, her hands dropping slightly behind her head as she took aim.

Two seconds

Every player on the Cougar bench was standing, screaming at Dawn to make some attempt to block the shot.

One second

Sherry, running at an angle to ensure she did not touch Gibbs, left her feet. Her body stretched as she reached her arm as far out to the side as it would go. Her fingers found the ball an instant before it left the post player's hand.

The game-ending buzzer sounded as the ball, deflected just enough by Sherry's fingertips, flew wide, bouncing off the backboard a foot to the side of the rim.

The Cougars were still celebrating when Pat took up a place at the front of the locker room. "Good game, ladies," Pat shouted to get the players' attention. Smiling, she waited for them to settle down so she could talk at a more reasonable volume. "It was close, but we won, and that is all I care about right now."

"You got that right, Coach," Val called out, and several players laughed.

"Of course, come practice tomorrow, I might feel different," Pat said to a chorus of groans. "Okay, I'm not going to stand up here and talk your ears off tonight, but I do have a couple of comments. We leave on a three-game road trip on Friday, and the teams we'll be playing are a lot tougher than the one you faced tonight. So think about that. We can't ever let one player dominate us. We have to be smarter than our opponents. Smarter. Faster. Tougher. Practice at eight tomorrow. Go home and get some rest. The time for celebrating is after we've won that," she pointed at the picture of the trophy, "not now."

The locker room was much quieter when Pat walked away than it had been just moments before, as the players took their coach's comments to heart.

Sherry was sitting near the door that led to Pat's office. It hadn't been intentional, but she was glad she was there when the coach walked toward her. The woman had not spoken to her outside of basketball since their hike the weekend before. She understood Pat's dilemma, but it was impossible to stop her heart from beating faster whenever the coach was near.

Pat smiled as she approached. "Nice play, Sherry. You sure saved our butts out there."

"Thanks, Coach," Sherry murmured. Pat walked past and closed the door behind her as soon as she entered the offices. Sherry sat for a few moments simply enjoying the memory of the coach's smile before moving to her locker. She had just pulled the locker door open when it was ripped out of her hand and slammed shut with a loud crash.

"You enjoy making a fool of me, rookie?" Dawn snarled, pressing her body against Sherry's and shoving her hard against the row of lockers.

Sherry struggled to free herself from the larger player. "Get off me."

"Dawn, back off." Pete had heard the commotion and had come around the end of the lockers to investigate. "Damn it, Dawn." She grabbed the player's arm, yanking her back. "Get off her."

"That's twice, rookie." Dawn poked a finger into Sherry's shoulder. "Don't make it three."

"What's the problem?" Marcie asked, hurrying to stand between Pete and Dawn.

"Nothing," Dawn snapped, spinning around. She stormed off to her own locker at the end of the row.

"Sherry?" Marcie asked. "What's going on between you two?"

"Got me." Sherry shrugged. "She's the one with the problem." *And I'm getting pretty tired of being on the receiving end of it.*

Marcie went to talk to Dawn, and Pete asked, "You okay?" all the while keeping one eye on the heated discussion between assistant coach and player.

"Yes, I'm fine," Sherry said, pulling her bag from the bottom of her locker.

Pete thought the tone of Sherry's voice told a different story. "You want to grab some dinner?"

"Thanks." Sherry smiled at the veteran player. "But I'm beat. I just want to go home, take a hot shower, and go to bed. Eight o'clock is going to come awfully early tomorrow."

"You sure?"

"Yeah." Sherry spun the lock dial and turned to leave.

Pete watched her walk away. "Great game tonight, rookie," she called after Sherry, then turned to walk down to Dawn, who was now sitting alone.

"Get away from me," Dawn growled.

"Listen, you idiot." Pete bent down, placing her hands on the chair arms, her face inches from Dawn's. "You better start getting some facts through that thick skull of yours. First, you're more ego than player right now, and I'm getting pretty sick and tired of it. Second, if you don't like looking like a fool on the court, then quit playing like one. And third, if you ever call Sherry rookie again, *rookie*, I'll reach down your throat and pull your shorts up so tight you'll talk funny the rest of the season."

"I'd like to see you try," Dawn challenged.

"If she don't, I sure as hell will." Terry slapped a hand down on Dawn's shoulder, squeezing tight. She and several other players had moved close to hear Pete's comments.

"Ow." Dawn tried to break Terry's grip but was unable to do so. "Get away from me."

Pete straightened up, motioning with her head for Terry to release the rookie. "Come on, Terr," she said, pulling her teammate away. "She's not worth you getting into trouble with Coach."

"You got that right." Terry chuckled, allowing herself to be led away.

CHAPTER THIRTEEN

Pat pulled some notebooks from her briefcase, stowed the bag in the overhead compartment, and then settled into her seat at the front of the plane, confident that Marcie and Kelley would make sure the players boarded and were seated. She opened the first notebook and studied the pages she had flagged, tuning out the activity going on around her so she could focus on what she was reading. The Cougars were embarking on a three-game road trip, and she had a lot of information about their opponents that she needed to review.

Marcie dropped into the seat beside Pat just as the plane backed away from the terminal. "We set?" Pat asked without looking up from her reading.

"Yeah. Where's Mac?"

"Business meeting in Seattle. She'll meet us in San Diego."

"You need to buckle up, Coach," the flight attendant said as she walked down the aisle, checking on all the passengers.

"Tulsa was tough on defense last year," Pat said of the team's first opponent as she complied with the request.

"And they should be again this year; all their starters are back."

"Peters had knee surgery over the off season." Kelley sat in the seat next to Marcie's, buckling her seat belt. "Some people are saying she's slow coming back from it."

"What about Daniels?" Marcie asked. "I heard she got married and might not be putting as much into the game any more."

"Doesn't seem to make much difference on the court," Pat muttered, flipping through pages. "Her last game, she missed a triple-double by one assist."

Marcie whistled softly. "No kidding?"

"Sixteen points, 12 rebounds, and 9 assists," Pat read off of the notebook page.

"Guess marriage hasn't affected her game."

From her seat a few rows behind them, her lover sitting beside her, Dawn listened to the coaches' discussion. Mandy twisted in her seat to slip her hand between Dawn's legs. Dawn grabbed the hand gliding up her thigh. "Knock it off," she grumbled, pulling it away from her.

"It's a long flight, Dawnie," Mandy pouted, dragging a fingernail up the player's arm and raising goose bumps in its wake. "I need something to keep me occupied."

Dawn yanked a magazine out of the pocket of the seat in front of her and tossed it into Mandy's lap. "Read this."

"I don't want to read."

"Then take a nap. Or do whatever the team pays you to do. Just leave me alone, I've got some stuff to think about."

"What stuff?" Mandy asked, twisting back around in her seat and flipping the magazine into the empty seat beside her.

"Nothing you need to be concerned with," Dawn said, turning to look out the window and placing her back to her lover.

The bus transport from the airport pulled up in front of the hotel just as the sun was setting. The Cougars had flown into Tulsa a day early so that they would have time to practice the morning of the game. Pat felt it was good for the players to get a feel for the court they would be playing on.

"Mandy, get up here," Pat called to the back of the bus where her assistant was sharing a seat with Dawn.

Mandy swayed up to the front of the moving bus. When she reached the coach, she placed her hand on the back of her seat. Leaning over to reveal her breasts under her loose-fitting blouse, she smiled suggestively. "What can I do for you, Pat?"

Pat frowned at her assistant's unveiled display. "I want you to get inside as soon as we stop and make sure everything is ready with the rooms."

"Anything for you, Coach," Mandy purred, slowly straightening.

Pat shook her head in disgust, leaned back in her seat and shut her eyes, effectively ending Mandy's effort to seduce her.

Sherry was watching intently, though she was more interested in Pat's reaction to Mandy's flaunting. She breathed a soft sigh of relief when the coach showed no signs of being interested.

"What a tramp." Pete chuckled beside Sherry. "How Coach keeps from knocking her flat is beyond me. I would have done it a long time ago."

"How long has it been going on?" Sherry asked, surprised that Mandy's conduct with the coach seemed to be common knowledge.

"Let's see: Mac dumped her on the coach two years ago, and Mandy has been doing her best to bed her ever since. You'd think by now she'd get a clue it isn't going to happen."

"You don't think so?" Sherry wasn't asking because she thought Pat would eventually succumb to Mandy's advances, but rather because she wanted to hear Pete's reasoning why it wouldn't happen.

"No way. Coach is too classy to take up with the likes of Mandy. She's looking for long-term, not some quick roll in the sack."

"You sound pretty sure of that."

"If a one-night stand was all she wanted, she could have her pick of any number of women willing to do just about anything to get into bed with her. We see them at every game. Far as I know, she's never given them more than a passing glance. I'm telling you, she's just not that kind of woman."

Dawn had also watched Mandy's overt display. Overhearing Pete and Sherry's conversation, she was beginning to understand why her lover had been so upset when Sherry had been invited to join the team. And why Mandy wanted the player off the team. She frowned. If she did as Mandy wanted, she quite probably would lose her position with the Cougars. If she didn't, she could lose Mandy. She turned in her seat to stare out the bus window as she tried to sort out her choices, which didn't seem acceptable whichever way she went.

"What's the problem?" Pat asked. The team was standing in the hotel lobby while Mandy argued with the desk clerk.

"They booked us one room too few." Mandy turned to Pat. "And this incompetent fool is trying to tell me there's nothing she can do about it."

Pat glared at Mandy. She had double- and triple-checked their travel itinerary over the past week. There had been the proper number of rooms booked, so if they were now one short, her assistant must have cancelled it along with Mac's room before they left Missoula. "Meaning what?"

Mandy lowered her voice to a sexy purr. "Meaning, I guess I'll just have to share yours."

Pat never shared a room; her assistant knew there'd be an unassigned bed in the coach's room.

"Don't count on it." Pat turned to the desk clerk. "Are these our keys?" she asked, smiling apologetically as she snatched up the stuffed envelope on the counter.

The receptionist returned the smile, relieved that the obnoxious woman was no longer doing the talking. "Yes, ma'am."

"They all have two beds?"

"Yes, ma'am."

"What floor are we on?"

"The fifth, ma'am."

"Thank you. Okay, ladies," Pat said to the players. "You heard, fifth floor. Everyone to the elevators, I'll pass out keys when we get there." She turned back to the young woman behind the counter. "You can call me Coach." Pat winked as the clerk blushed.

"Wait a minute," Mandy said as Pat followed the players to the bank of elevators at the side of the lobby. "Where am I going to stay?"

Frowning, Pat looked at Mandy for a moment, then turned to survey her players. "You bunk with Pete," she told her assistant. "Sherry, you're with me. There, now you have a place to stay," Pat informed her assistant. "Happy?"

Mandy glared at Pat. Lowering her voice so only the coach could hear, she said, "You can't have a player sleep in your room. You know the rules."

"There's no rule about that, Mandy, only about me sleeping *with* a player."

"Mac isn't going to like this."

"Probably not, but this isn't my doing. So, like it or not, she'll have to accept my judgment on the matter."

"We'll see about that," Mandy threatened, brushing past Pat to get to the elevators.

Pat reached out to stop her. "Wait a minute."

"What?"

"When you call Mac, be sure to tell her that *you* cancelled *your* room. I'm sure she'll be happy to hear that you thought you could force your way into my bed by doing so."

Mandy shook Pat's hand off her arm. "Don't flatter yourself."

"You're some piece of work, aren't you?"

"Are we done?" Mandy snapped.

"Yeah. You can go. By the looks of it, you have some explaining to do."

Mandy stormed away but pulled up short when she saw Dawn leaning against the wall next to one of the elevator bays. "Shit." She spat the word out, resuming her walk toward her unhappy lover.

"Um." Sherry stood just inside the room looking around. "Which bed do you want?" she asked as Pat walked into the room.

"Take your pick." Pat set her bags down on the floor next to the small table under the window. "I've got to go down and make sure Mandy didn't do anything to screw up the restaurant reservations," she said, pulling her notebooks free. "After dinner, I'll be going over game plans with Marcie and Kelley in their room, so make yourself at home. I won't be back until after curfew," she told Sherry as she walked out of the room.

"Guess that answers that," Sherry muttered, dumping her bags on the bed closest to the window.

"I want to thank you for the most pleasant evening that I had last night," Pete sarcastically told her usual road trip roommate as they walked onto the court for practice.

Sherry snickered, imagining what kind of foul mood Mandy must have been in the night before. "Oh, really?"

"Can you believe she asked Stacy to switch rooms so she could stay with Dawn?"

"Why didn't she?" Sherry asked. "I'll bet Dawn wasn't much better to be around."

"Actually, it was Dawn who vetoed the idea."

"Uh, oh. Trouble in paradise?"

"I doubt it." Pete laughed. "They seem to have a real love-hate thing going on. They love to hate that they love each other."

"Huh?"

"Yeah."

"Come on, ladies," Pat called to the players. "We've got a lot to do in the limited time we have the court."

Practice consisted of the team taking open shooting practice for a half hour before Pat called them together to run through a couple of plays. She wanted them to get used to the arena surroundings so they wouldn't be caught off guard by anything during the game. Although all basketball courts were the same dimensions, the arenas varied greatly as to where things like scoreboards and team benches were located and how close the fans were seated in relation to the floor. It wasn't unusual for a player in the heat of the game to spot an unusual structure out of the corner of her eye and react to it because she wasn't used to it being there.

"Sherry, Pete, you need to take it to the key tonight," Pat was telling the players. "They play a sagging defense so take advantage of that by drawing them to you and then passing to whoever's left open. Okay, let's run through some plays from half court. Just work on getting your game legs, nothing fancy," she added. "Sherry, Pete, Val, Terry, Tonie, you take the offense. Wendy, Amie, Latesha, Ashley, and Dawn, you're on defense. Remember, you're playing a sagging pocket focusing on the ball."

Sherry trotted to mid-court, dribbling the ball between her legs and switching it from hand to hand to loosen up. When Pat blew her whistle, she headed up court. Pete was several feet off to her right, beginning a move across the court between Sherry and Val positioned at the top of the key. Sherry snapped the ball to Val, who flicked it to Pete as she ran past.

Pete dribbled around the corner, pulling up when Latesha and Wendy double teamed her. She passed the ball back to Val.

Sherry was cutting to the right side of the court, hoping to get behind a screen being set by Tonie.

Val caught the pass, turned toward the key, and saw Sherry racing for the end of the court. She thought about passing to her, but Wendy moved in to help cover her and blocked the passing lane. Val spun back the opposite way, dropping the ball off to Pete.

Sherry saw the ball go to the other side of the court and made a cut that would take her across the middle of the key, jamming her guard, Amie, into Dawn and Ashley as they sagged on defense. If the players reacted as expected, she should be able to make a second cut to the top of the key, where she should be open for a 15-foot turnaround jumper.

Val faked a pass to Pete, giving Sherry time to make her second cut, then dropped a bounce pass to the point guard moving to the top of the key.

Sherry grabbed the ball. Planting her feet, she leaped into the air, twisting as she rose. She sensed someone closing in on her, but she expected them to pull up in order not to cause any unnecessary injury to a teammate. She didn't suspect Dawn would be the player, nor did she anticipate that the post player would purposely charge into her.

Dawn, still fuming over Mandy's attempted seductions of Pat and over the memories of the two games the point guard had been hailed a hero at her own expense, decided to do what her lover had been begging her to do — take Sherry out. Dawn saw her opportunity, and she wasn't about to let it pass. Shoving Tonie aside, she rushed to intercept the point guard. Running at full speed, she plowed into Sherry, taking her legs out from under her.

Sherry wasn't sure what had happened. One minute, she'd been rising off the court to execute an easy turn-around jump shot and the next everything went black.

Pat watched in horror as Dawn failed to pull up. She was already running toward the players before Sherry had been knocked into an airborne somersault. The players froze when Sherry hit the floor, head first, and remained still.

Lizzie, who had also watched the play unfolding, raced onto the court, screamed, "Don't touch her!"

"Move back," Marcie ordered the players crowding around Sherry. "Move back, now."

Kelley grabbed hold of Dawn's arm, yanking her out of the crowd of players and to the side of the court. "What the hell were you thinking?" She pushed the player back into a row of seats, causing her to fall into one of them.

"I was just—"

"Shut up," Kelley growled. "Shut up and stay here until we find out if she's all right."

Dawn slumped back in the seat.

"Ugh..." Sherry groaned, reaching for the back of her head.

"Welcome back," Lizzie said as she continued to determine the extent of the player's injuries.

"Is she going to be okay?" Pat asked anxiously.

Lizzie didn't answer. She was concentrating on Sherry, asking her a number of questions and judging her responses.

"She should be fine. I think she has a concussion. We should take her to the hospital and have them check her over. At the very least, she's going to have a whopper of a headache for a day or two." Lizzie patted Sherry on the arm. "And she definitely won't be playing tonight."

Hearing that, Sherry struggled to sit up.

"Lay still." Lizzie forced the point guard back down. "You try to stand up right now and you'll take another header."

Pete ran up to the coaches. "Ambulance will be here in a few minutes." She had gone to have one called as soon as she realized Sherry had lost consciousness.

"Good." Pat nodded, fighting the urge to drop to the floor and wrap the injured woman in her arms. Slowly she knelt down, placing a gentle hand on Sherry's shoulder. "You doing okay?" she asked, concern clouding her voice and eyes.

"Think so." Sherry tried to smile, but even that caused her head to hurt.

"Take it easy. Lizzie will go with you to the hospital."

"I'll be okay, Coach." Sherry blinked, attempting to focus on the woman leaning over her. "I can play."

Pat smiled. "I think it's okay if you sit this one out, Sherry." She looked up when two EMTs rolled a gurney onto the court. "Here's your ride now. You take it easy and do what the doctors say. I'll see you later, okay?"

Sherry's eyes never left Pat as the coach stood up to make room for the EMTs.

Mandy was sitting on the end of the bed watching cartoons, the television turned up loud as she laughed at the antics of the animated characters.

"Would you mind turning that down?" Sherry moaned. She was lying on her side, staring out the hotel room window. It was dark outside, and she wondered how late it was. And how her teammates were doing in the game she had been forced to miss. Her head hurt like the blazes, but the doctors had agreed she could return to the hotel as long as someone stayed with her at all times. Lizzie needed to be at the game, so Mandy was volunteered to stay with the injured player.

"I can barely hear it as it is," Mandy grumbled. It wasn't the first time she'd been asked to lower the volume.

Sherry was in no mood for the administrative assistant's well-practiced pout. "Then why don't you go watch it in your room?"

"Can't leave you alone." Mandy shrugged. "Otherwise, I would."

The door to the room swung open, and Pat marched in, followed by Lizzie. Sherry rolled over on her back, groaning at her throbbing head. She was about to ask about the game, but the look on the coach's face told her everything she needed to know. Obviously the game had not gone well for the Cougars.

Hearing the noise from the television, Pat switched it off as she walked by on the way to her bed, where she collapsed. "You can leave, Mandy. Lizzie and I'll take over."

"'Bout time." Mandy stood. "I never signed on to be a babysitter."

Lizzie sat on the edge of Sherry's bed, careful not to cause the player any more discomfort. "How you doing?" she asked, taking careful note of the player's reactions.

"Head hurts," Sherry said.

"Have you taken the pain pills the doc gave you?"

"No. They make me sick. Can't I just have a couple of Advil?"

"Sure." Lizzie reached into her bag, pulling out the requested analgesic. "Let me get you some water."

"I'll do it." Pat pushed off her bed and went into the bathroom to find a glass.

"That bad?" Sherry whispered so the coach wouldn't hear. She'd seen the slump of Pat's shoulders and the frown that seemed permanently affixed to her face.

"It was nasty," Lizzie whispered back. "Lost by 27. I think everyone was worried about you, especially Coach."

"What she'd do with Dawn?"

"I benched her ass for the next two games." Pat walked back into the room with a glass of cold water. "Would have thrown her off the team if I thought Mac would let me get by with it."

"That's kind of severe, don't you think, Coach?" Lizzie took the glass from Pat. "She said she was just going for the block. These things happen."

"Hard to block the ball when you're aiming at the knees." Pat dropped back onto her bed. She flopped onto her back, exhausted by the day's events.

"Thanks." Sherry downed the pain pills and emptied the glass.

"Well, you seem to be doing pretty well for having landed on your head. I'm going down to the restaurant for something to eat as soon as I grab someone to keep an eye on you."

"I'll stay," Pat said. She knew she shouldn't, but she selfishly wanted some time alone with her player.

"You sure? I could get Pete or one of the others to stay with her."

"I'm sure. I'm too tired to move right now anyway."

"Want me to bring you something back?"

Sherry turned a little green just thinking about eating. "Not for me, I don't think I could hold anything down right now."

"Pat?"

"Nah. I'll just order room service in a bit, if I don't fall asleep first."

"Don't fall asleep too soon. You're supposed to be watching Sherry, you know."

"I know." Pat sat up, swinging her long legs over the side of the bed. "I'll stay awake, I promise."

"Okay." Lizzie stood, walking to the door. "Page me if you need me."

"Will do."

The room was silent for several minutes after the trainer left. Pat and Sherry looked at each other, but neither seemed to know how to break the silence. Finally, Sherry could take it no longer. "Rough game, huh?"

Pat sighed. "Missed my point guard."

"Sorry."

"Not your fault." After spending a few heartbeats thinking about it, Pat stood up and moved over to sit on the edge of Sherry's bed. "How are you feeling?" she asked, brushing a few stray hairs off the guard's forehead.

"I'll be fine," Sherry whispered. Clasping Pat's hand with her own, she held it to her cheek, softly rubbing against it.

Pat's heart rate skyrocketed. "Sherry..."

"I know." Sherry released the hand. "I just needed to know what that felt like."

Pat smiled. "Nice."

"Very nice."

"You should get some sleep. Let that hard head of yours rest."

"You, too. You look beat." Sherry's hand started upward to caress the coach's face, but she withdrew it when she saw the look of regret in Pat's eyes. "Promise me something?"

"If I can."

"When the season is over, we take the time to figure all this out."

"I can't—"

"No." Sherry reached up and placed two fingers against Pat's lips. "You don't have to say yes; just don't say no."

Pat nodded. She gently wrapped her fingers around Sherry's wrist, pulling the fingers away from her mouth. "Go to sleep," Pat said softly, placing Sherry's hand back on the bed.

CHAPTER FOURTEEN

Cougar Arena: late Second Half — New York 62 Cougars 73

Sherry dribbled down the right side of the court, passed the ball to Terry at the top of the key, then circled back out to the 3-point line.

Terry looked over her shoulder to see Pete tied up on the left side of the court and Tonie and Val having trouble getting free under the basket. She flipped the ball back out to Sherry.

Sherry caught the pass, taking a stutter step to freeze her defender, then charged for the top of the key where Terry was setting a pick. She dribbled close, brushing past Terry to dislodge her defender. Two steps further into the corner of the key, she turned toward the basket, an opportunity for an open jump shot clear to everyone in the arena. Her defender spun around Terry, then ran to regain her position. Seeing the movement, Sherry hesitated, then backpedaled several feet from the key.

Unhappy with Sherry's repeated unwillingness to take a shot, the fans let loose a chorus of boos.

"Damn," Pat muttered.

Since the point guard had rejoined the team for the San Diego game, the coach had watched her pull up on shot after shot whenever a defender was close enough to offer any pressure.

Marcie leaned over close to the coach to be heard above the crowd. "You need to take her out."

"No, she needs to work out of it."

"She'll hurt us if you leave her in there."

Pat knew Marcie was right. The Cougars had won in San Diego and in Los Angeles the next night, but not by much. And Sherry's stats for both games were way below normal for the jittery player.

Sherry dribbled around the top of the 3-point circle, looking for an open teammate.

Pete made a cut across the top of the key, running for a screen Tonie was setting.

Sherry's defender bit on her fake pass to the other guard, leaving Sherry open. Effortlessly, she pumped the ball into the net from behind the arc.

The boos from a moment before turned to cheers.

"Time!" the New York coach yelled from the sideline.

"That's why she's staying in." Pat smiled, shouting above the crowd to her assistant coach, "She's still got her shot; all she needs is her confidence."

Pat sat a few rows up in the first tier of seats, watching Sherry practicing free throws. The Cougars had finished the home game against New York on the winning side of the score, but the point guard had been absent from the celebration in the locker room. When the coach went searching, she had a pretty good idea where she'd find her. She knew she was right when she heard the recognizable pattern of two bounces, pause, one bounce, pause, echoing down the corridor followed by a ball rattling the basket rim.

The point guard barely noticed Pat climbing up into the stands to watch her.

Pat knew what Sherry's problem was. What she didn't know was how to help her overcome it. She considered several options as she watched the player practice.

It was almost two hours after the game's end when Sherry sank her last practice shot. She retrieved the ball and headed for the locker room, her path taking her near to where her coach was sitting.

"You have a few minutes?" Pat asked. "Or do you have to get someplace?"

Sherry shook her head. "No. I'm okay."

"Good." Pat stepped down to the arena floor. "Thought we might talk."

"Um, Coach," Sherry said hesitantly; she knew what the conversation was going to be about. "I'm really sorry. I know I'm choking in the key..."

Pat reached out, tapping the ball out of Sherry's hands. She let it bounce once before catching it on the rebound. "I'm not worried about that."

Sherry stared at her coach. She'd been sure that Pat was about to chew her out for her play in the last three games. "You're not?"

"Nah." Pat barely glanced at the basket before releasing the ball in its direction. They were standing on the sideline, but the ball dropped through the center of the basket, scarcely ruffling the net. "We all go through spells where we're afraid to trust our instincts," she said as she went to retrieve the ball.

Sherry followed her coach back onto the court. "Even you?" she asked doubtfully.

"Oh, yeah." Pat popped into the air to sink a 10-foot jumper. This time, she flipped the ball to Sherry after retrieving it.

Without thinking, Sherry caught the pass and duplicated Pat's shot. "What happened?" she asked, as she trotted for the ball, then passed it to her coach.

"My junior year in high school, a player from another school thought she should have been named state player of the year. So, the next year she took my legs out from under me on a lay-up. I landed on my head."

"No shit?" Sherry gasped. "That hurt."

"Sure did. You must have a harder head because you got off lucky compared to me." Pat took a couple of steps into the key before popping up in the air for a 5-footer. "I spent two days in the hospital with my concussion."

"Damn." Sherry caught Pat's pass, took three steps toward the basket, and cut left around Pat, who was offering a little pressure, before taking a jump shot. "Messed up your shooting?"

"For a few days. I kept hearing footsteps whenever I thought about leaving my feet."

"How'd you get over it?"

"I've been making baskets since I was old enough to pick up a ball." Pat smiled at the memory of all the hours spent shooting baskets in the driveway of her parents' house. "I wasn't about to let one dirty play ruin my dreams. When my coach finally let me back into a game, I forced myself to ignore the footsteps. Won't say I didn't get a scare or two, but I bulled my way through them."

As they exchanged baskets, Pat gradually put more pressure on her player, guarding her a little tighter each time she had the ball. Pat's un-braced knee was screaming in pain, but she sensed she was on the right track with Sherry so she ignored the warning signs. She would deal with the knee later. Right now it was more important to get Sherry back on track.

"What happened to the girl?" Sherry asked as she feigned a move into the key, then pulled up for a quick jump shot.

"Her coach benched her for the rest of the season, which was basically the whole year since she'd hit me in only the second game." Pat caught the ball after it dropped through the net, immediately flipping it back up against the backboard to drop in again.

"Ouch," Sherry grunted. She had the ball, and when she stepped toward the basket for a lay-up, she found Pat moving in on her. A quick step to the right opened a path to the basket, and she banked the ball off the backboard.

"She didn't suffer too long." Pat laughed. "Her parents moved out of state, and she transferred to a school that didn't care what she'd done and let her play."

"Guess that was the last of her, huh?"

"No. I ended up playing against her again in college."

"You get even?" Sherry asked as she caught a pass, then pivoted to drive down the lane.

"Sure did." Pat slid into Sherry's path, blocking her. "It was the first round of NCAA tournament, and I had my best game ever."

Sherry grunted as she tried a head-fake against her coach. When Pat seemed to fall for the fake, Sherry tried to dribble around her, but she found her path blocked again. Instinctively, Sherry feinted left, made another head fake, then spun a 360 around Pat, giving her nothing but empty floor to the basket. A quick step before she left her feet and the ball kissed the backboard before dropping into the basket.

"Think you can do that in our next game?" Pat asked.

Sherry grinned. Somehow, without her even realizing it, Pat had put her demons behind her. "I can give it a try."

"Good."

"Hey, first round of the NCAAs? The year you were voted MVP and set the scoring record? I was at that game," Sherry said excitedly, remembering being in the stands the night Pat put on a scoring demonstration that had never been equaled and quite possibly never would be. "You scored 49 points that game."

"You were there?"

"I was a freshman at Western Arizona, and the entire team made the trip to Arizona State to see those first-round games." Sherry wasn't about to tell Pat she had gone more to see her than to watch the teams play. "I couldn't believe the way you played that night. Everything you threw up went in. It was awesome. So, which player was it?"

"I probably shouldn't say." Pat grinned. "She plays in the league."

"Come on," Sherry whined. "I won't tell, I promise."

Laughing, Pat shook her head. "It's getting late. Hit the showers, and get some sleep. Practice starts at eight tomorrow."

Sherry groaned. "Eight?"

"Yes. Don't be late," Pat called after the player running for the locker room. Retrieving the ball, she groaned as she took the first step. "Looks like I'll be spending the next few hours with an ice pack." She grimaced at the pain radiating from her knee, knowing she had stressed the joint way beyond anything she should have attempted without wearing her brace. But she figured it was worth it, given the look on Sherry's face when she ran off the court. She smiled. When she'd asked the player to stay and talk, she'd had no idea how to address Sherry's problem. But a solution had worked itself out naturally. "Seems I have a knack for this coaching thing, after all." She whistled happily as she limped across the court.

Smiling, Mac turned away from the wall of glass at the front of her office. Noticing that the lights over the court had been left on long after the building should have been cleared of fans, she had left her desk to investigate. She saw Sherry practicing free throws, but it had taken a few moments for her to spot her coach sitting in the stands. She had continued to watch when Pat joined Sherry on the court, wondering why the two hadn't yet left for home. It hadn't taken her long to realize what the coach was accomplishing.

"Want to tell me again why you don't put the uniform back on?" Pete was sitting on a chair in the medical room watching Lizzie wrap an ice pack on the coach's knee.

"Don't start," Pat warned the veteran player.

"It's a fair question." Lizzie tucked the end of the elastic bandage under the edge of one of the folds.

"Don't you start, either," Pat repeated.

"You've still got the moves and the touch." Pete approached her coach. Hidden in the shadows of the corridor to the locker room, she had watched Pat work with Sherry. "The only thing stopping you is you."

"I'm tired of this conversation," Lizzie said as she checked to make sure the ice pack was secure. "You know the drill. Take it off when you're ready. I'll check on you tomorrow."

"Good night, Lizzie," Pete said as the team trainer walked away.

"Let it drop, Pete," Pat warned.

Pete shrugged and returned to the chair. "Too bad Mac didn't put those cushy chairs in here." She squirmed to find a comfortable position on the metal folding chair. "Remember when you joined the Cougars?" she asked casually. "You were nothing but a punk out of college, still hobbling around on crutches."

"I remember," Pat said, wondering where the player was headed.

"Remember what you told me that day?"

"No."

"Sure you do."

Pat looked at the woman who wasn't just a player she coached, but one of her closest friends. That fact was not well known, as the women kept their relationship strictly on a business level during the season. She thought back to that first day she had entered the Cougar arena as a newly hired assistant coach.

It was early and the place was empty, or so she had thought. As Pat walked across the basketball floor, a slight movement caught her attention.

"So, you're the new coach." A black woman was sitting in a seat a few rows up from the floor. She wore a set of Cougar sweats and had her feet propped up on the seat in front of her. Her dark hair was divided into neat cornrows, the braids pulled back with an elastic band holding the ends together. She sat calmly observing the woman standing below.

"That's what my contract says."

"What do you say?"

"I'm the new coach."

"You don't sound very convincing."

"Oh?"

"Probably because you're not too comfortable in the role."

"Is that what you think?"

"Not important what I think. What do you think?"

Pat gazed at the woman for several minutes. *"I think...I'm scared to death,"* she admitted, not knowing why she trusted the woman.

"I figured. Come on up and sit."

Pat did as she was instructed.

"Hi." The black woman held out her hand when the coach was settled beside her. *"Diane Sunndee. But everyone calls me—"*

"Pete. Yes, I know." Pat smiled, clasping the offered hand. *"Pat Calvin."*

"I've seen you play. You're good."

"Was," Pat corrected.

"Surgery went well?"

"Yes."

"Rehab going okay?"

"Yes."

"So what's the problem?"

"Can't play on this." Pat looked down at the knee, still swollen and stiff.

"Not today. But give it a couple of months and you'll be fine."

"No."

"No?"

"I can't play," Pat said softly. *"I can't..."*

"Afraid of it happening again?" Pete asked, her voice caring, not critical.

Pat sighed. *"Yes."*

"Give it time, Pat. Don't let your dreams die so easily." Pete stood. *"I've got to get ready for practice. Hear we have a new coach arriving today."*

"Why?"

"Sorry?"

"Why did you do this?"

"Like I said, I've seen you play. Always wondered what it would be like to share the court with you. I hope someday I'll get the chance to find out."

"It's not going to happen."

"Maybe. But at least I can say I shared a team with Pat Calvin."

"Thank you."

"I wouldn't go thanking me yet. You don't know how much of a pain in the butt I am to coach." Pete laughed as she climbed over the seats to reach the arena floor. *"Oh, and Pat,"* she turned to face the rookie coach, *"one thing I know for sure — unless you have confidence in yourself, there isn't a player on this planet who will have confidence in you. So you want to try and answer my question again?"*

"What was the question?" Pat asked.

"Are you the new coach?"

Pat smiled. *"Yes, damn it. I* am *the new coach."*

Pat tucked her memories away. "Why did you do that?" Pat asked.

"I'm not sure. It just seemed the right thing to do."

"You saved my career."

"No." Pete shook her head. "You're a good coach. You just needed a nudge to get you to see it. Just like the knee. You can play, Pat. But until you're willing to put on the uniform and prove it—"

"I can't."

Pete rose off the chair and stood beside the examination table where Pat sat. "You can," she said placing a comforting hand on Pat's thigh. "And some day you will. You just haven't found the right reason yet." Not waiting for a response, Pete walked out of the room.

"It was an accident," Dawn lied. There was no way she was going to admit to purposely trying to injure a teammate to the woman on the other end of the phone.

"I guess I'll have to take your word for that. But I'm telling you right now, if anything else like that happens..."

"It won't. I promise."

"Make sure it doesn't."

The phone line went dead, and Dawn flipped her cell phone closed.

"Who was that?" Mandy asked from across the bedroom where she was looking through the closet for something to wear to dinner. Dawn had offered to treat her to a meal at a restaurant rather than ordering pizza as was their usual habit.

"Doesn't matter," Dawn said dourly.

"Oh, Dawnie." Mandy looked at her gloomy lover. "I thought you'd be happy. You took care of Sherry—"

"Will you stop acting like that was a good thing?"

"It was a good thing. Stupid bitch deserved to be dropped on her head."

"Mandy, are you really that..."

"That what?"

"Don't you understand she could have been seriously injured?" Dawn had been petrified when she saw Sherry hit the hardwood floor. She hadn't thought how her actions could permanently affect the other player. "It's lucky she wasn't." She shook her head in an attempt to dispel the awful memory of Sherry's prone, unmoving body.

"So? What do you care?"

"I care."

"If you're so concerned, why'd you do in the first place?" When Dawn didn't answer, Mandy stormed across the room to confront her. "Why? You didn't do it for me. Remember? You said you wouldn't. You couldn't be bothered. So, why? What changed your mind?"

Dawn stared at her lover. "You."

"I what?"

"You changed my mind; you throwing yourself at Coach, and right in front of me. Is that what all this has been about? You're just using me as a way to get into Coach's bed?"

"Don't be silly." Mandy laughed nervously. "Of course not."

"Talk about a bitch." Dawn pushed Mandy aside. Grabbing the keys to Mandy's car off the dresser top, she stormed toward the apartment door.

"Where are you going?"

"Don't know."

"When will you be back?"

"Don't know."

"What about dinner?"

The door slammed behind Dawn.

"Shit."

Cougar Arena: Second Half — Eugene Rafters 72 Cougars 87

Pete dribbled the ball across the 3-point line as Sherry kept pace about six feet off her left shoulder. Dawn and Terry were jockeying for position under the basket, and Val was drifting off to the left side of the court, taking her defender with her. Sherry charged for the key, her defender a half step behind.

Pete rifled a bounce pass, leading Sherry into the key. Snatching up the ball, Sherry took one long stride into the paint, planting her foot to push herself upward.

Dawn and Terry's guards released, converging on the point guard. Sherry head faked a shot, sending the two taller defenders into the air. Twisting her body sideways, she thrust upward, slicing between the defenders. The ball, curling off her fingertips, floated over the rim to drop neatly into the basket. Whistles blew as a Eugene player was called for a foul.

Taking her place at the free-throw line, Sherry glanced over to the sideline and the Cougar bench and saw her coach smiling at her.

As she trotted past to her position behind the 3-point line, Pete nudged Sherry's shoulder. "Nice shot."

"Thanks," Sherry mumbled, smiling at Pat.

"You ready?" an official asked Sherry, who was standing with her back to the basket.

"Yes." Sherry nodded, turning around to accept the ball from the official.

"One shot," the official alerted the other players.

Sherry planted her feet shoulder distance apart, the toes of her shoes just behind the stripe, then began her normal routine. *Look at the basket. Two bounces. Deep breath. Bend knees. One bounce. Deep breath. Bend knees. Push up while raising arms until hands are just over head. Flip wrists.*

Sherry was already backpedaling when the ball dropped through the center of the rim.

"Good game, ladies," Pat said, standing at the front of the locker room. "Nice to have you back, Sherry." She smiled at the point guard as several of her teammates congratulated her on the return of her game. "We can notch up another W." Pat added a tick mark on the marker board behind her; the Cougars had six wins to their one loss for the season. "Go home and get some rest. Tomorrow, we start getting ready for Little Rock." Arkansas was the team the Cougars would face in two nights on their home court.

Pat went into the training room to talk with Lizzie. Except for the fall Sherry had taken, the Cougars had suffered few injuries, and she wanted to make sure no one's status had changed. She was very aware that players didn't always let their coach know when they were injured, but it was a little harder to keep that information from the trainer.

"Nice game, Coach," Lizzie said when Pat approached.

"Thanks." Pat smiled. "It's nice to have Sherry back."

"I think everyone feels that way. Fans sure like to see the extra points on the scoreboard. What'd she end up with tonight?"

"Twenty-six."

"Good night."

Pat nodded. "Anything going on I should know about?"

"Couple of sore ankles, one slightly twisted wrist, more bruises than I can keep track of, but nothing major."

"Good."

"I don't know." Lizzie said. "It's kind of boring around here. I think I'd prefer a few broken bones."

"Hush," Pat warned. "I don't want you jinxing us."

"Don't worry, Coach." Lizzie laughed. "I wouldn't complain if we went all season with nothing more serious than what we've got now. Mac pays me the same either way."

"And don't you forget that." Pat smiled. "Just keep them healthy for me, Lizzie. I'm going to need all of them to get where we're going."

"Even Dawn?"

"Even Dawn."

Lizzie tone turned serious. "She seems to have undergone an attitude adjustment this past week."

"Yeah."

"Any ideas why?"

"Not really."

Pat passed through the locker room on the way to her office. Most of the players were gone, but she spotted Sherry and Pete talking at the front of the room and decided to join them.

Her feet propped up on the wall, Sherry was sitting and listening to Pete tell her about the Little Rock guards. She was trying to spend as much time as she could with Pete and Marcie, learning everything they could teach her about the game and the other guards in the league. She was sure she was driving the two women crazy with all her questions, but it was a way to keep her mind off the woman she really wanted to be spending her time with.

"You two plan on ever going home tonight?" Pat asked as she walked up.

"Oh, sure, Coach." Pete smiled. "Just as soon as my husband gets here. My car is in the shop, and he had to work late."

Pat glanced up at the clock. "Puts in longer hours than you do," she said when she saw how late it had gotten to be.

Pete laughed. "Good thing we don't have kids yet."

"I'd prefer you leave 'yet' out of that comment," Pat teased.

Marcie poked her head into the locker room. "Pete, your hubby is out here."

By order of Pat, no one was allowed in the team's locker room except players and female members of the Cougar organization.

"Thanks." Pete leaned down to grab her bag. "I'll see you tomorrow."

"'Night, Pete," Sherry called as the player rushed to meet her husband. "Thanks."

"What about you?" Pat asked after Pete left. Absently, she dropped her hand onto Sherry's shoulder.

"I'm leaving now," Sherry said, but she refused to move, enjoying the feel of Pat's hand where it was.

"Good." Pat smiled warmly at the point guard. "You played a good game tonight, Sherry."

"I wouldn't have been able to do it without your help."

"Just doing my job."

"Well, it felt good," Sherry said.

"What the hell are you doing?"

The women looked up to see the Eugene coach, Michael Palmer, standing just inside the locker room door.

"I could ask you the same thing," Pat snapped, her hand falling away from Sherry's shoulder when she turned to face the other coach. "You know that this room is off limits."

"Now I know why. I've warned the league about you and your kind!" the man shouted. "It's disgusting that they let you near young women like her."

"What the hell are you talking about?" Pat shouted back at the man, who had been very vocal in his wish to ban all lesbians from the league — players and coaches.

"I saw you. I saw what you were trying to do."

"You didn't see anything, because there was nothing to see."

Marcie ran into the locker room from the offices, followed by Kelley. Lizzie also ran in from the trainer's room when she heard the angry voices.

Marcie rushed up to the Eugene coach. "Get out of here, Palmer."

"Don't try to protect her." The man fought Marcie's attempts to force him out of the room. "You can't deny what she was doing."

"It doesn't need denying, 'cause I'm sure it never happened if you're saying it did." Marcie grunted, digging her heels in and pushing the man toward the doorway.

"Nothing happened!" Sherry cried out, jumping to her feet, ready to defend Pat against all comers. "Nothing."

With Kelley's help, Marcie was beginning to have some success in moving the agitated man out of the room.

"I'm going straight to Mac. I told her you were nothing but trouble. Now I have the proof."

"*Nothing* happened!" Pat yelled at the coach. "But if you want to go running to Mac about me congratulating a player for a great game, I'm sure she's in her office."

"Get the hell out of here, you stupid fool." Kelley shoved the man out into the corridor.

As soon as her accuser had been forced out of the room and the door slammed shut behind him, Pat slumped against the wall.

"Pat?" Sherry whispered.

Marcie dropped into a chair, exhausted from her struggle with the other coach. "Now what?"

"Anyone know what he was here for?" Pat asked.

"Didn't think to ask," Kelley grumbled, rubbing her arm where a bruise was forming.

Pat blew out a long breath. "Well, someone probably should go see if his team needs something."

"To hell with them," Lizzie said. "What are you going to do about him and Mac?"

"Nothing."

"What!" Kelley, Lizzie, and Sherry all asked at the same time.

"Coach, you can't just let him go to Mac with his lies," Kelley said.

"Mac knows he's a bigoted, homophobic idiot." Pat looked at Sherry, who appeared to be on the verge of tears. "Go home," she said softly.

"But—"

"Go home. You did nothing wrong; I did nothing wrong. Mac will know that. The most he can do is spread more of his hateful lies around the league."

"I've yet to figure out why he even coaches women's basketball, considering how he feels." Marcie sighed. "Geez, if he hates lesbians so much, why surround himself with them?"

"Who knows?" Lizzie muttered. "Pat, what do you plan to do?"

"I'll try to give Mac a call. Maybe I can catch her before he gets up there." Pat pushed off the wall. "Go home. It'll be okay," she told Sherry again before walking toward her office.

"She's right, Sherry," Kelley said sadly. "It's not the first time someone's openly accused her of being a lesbian."

Lizzie snickered. "Sure won't be the last, either."

"Mac knew Pat was gay when she hired her, so it's not going to be any life-shattering outing. She'll be okay."

"But nothing was going on," Sherry said, her voice cracking.

"We know," Marcie chimed in. "Pat's no fool. She would never try anything with a player."

"Come on." Lizzie walked up to Sherry. "I'll give you a ride. This night has been long enough for all of us."

"Shit," Marcie muttered after Lizzie led Sherry out of the locker room.

"You can say that again," Kelley said.

"Shit."

"Now what?"

"Let's go wait with Pat."

"Yeah."

Mandy scurried back behind her desk. She didn't want any of the coaches to see she'd been listening to the confrontation and its aftermath, especially not Pat. "Well, this could be just what I need," she said to herself as Pat walked past into her office.

"What?"

"Oh, nothing."

"Go home, Mandy."

"Are you sure, Pat? I don't mind waiting."

"Go home."

"Mandy, don't cause any problems tonight," Kelley said as she entered the office area. She had heard Pat order the assistant to leave.

"No problems," Mandy said, standing. "I'm leaving."

"Trouble," Kelley mumbled, watching Mandy leave.

"With a capital T," Marcie added, pushing open the door to Pat's office.

Mandy giggled, turning the key in the car's ignition. "My, my, my."

"What?" Dawn asked. She had been waiting in the car and was perturbed Mandy had taken so long to appear.

"Do you think there's something going on between Pat and Sherry?"

"Who cares?"

"I care," Mandy snapped. "Do you?"

"Who cares?" Dawn repeated, turning her head to look out the window as Mandy jammed her foot against the gas pedal, spinning tires as they left the parking lot.

"All right, Pat," Mac said into the speaker phone on her desk. "I want you to go home. And make sure everyone else is gone, too. I'll have Mandy go over to the other locker room and see what, if anything, the Rafters needed."

"Too late for that, Mac," Pat said, watching Mandy's car speeding away from the arena. "She just took off. I can go over there."

Mac thought a few choice words about her niece but stopped herself from saying them. "No. I'll find somebody to check on them."

Pat didn't argue. She wasn't much in the mood to face the visiting team. "Okay."

"Someone is beating on my door. I'll bet it's Palmer."

"Sure you don't want me to stick around?"

"Go home, Pat." Mac stood up. "That's an order." She punched a button ending the call. "Hang on!" she yelled at the persistent knocker on the other side of her office door. "I'm coming." Pausing long enough to take a deep breath, she pulled the door open and found Coach Palmer, red-faced and sweating profusely. "Geez, Palmer, calm down before you blow a gasket or something," she said, stepping aside as the enraged coach rushed into her office.

Palmer spun around. "You have to fire *that*—"

"That what?" Mac slammed the door shut. "That what?" Her tone was icy, challenging the coach to complete his epithet. "Sit down, Palmer," Mac ordered. "I've got a call to make before I listen to your newest batch of lies."

When Mac had released the announcement naming Pat as the Cougars' head coach, Michael Palmer had been the first person to call her. Instead of the usual supportive niceties she'd expected to receive, she had been subjected to an hour-long tirade filled with innuendo and lies that only ended when she'd slammed the receiver into its cradle, disconnecting the call. Since then, she'd never been in the same room with the Eugene coach without getting another earful of his hate-filled spewing.

Returning behind her desk, Mac glared at Palmer, who was pacing about the room. "Sit down," she ordered. "I just had this carpet put in, and I don't need you wearing a hole in it tonight." Palmer dropped into a chair, glaring at the Cougars' owner. Mac punched buttons on the phone pad and waited for someone to answer.

"Security," a male voice said after the second ring.

"Tom, this is Mac."

"Kinda late for you to be here, Boss. Is there a problem?"

"No. At least, nothing I can't handle. I need you to send someone to the visiting locker room and find out what the Rafters needed that would cause their coach to barge into our locker room. Chances are they won't know anything, so go easy on them."

"Will do, Mac. Anything else?"

"Make sure they get the hell out of here tonight." While Mac made her requests, she studied the reaction of the man sitting across from her and grinned when his anger turned to shock.

"I'm on it."

Ending the call, Mac smiled smugly. "Did you really think you could pull a stunt like that in my arena and I wouldn't know about it? Tell me, Palmer, why did you go into the Cougar locker room? There are several signs stating it's off limits, so your mission must have been very important for you to ignore them."

Palmer continued to glower at Mac, refusing to answer.

"That's what I thought," Mac said, leaning back in her chair. "All right, you're here, and you obviously have something to say. Spill it so I can go home."

"In the morning I'm filing an official complaint with the league on behalf of the player *that woman*," he shivered, "was forcing herself on."

"And that player would be?"

"Sherry Gallagher."

"And just how was Coach Calvin forcing herself on Sherry?"

"She had her hand on her shoulder, and she was leaning over her. I could tell what she was trying to do," Palmer said, disgusted by what he imagined he had seen.

Mac chuckled. "Did you, by chance, happen to take the time to ask Sherry her take on the subject?"

"Why would I? She wouldn't tell me the truth; her career depends on giving that woman what she wants."

"Why would you, indeed?" Mac said calmly. She sat for a moment gathering her thoughts, then...*SLAP!* The sound of Mac's hand slamming down onto her desk exploded in the room, the force of the blow causing everything on top of the heavy piece of furniture to clatter.

Palmer's head snapped up, his eyes going wide when he saw the look on the owner's face.

"Let me tell you something in terms that even you can understand." Mac's body shook with anger. "I've put up with your crap as long as I plan to. The league may not want to rock the boat when it comes to you, but I plan to sink the bloody thing."

"You can't talk to me like this."

"You came in here with your lies, remember. I'll talk to you any damn way I please, *and* you'll listen to me.

He lumbered to his feet. "I don't have to—"

"Sit down, you self-righteous, hypocritical, homophobic waste of a human being. You hate lesbians, and you make sure everybody knows it. Yet you hire them as your assistant coaches, and you recruit them to play for you. Why? Because about the only thing you're smart enough to have figured out is that you can't win without them. And still you continue to do everything you can to make their time in the league as miserable as possible. You've made accusations against Pat and others that have absolutely no basis in fact, and you feel free to spread your shit as far and wide as you can."

"She's a dyke!" the coach screamed. "A filthy dyke."

"A dyke, yes." Mac nodded. "But she's not a 'filthy' anything."

"So you condone her behavior of seducing players."

Mac chuckled. "Pat has never seduced or attempted to seduce any player while she's worked for me. Although there've been plenty who have tried to seduce her."

"How can you be so sure?"

"Because if I had even the smallest suspicion of something like that happening, I'd fire her."

"Then explain why she was touching that player."

Again Mac chuckled. "Don't you touch your players, Palmer?"

"No."

"Never?"

"Only in my official duties, when I'm coaching. Maybe to make a point or offer encouragement."

"As would be expected." Mac nodded. "Just as I would expect it of Pat when a player that's been having trouble on the court finally managed to regain her confidence. Sherry broke out of a slump tonight, Palmer, a slump she's been in since being dumped on her head. I'm sure you're aware of it; it was in all the papers. The very least I would anticipate of my coach in that situation would be to acknowledge the player's accomplishment. Even if it meant an encouraging squeeze of the shoulder. That's *not a seduction*, Palmer." Mac slammed her hand down on her desk a second time.

The coach stood. "Just because you're willing to turn a blind eye to what *that* woman is doing doesn't mean I will. Whether you like it or not, I'm taking this to the commission."

Mac waited until the man had almost reached the door. "One more thing, Palmer."

"What?" the coach barked, not looking back.

"If you do go to the league with this, it will be the end of *your* career, not Pat's."

Palmer laughed. Slowly, he twisted around to stare at Mac. "Is that a threat?"

"A statement of fact." Mac shrugged. "You see, I find it very odd that someone with your history would be so willing to make accusations of seduction against another coach."

Palmer took a step back into the room. "What the hell does that mean?"

"It means that coaches who sleep with their players generally don't have a very long career ahead of them once the word gets out."

"What the hell are you talking about?" Palmer took a few more steps back into the room, but each step was a little more hesitant than the previous one.

"I'm talking about an eighteen-year-old girl you recruited out of high school when you coached for Middle State College." Palmer turned white as the blood drained from his face. "A young girl who had quite a future in basketball to look forward to. Or so you told her. What ever happened to her, Palmer? Funny thing, she only played for you that one year. Then she disappeared, and you left Middle State behind to coach in the league. One didn't have anything to do with the other, did it?"

"You bitch," Palmer spat. "You wouldn't dare."

Mac smiled, but her eyes and voice were hard as steel. "Try me."

Palmer spun around. "This isn't over!" he shouted, storming out of the room.

"It had better be!" Mac yelled after him.

CHAPTER FIFTEEN

Pat wasn't surprised when Mac walked into her office the morning after the confrontation with Michael Palmer. She watched patiently as the team owner carefully shut the office door behind her. Instead of sitting in one of the chairs opposite Pat's desk, Mac walked to the window and looked out across the parking lot.

"How bad is it?" Pat asked.

"He said he was going to the league, but I just checked with a friend of mine there. They haven't heard from him. Yet."

"Nothing happened, Mac."

Mac turned slowly, leaning against the narrow ledge under the window. "What's going on between you and Sherry? Give it to me straight." Mac smiled. "Guess that's not the best word to use under the circumstances."

"Probably not." Pat blew out a long breath. "Officially, nothing. We've met a few times to go hiking. Strictly hiking, nothing more," she explained. "That's it."

"Nothing else outside of the team?"

"Nothing."

"And unofficially?"

"I'm not sure. There's an attraction, Mac. I can't deny it."

"Does Sherry feel the same?"

"Yes. But I've made it clear it can't go any further. Not now. Not while we're both with the Cougars."

"She agreed?"

"Yes."

"And the room situation in Tulsa?"

"There wasn't anything I could do about it."

"You could have picked a different player."

"I could have."

"What would have happened if Sherry hadn't been injured?"

"Nothing."

"You sure?"

Pat's answer came in a quiet whisper. "No."

"This is a nasty situation, Pat." The room became deathly quiet as Mac turned around to again stare out the window. She had some options, but they were limited, and she couldn't make a mistake.

Because of Mac's own beliefs, and at the league's insistence, the contracts Cougar coaches and players signed contained conduct clauses. Immediate termination was the penalty for breaking them. But should two women having feelings that had yet to be acted upon be grounds for destroying their careers?

"No more hiking. Concentrate on basketball," Mac told her coach, walking to the door. "And no more shared hotel rooms, understand?" she asked, her hand resting on the doorknob as she looked at Pat.

"Yes."

"We'll talk again at the end of the season."

Pat went through the motions at practice, but her mind was on her conversation with Mac. She knew the owner was right. She had to stop taking chances with Sherry, stop seeing her outside of the team's activities. The reality was that there wasn't any hope of something developing between them as long as both were on Mac's payroll. She had to concentrate on the Cougars and the goal of the championship that she herself had set for the team.

"Sherry," Pat called. Since Sherry had been in the locker room when Coach Palmer had barged in, Pat felt it was only fair to tell the woman she dreamed about every night what had happened and how it would change the way they interacted.

Sherry stood at mid-court with Pete, watching Wendy and Amie run through plays. She looked over when she heard her name. "Yeah, Coach?"

"Give me a minute."

"Sure." Sherry jogged over to Pat. "What's up?"

"Let's walk down to the other end of the floor." Pat wanted to talk to Sherry privately, but she also needed it to be public enough so there could be no further misunderstandings.

Sherry felt her stomach ball up into knots as she followed the coach. Guessing that Pat wanted to talk about the events of the previous night, she remained silent, too afraid of what might have resulted from the incident to say anything.

"Let's sit," Pat said, dropping into a seat in the first row and stretching her legs out in front of her. "I'm beat. Didn't get a whole lot of sleep last night."

"Me either." Sherry began to sit in the adjoining seat.

"Move down one, please." Pat smiled apologetically.

"What's going on, Coach? Did Mac believe what Palmer said he saw? Because if she did, I'll go tell her myself that nothing happened."

"Sit down," Pat said quietly. "Mac wouldn't believe Palmer if he said the building was on fire and she could see the flames." Sherry sat and waited. "Look, I'm just going to tell you what the score is. Okay? It's not necessarily the way I want things to be, but it's the way they have to be until the season is over."

"Okay."

"Palmer is threatening to file a complaint with the league against me on your behalf."

"He can't do that," Sherry sputtered. "I won't go along with it," she said loudly.

"Sherry, please," Pat said, the pain of the situation written in the grimace on her face. "Just listen to me. Please."

Sherry took a deep breath, trying to relax. "All right."

"Thank you," Pat said quietly. "Mac doesn't think he'll go through with it, but it's pretty irrelevant anyway. This isn't the first time I've been accused of something with one of my players, one of the drawbacks of being gay and single." She shrugged. "But it's the first time that there's been some truth behind the accusation."

Sherry looked at Pat, the corners of her mouth rising into a small smile at the coach's declaration.

"I told Mac about us."

"What about us?"

"The feelings we're having."

"But we haven't done anything."

"I know. I told her that, too. But some of what *I've* done hasn't been right, Sherry. I'm your coach, and I'm supposed to know better than to put you into situations where things could happen."

"Like the hiking?"

"Yes. And the hotel room. You never should have been in there. I knew it, but I..."

"I'm glad I was," Sherry whispered, looking into Pat's eyes.

"It can't happen again."

"So what do we have to do?"

"Play out the season. Keep everything, and I mean *everything*, between us professional and nothing more. We don't see each other off the court. We're never alone together. We never touch."

"That's going to be hard," Sherry murmured. "Especially the never touching."

"I know. But we can't let whatever there may be between us hurt Mac or the team. And we have to remember the contracts we both signed. We agreed to the terms, and we need to respect them."

"I can quit," Sherry offered. She knew she was falling in love with her coach, and if she had to give up basketball to have a chance at a relationship with her, she was ready to do it.

Pat shook her head. "No."

"Pat."

"No," Pat said again, more forcefully than the first time. "I'm not willing to have you give up something you've worked so hard to achieve. Not on a 'what if'."

"I think it's more than that. And so do you."

"If it is," Pat looked into Sherry's eyes, "then it'll still be there at the end of the season."

Sherry slumped against the seat back and groaned. "I guess I can stand to ignore you for the next three months."

"Gee, thanks."

"You set the rules; don't complain to me about them now."

Mandy observed the private conversation between Pat and Sherry and wondered what could have been so important that the coach would pull the player out of practice. Later she watched as Pat locked up her office shortly after practice ended, something she almost never did. When she noticed Sherry also preparing to leave the arena immediately after practice, thoughts raced around in her head. She pushed open the outside door and hurried out into the parking lot where she could see Pat getting into her pickup.

Mandy opened the door to her car, her eyes following Pat's pickup as it moved across the mostly empty parking lot to an exit. She jabbed her key into the ignition, starting the engine before she had both feet inside the car.

Dawn dropped into the seat beside Mandy. "What's so damn important? I really could use a shower."

"You can take one later," Dawn said, her eyes still on the Pat's pickup. "This is more important." She threw the car into gear, racing out of the lot in chase of the coach.

"What is?"

Mandy pointed down the street. Pat's pickup was a half block ahead of them. "Where she's going."

"Why do you care?"

"I want to see if she's meeting Sherry somewhere."

"Sherry? Oh, come on." Dawn grabbed the shoulder harness, clicking the belt into place. She was sure Mandy would kill them some day with the way she drove. "Coach is not that stupid."

"Palmer claimed he saw something."

"The guy's a homophobe, everybody knows that."

"Won't hurt to check it out."

"What makes you think she's going to see Sherry?"

"They were talking earlier during practice."

"Yeah, everybody saw them. So what?"

"They both left right after practice."

"Again, so what?"

"I want to know what's going on, that's so what."

"Let's just go home, Mandy. I'm tired and I need a shower." Mandy sped up, switching into the other lane by cutting off another car. "Geez, will you slow down before you get us killed?"

"Don't you even care if they are getting together?"

"No. Right now I don't care about anything but a hot shower."

"Think what we can do with that information if it turns out to be true."

"Damn it, Mandy!" Dawn screamed when they almost rear-ended the car in front of them. "Turn around, and let's go home."

"I want to know. And so should you."

"Shit." Dawn looked out the side window. The car was moving too fast to jump. "Look, Mandy, Coach can sleep with whoever she wants. I don't care."

"It's against the rules for her to sleep with a player."

"It's against the rules for *you* to sleep with a player. If you're not going to go home, stop the car so I can get out."

"No. You're going with me. I'll need a witness."

"Like hell I am. I'm working on something good here, and I'm not going to ruin it because of your obsession with Coach. Now stop the damn car!" Dawn shouted.

"I think you owe me this little favor."

Dawn looked ahead to the next intersection, smiling when she saw the signal turning yellow. "I hate to break this to you, bitch. But if you think getting me on the team is something I plan to pay for forever, you're crazy. I did what you wanted, I took Sherry out, and she bounced back. We're even." As the car rolled to a stop, she released her seat belt and pushed the door open, jumping out. "You want to chase shadows, go ahead, but I'm not helping you ruin Coach's career just so you can sleep with her." She slammed the door and trotted over to the sidewalk.

"Get back in here, you bitch!" Mandy screamed. She turned around in the seat to see Dawn walking in the opposite direction, her hand held high and her middle finger pointing skyward.

The driver of the car behind her honked his horn when the light turned green. "Hold on to your shorts," Mandy snarled, turning back around in the seat. The car lurched forward when she stomped on the gas pedal. She squealed around the corner of the intersection, sped down to the next street, and squealed around that corner. An identical turn at the next cross street, and she started searching for Dawn. She looked in the direction the player had been walking. The sidewalk was empty for as far as she could see. She looked in the opposite direction for any sign of Pat's pickup. "Shit," she muttered, slamming her hand against the steering wheel when she saw neither.

"Thanks for the ride, Pete," Sherry said, getting out of the car.

"Sure you don't want to come over to my house for dinner? Hubby's working late, we could talk," Pete offered. Sherry wasn't the first player she'd seen looking devastated after a having private talk with the coach. The difference was, this time Pat had looked devastated as well. She wasn't blind to the fact that her coach and friend was falling in love with the rookie guard.

"Thanks, but I'm not really hungry. I think I'll hit the sack early tonight."

"You sure you're okay?"

"I'm fine. I'll see you in the morning."

"Okay, good night." Pete waved, pulling away from the curb in front of the house where Sherry had rented a basement room. "Looks like the season is going to be a lot longer for some of us than others," she said as she drove toward home.

"Can you handle it from here?" Pat asked Kelley. It was near the end of practice, and the team was alternating between running wind sprints and completing passing drills. "I've got some stuff to go over in my office." The Cougars would be leaving the following morning for a five-game road trip, and Pat wanted to review her notes on game plans. That's what she told herself.

Kelley spoke for both herself and Marcie. "We can handle it, Coach."

"Okay. I'll be in my office if you need me."

Kelley watched Pat go. The coach's normally erect posture was slumped, and that told the assistant coach all she needed to know about Pat's emotional state.

Since the accusations made against her and her talk with Sherry, Pat had withdrawn from any contact with the team except for what was demanded for her job during practice and games. She rarely entered the locker room and always retreated to her office before the team was released from practice. Any contact she had with players off the court was friendly, but no one, especially Sherry, failed to notice the invisible wall that the coach had built around herself.

Marcie trotted up to stand beside Kelley. "This season can't end fast enough for me."

"Bet it seems a lot longer for the two of them," Kelley said, not having missed the look on the point guard's face when the coach left the court.

Sherry was handling the frustrating situation completely differently than the coach was, delving into the details of the game, endlessly badgering Marcie and Pete for every piece of advice their experience in the league had taught them. She spent hours reviewing film of past and present point guards, picking up a move here and there and discovering tricks she had never thought of. All her work was showing on the court, where she was proving to be the premier player in her position and a dominant force behind the Cougars' 18-3 record.

Pat had barely sat down at her desk when Mandy buzzed the intercom.

"Pat." Mandy's tone gave away her feelings about announcing the call. "There's a Karen something-or-other on the phone. Should I tell her you're busy?"

"No, I'll take it." Pat reached for the phone, wondering why her ex would be calling. "Karen?"

"Hi, Pat. Is this a bad time?" Karen asked cautiously. She was unsure of the response she would get from the woman whose heart she had once broken.

"Not too many good times around here lately," Pat muttered, leaning back in her chair.

"So I've heard. Palmer's been busy."

"Still hasn't gone to the league yet. At least, not officially." Pat swiveled around to look out the window.

"You doing okay?"

"Yeah." Pat sighed. "Is there a point to this call?" she asked, never really comfortable talking to her ex-lover. She still carried a lot of pain over their breakup.

"I'm spending a few days in Spokane. Debbie had a conference to attend and I decided to tag along. I thought you and I might be able to have an early dinner."

"When?"

"Tonight. I drove over."

"That's a long drive to make without calling first," Pat said. Spokane was two hundred miles away and even though it was interstate the whole way, it was mountainous, with a handful of high passes to cross. "What if I say I'm too busy?"

"I'm hoping you won't. I thought you might like to talk about what's going on."

"I have people here to talk to, Karen."

"I know, but considering our history..." Karen hesitated, unsure of how she wanted to finish her offer. "Look, I just figured at one time we talked about everything. I'm offering that again."

Pat didn't respond. Her heart skipped several beats as she watched Sherry walk across the parking lot on her way home. The apartment Sherry had leased for the duration of the season was less than a mile from the arena and she often walked the distance.

"Pat?"

"Sure, why not. I'll meet you at Creekview in a half hour." It was her favorite restaurant; she might as well have a good meal.

"I'll be there. 'Bye."

"Yeah, 'bye." Pat continued to hold the phone long after the line went dead; she was too captivated watching Sherry to notice.

"Hi," Karen said as she slipped onto the bench seat across the table from Pat. "Nice view," she added, looking out the window to the creek flowing beneath the restaurant.

"I like it." Pat smiled, but her eyes betrayed her sadness.

"You look tired."

"It's the middle of the season." Pat studied her reflection in the window. "I should look tired."

"The Cougars are playing extremely well," Karen said, picking up the menu. "Sherry, especially," she added, trying to sound casual.

"She's very talented," Pat said absently, suddenly wondering if it had been a mistake to agree to meet her ex. The last thing she wanted to do was talk about Sherry. Pat was grateful for the short interruption provided by the waitress arriving to take their orders.

"Do you think the Cougars will make it to the championship?" Karen asked as soon as the waitress left.

"We're going to give it our best shot." Pat lifted her coffee cup to her lips, staring over its rim at Karen. After a few sips, she replaced it on the table. "I'm sure you didn't make a four-hour drive just to ask me if I thought we could win. You could have done that on the phone. So, do you mind telling me why you're here?"

"I was worried about you."

Pat remained silent, waiting for the rest.

"All right. When I heard what Palmer was saying about you and Sherry, I guess I felt—"

"What? And please don't say jealous," Pat said bitterly.

Karen's eyes flashed, but she quickly contained the anger. "No, I'm not jealous." She laughed. "But I am concerned about you. And about Sherry," she said of the guard who had been recruited from her team. "Are you in love with her?" she asked bluntly.

"You know that's against the rules," Pat said quietly.

Seeing the pain in Pat's eyes, Karen softened her own tone. "Are you?"

"Don't ask me questions I can't answer."

"If you didn't have basketball between you, what would you say?" Karen asked, refusing to let the subject drop.

"Karen, you're a coach. Don't put me in this position."

"I'm a coach in a long-term relationship. I'm not looking for anything else."

Pat stared at her ex-lover, no longer thinking of Sherry. "You told me that once before, remember?"

"I'm sorry, Pat. I handled things really badly when it came to you. But by the time I realized what was happening between Debbie and me, I was in too deep."

Pat remained silent for a long time, then finally asked the question that had haunted her for years. "Did you sleep with her?"

Karen hesitated, thinking about lying. The look on Pat's face demanded the truth. "Yes."

Pat released her held breath, lifting the napkin off her lap and carefully folding it before placing it on the table. She stood, pulling her wallet out of her pocket. Tossing enough bills on the table to cover the cost of their meal, she said, "I wish you well, Karen. But this is the last time I ever want to see you." Without waiting for a reaction, she turned and walked toward the exit.

"Pat, wait," Karen called after the coach. When people at the tables around her looked to see what the problem was, she forced a smile, turning toward the window. From her seat, she watched Pat walk to her pickup and drive out of her life.

As Pat pulled into traffic, it was all she could do to contain her emotions. The last slim thread of trust she had clung to regarding her relationship with Karen had just snapped. It was like a slap in the face. Holding her emotions in check, she drove home.

Entering the empty house, she felt an unbearable ache in her heart. She needed someone to console her. And the person she needed...was Sherry. Pulling her cellphone from her pocket, she dialed the number. "Do you have any plans tonight?" Pat asked, fighting to rein in her emotions while she spoke to Sherry, the phone trembling in her hand.

"No, Coach, I'm just watching some TV." Sherry was more than a little surprised by the call.

"Take a drive with me?"

Sherry glanced over at the clock, which read a little past six. "I don't think I can arrange to borrow Val's car this late."

"I'll pick you up. Walk to the park down the street; I'll be waiting at the corner behind the bandstand." She had driven past the point guard's apartment enough times to be familiar with the neighborhood.

"Okay." Before Sherry could say more, the line went dead.

Sherry quickly pulled on her hiking boots and grabbed a jacket. She walked to the park, her steps steady but not too fast; she didn't want to draw any unnecessary attention. Walking through the park, she looked for Pat's pickup and was surprised when she didn't see it. An older model Oldsmobile was sitting alongside the curb with its engine running, and she assumed it to be a mother waiting for her children. As she walked alongside the car, the passenger window rolled down and she heard Pat's voice from inside.

"Get in."

Sherry pulled the door open and literally fell into the seat when Pat drove away from the curb before she could get properly seated. The window was already being rolled up when she pulled the door shut.

Sherry turned to face the coach. "Pat?"

"Not here. Let me get to someplace we can talk."

Seeing how upset Pat was, Sherry nodded, yielding to her wishes. She adjusted herself comfortably in the seat, pulling the shoulder harness into place.

Pat drove along residential streets, working her way to the east end of town. She swung onto a freeway on-ramp and accelerated, the Oldsmobile smoothly picking up speed.

Sherry had to say something, the heavy silence too much for her to handle. "I didn't know you had another car."

"Most people don't. I inherited it from my mother when she passed away. Don't really know why I keep it, except it reminds me of her." Pat smiled at her memories. "It spends most of the time in the garage. I take it out once in a while, just to keep it running."

The women made small talk as Pat took the off-ramp to Highway 200, slowing her speed to drive through the twin logging towns of Mill Town and Bonner, then accelerating again when they entered the canyon of the Blackfoot River. Pat described points of interest as they drove through the Potomac Valley on their way to the Clearwater Junction, where Pat turned at Stoney's Corner, taking the highway to Salmon

Lake. It was dark when she pulled into the state park along the lake shore. Glad to see they had the place to themselves, she parked near the picnic area.

"Do you mind?" Pat asked, getting out of the car. "I have to..." She indicated she wanted to sit beside the water.

"Sure." Sherry climbed out of the car, zipping up her jacket against the brisk evening air. "I'd like that."

Pat led Sherry to the picnic table closest to the pebbled shoreline. Sitting on top of it, she pulled her long legs up to rest her feet on the bench as she stared out over the water. The surface of the lake was beginning to ice over with the colder temperatures of fall, but there was still plenty of open water to be disturbed by the occasional trout breaking its surface.

Sherry sat on the table, leaving a respectable space between herself and the coach. Pat remained silent. "Pat?"

"Hold me?"

Sherry didn't stop to think of the propriety of doing what Pat asked. She scooted next to the coach, wrapping her arms around her and hanging on tight when the sobs began.

It took some time for Pat to cry herself out, but she eventually did, and then she told Sherry of her conversation with Karen.

"I'm sorry, Pat." Sherry wiped at the tears that stained her own face. "You must have really loved her."

"I thought I did. I was planning to ask her to marry me when we finished our senior season. I thought we could find a team to play on together. I guess I didn't know her at all. I sure didn't know she was sleeping with Debbie." Pat felt Sherry shiver as the evening breeze rippled the lake's surface. "We should probably get back."

"Pat?"

"Hmm."

"Why'd you call me? Why not one of your friends?" Sherry knew the chance Pat was taking by being together with her. If they were seen, it would mean the end of her coaching career.

"Because I wanted *your* arms around me," Pat explained in a voice soft with longing. "I'm sorry. I shouldn't have done it. It just complicates—"

Sherry reached out, cupping her hands around Pat's face. She leaned forward, pressing her lips against the coach's and showing her just how much she loved her. When Sherry pulled back after several moments, she left her hands where they were. Pat smiled.

"Pat, I lo—"

"Don't." Pat pulled away from Sherry's caress. "Don't say it."

"But it's true."

"I know. But the only way I can deal with this is if we don't say it."

"Then you feel it, too?"

"Yes." Pat smiled, and for the first time in a long time, she actually felt good about something. "Come on, I'll take you home." Pat held out her hand, and Sherry immediately grabbed hold of it, letting go only when they reached the car.

Neither spoke on the drive back to Missoula, but their hands never separated.

CHAPTER SIXTEEN

"Gallagher is on fire tonight!" the television announcer shouted into the microphone. "Seventeen points, 12 assists, and 4 steals in the first half. Those are pretty good numbers."

"And the way she runs the Cougars' offense, she is definitely on her way to a Rookie of the Year season!" the second announcer shouted above the crowd. "It will be interesting to see if Kansas City can contain her in the second half."

"If they don't, the Cougars will win their fifth game of this road trip and return to Missoula with a 23-3 record. That's a tremendous lead over the rest of the league."

"Coach Calvin has not been secretive about wanting to win it all this year."

"No, she hasn't. And it looks like Gallagher is going to help her do just that. Here come the teams." The rest of the announcer's comments were drowned out by the screaming fans as the teams reappeared from their respective locker rooms.

Sherry stood at mid-court, bouncing the ball in place as she studied the defense. She smiled. The Kansas City players were slowly inching toward her, so concerned were they about her again faking a drive and attempting a long 3-point shot. She caught the movement of Pete slipping behind her defender and running her into the corner of the court. At the same time, Tonie stepped into the key, raising her hands for the ball.

Sherry began a half-trot, half-walk movement forward. Reaching the 3-point line, she charged forward two steps, then abruptly stopped. Four defenders converged on her. Faking a jump shot put all the defenders into the air, and Sherry waited until they were on their way back down to the floor to make her move. She jumped up between them, easily dumping the ball off to her unguarded teammate.

Tonie caught the ball. Turning toward the basket, she scored on an uncontested hook shot.

"Time!" the Kansas City coach yelled from the sidelines.

Pat waited for the Cougars to trot to the bench. A glance at the scoreboard showed they were almost 30 points ahead with less than five minutes to play. She looked at the players on the bench, "Wendy, Amie, Latesha, Ashley, Dawn, you're in. Take a rest, ladies," she said to the five players coming off the court. "Let's give the rest of the team some playing time."

"Sherry is one rebound shy of her first triple double," Marcie said, looking at her list of stats.

"Risking getting her injured isn't worth a record." Pat turned to her assistant coach. "The way they've been playing her, someone's going to get frustrated before the night is out and do something stupid."

Marcie nodded. It was her job to keep the head coach aware of stats during the game, but she agreed with Pat — it was time to rest the guard.

The crowd let out a collective sigh of relief at seeing a complete changeover of Cougars trot onto the court. Even the Kansas City players appeared happy at the prospect of not facing the Cougars' best point guard any more that night.

"How's it feel?" Pete chuckled, handing Sherry a cup of water.

"How's what feel?"

"Being the big, bad player everyone in the place is afraid of?"

Sherry drained her cup. "I'm hardly that."

"Oh, really?" Tonie laughed. "Not too many players I know of in the league get quadruple-guarded every time they touch the ball."

Sherry frowned at the teasing. "I was having a lucky night."

"I'll say." Pete was looking up at the overhead scoreboard as Sherry's stats for the night were displayed. "Twenty-nine points, 14 assists, 9 rebounds. I wouldn't mind having a few lucky nights like that myself."

"Geez." Tonie read the scoreboard. "Perfect from the line and 87 percent from the floor. No wonder they were throwing everything they had at you. Keep that up, rookie, and you'll make everyone in the league look bad."

"Just doing what Mac pays me to." Sherry tried to growl, but she couldn't control the grin developing on her face.

"Right." Tonie leaned over close to the guards so she wouldn't be overheard. "I'd say it's more because of all the pent-up energy you have to find an outlet for."

Sherry's grin faded. "Excuse me." She stood, then walked down to the end of the bench to sit alone by the small table that held cups of water and sports drink.

"Shit, Tonie." Pete frowned at the post player. "Don't you think the situation is hard enough for her without you throwing it up in her face?"

"I was just teasing," Tonie muttered.

"This isn't the time or the place." Pete looked down to the end of the bench and sighed. "I'm not sure there's ever going to be a time or place for that."

Sherry was sitting with her elbows on her knees, her lowered head covered by a towel. Pat was standing further down the sideline, also looking at the point guard. Though the coach's face was impassive, it didn't take much imagination to read the emotions in her eyes.

Eight weeks later

Dawn turned onto a side street, looking for an out-of-the-way place to park Mandy's rental car. Seeing the lot for the public library, she drove into an empty parking spot under the overhang alongside of the building. Looking around, she turned off the engine. From there she could walk the block to the hotel. If anyone happened to spot the car, they would just wonder what the non-reading Mandy was doing at the library.

It didn't take long for Dawn's long legs to cover the distance to the end of the next block. She skirted the hotel lobby, looking for the back stairway she had been told about. Locating it, she quickly made her way up two flights of steps and hurried down the balcony lined along one side with numbered doors.

"Just a second," a voice called from inside the room when Dawn rapped on a door.

"Hurry up," Dawn called back, looking around to see if anyone was watching her. As soon as the door opened, she shoved her way inside.

"Good to see you again, Dawn." The woman pushed the door closed, making sure the security latch was in place before pulling the heavy drapes across the window.

"You too, Coach Buttram." Dawn looked across the room where another woman sat at the corner table in shadows. "I thought you were going to be alone."

"Oh? I thought I'd mentioned that Miss Tomkins would be here."

"Tomkins?" Dawn asked, squinting into the shadows at the woman. "As in..."

"Teresa Tomkins," the woman said, stretching an arm out to flip on the light over the table, "owner and general manager of the Los Angeles Beachcombers and your prospective new employer, if things work out."

"Miss Tomkins wanted to meet you," the coach of the LA team explained. "Why don't you sit down?"

"I rarely agree to sign a player I haven't met." Tomkins smiled as Dawn sat in the other chair. "I must say I had my doubts about you when Coach Buttram first approached me with the idea of you joining the Beachcombers. You've given me a couple of jolts since then, too."

"I've held up my end," Dawn said suspiciously. "And done everything you asked. Now I want to be sure you're going to come through with what you promised." She turned to look at the coach, who had taken a seat on the side of one of the room's beds.

The owner chuckled. "I said I *had* my doubts. And I still do, but Coach Buttram is convinced you'll be an asset to my team. Your performance on the court has improved since the start of the season. Pat has done well by you." Dawn frowned. "Ah. I see you don't think she deserves any credit for the improvement in your playing skills," Tomkins commented. "That surprises me."

"I had talent before I met her," Dawn grumbled.

"Talent, maybe. Potential, yes. But you did little to use either. I believe you owe a debt of gratitude to Coach Calvin for bringing out both. Without her, you wouldn't be sitting here right now. You know..." She paused to study the player. "I'm actually surprised she kept you on the team the full season, especially after that stunt with your teammate."

"It was a good play," Dawn muttered, but even she wasn't convinced of the truth of her contention.

"It was a cheap shot that could very possibly have injured a valuable talent. Had it been me, I would have released you right then and there."

"It was a mistake, Teresa," Coach Buttram quickly interjected. "Dawn learned her lesson."

The Beachcombers owner looked at her coach. "Good thing. At least it proves she takes direction. You'll be a starter for us, Dawn. That means more responsibility. I hope you're as ready for that as you claim."

Dawn squirmed under the scrutiny of the two women. "Look, can we get this over with? I need to be at the arena in an hour."

"You must be nervous," Tomkins looked back at the player, "playing in the championship game your rookie season."

"A little."

"All right." Tomkins smiled. "We do want you to be at your best tonight."

"Here's the deal, Dawn. Everyone knows Mac only signs one-year contracts with rookies," Coach Buttram said. "She's been burned one too many times with players who didn't perform once they got into the league and had a multi-year contract to fall back on. So as soon as the last game of the season is played, in your case, tonight's championship, you become a free agent, if Mac hasn't already re-signed you. Has she made an offer?"

Dawn nodded.

"And you want to know what our offer will be so you can choose the best one?"

The player shrugged.

"Miss Tomkins is ready to offer you a contract, but only with the stipulation that you continue to show improvement. Both in your play and your attitude."

Dawn waited.

Tomkins slid a piece of paper across the surface of the table. "Is this what you're waiting for?"

Dawn looked at the figures written on the paper and smiled. "That's it. Where do I sign?"

"Sorry." Coach Buttram stood up. "Can't do that until tomorrow. League rules, you know." She picked the paper up from the table, handing it back to the Beachcombers owner without looking at it.

"What guarantee do I have you'll still be here tomorrow?" Dawn asked, watching the paper disappear into the woman's pocket.

"We'll be here," Buttram said, walking to the door. "You just be sure that tonight you show us how you plan to play when you're wearing a Beachcombers uniform." She unlocked the door.

Dawn stood. "I'll do that," she assured the women as she walked to the door.

"Dawn," Tomkins said to the departing player.

The player turned around. "Yes?"

"Good luck tonight."

Dawn smiled. "I'll see you in the morning," she said as she stepped outside. The bright sunlight was harsh on her eyes after the time in the dark room; she raised her arm to shield them as she made her way back to the stairwell. "Tomorrow, Dawn, my dear," she said out loud, "you'll be on a plane with a big fat check in your pocket. I can't wait to see Mandy's face when I tell her we're going to L.A." She grinned with delight.

Denver Arena: Championship Game between Miami Surf and Missoula Cougars

"Good evening, basketball fans, and welcome to Denver Pioneer Arena for the Women's Professional Basketball League championship game between the Miami Surf and the Missoula Cougars. This is going to be one heck of a game."

"That it is. A lot of people would not have given Missoula much of a chance at the beginning of the season, but they have plowed their way through the league, leaving most opponents wondering what hit them."

The television announcers were standing at mid-court, waiting for the teams to emerge for the pre-game introductions.

"Well, after losing in the quarter-finals last year, Coach Calvin did promise the Cougars would be here."

"Yes, she did. And tonight we'll see if she will be going home with the trophy that eluded them last season."

"It hasn't been an easy year for Coach Calvin, starting with the unexpected retirement of Kinsey Donaldson, the point guard who had captained the Cougars the last four years. Coach Calvin really had to scramble to find someone to replace her — not an easy task."

"I would say she did quite well in that department. Kinsey, incidentally, is here tonight and we're told she will be on the Cougars' bench and suited up. Coach Calvin found Sherry Gallagher playing amateur ball in North Carolina, a completely unknown player with a mediocre college record. Calvin brought her to tryout camp and turned her into a point guard with some of the most unbelievable moves you'll ever see on a basketball court."

"And we're not the only ones to think so. Earlier this week, Gallagher was named Rookie of the Year, something never before achieved by a player at that position."

"That's because it's almost impossible for a rookie to come into this league and play point guard, a position that is the heart and soul of every team."

"We'll be right back to get things started after a commercial break. Don't go away. You don't want to miss this one."

Pat stood leaning casually against the wall at the front of the locker room. The players were scattered out on the benches in front of her making last-minute adjustments to their shoes and uniforms. "Ladies," she said quietly, then waited until she had the attention of every player. "It's been a long season, but we are where we said we wanted to be. We have only one game left between us and this." She pointed to the picture of the championship trophy, which had traveled with the team to Denver and was taped to the wall next to her. "One game to prove that you are champions. One game to put an end to any remaining doubts. You've worked hard, and you've come together as a team. Tonight you will face your most difficult challenge. Tonight you will face yourselves. None of you have been here before, so it's all going to be new. And scary. The basket will look smaller, and the ball will feel bigger. The court will seem longer, and the crowd will seem louder. Your opponents will seem quicker and faster and smarter." Pat pushed away from the wall.

"But they're not. Nothing you see, hear, feel, or touch out there will be any different than what you've dealt with all year. *Nothing.* The only difference will be what you create up here." She tapped the side of her head. "There's only one thing that can turn you into losers tonight, and that's you. Don't become a loser. You're winners. You've proven it over and over again these past several months. *Think like winners,* and *this* will be your reward." She pulled the photograph off the wall, holding it out for the players to look at.

"One game. This is it. You go out there, and you leave everything you have to give on the court. You hold nothing back. There's no tomorrow, no next game, no second chance. This is it. *Are you ready?*"

The players responded by jumping to their feet and shouting their affirmations.

"Then let's go out there and show them who the Missoula Cougars are."

Marcie pulled the locker room door open, quickly backing away to avoid the rush of players charging through it.

Kelley started gathering up the clipboards and notebooks to carry out to the court so the coaching staff could refer to them during the game.

"Leave 'em," Pat instructed. "If we don't know what they say by now, we haven't been doing our jobs."

"Good." Kelley let the collection fall back onto the bench. "I think I'll be too nervous to use them anyway."

Pat turned to her assistant coaches. "Kelley, Marcie, listen up. The one thing we can't be is nervous. The players are going to be taking their cues from us. If we're nervous, they're going be. If we're confident, they're going to be. Got it?"

"Yeah, Coach."

"It's just one more game," Pat said.

"That's easy for you to say, Coach." Marcie grinned. "You've competed for national championships before — and won two. The rest of us haven't."

"Then believe me when I say, keep the nervousness for after the game." Pat smiled. Her college career had prepared her well for the emotions everyone was experiencing. "Right now, we need the confidence." Both Marcie and Kelley nodded. "Good. Let's go join our team."

Sherry stood beside the row of chairs that would serve as the Cougars' bench for the game. She bounced nervously as she waited for the pre-game festivities to end and the game to begin.

Pete walked up to the anxious rookie. "Calm down." She placed both hands on Sherry's shoulders, gently exerting pressure until the rookie stilled.

Sherry looked at her teammate. "Aren't you nervous?"

"Terrified."

"Then how can you be so calm?"

"Because I trust Coach. If she says we can win, then we can win. Besides, the worst thing you can do is let them," she looked over her shoulder at the Miami players gathered at the other end of the court, "know you're nervous. Look at Coach. See how calm she looks?" Sherry nodded. "Don't you think she's nervous? I bet she's got butterflies inside her butterflies. But she's not going to let anyone else know that. Now, look at the Miami coach. I bet he's had to change his shorts three times already."

Sherry laughed, but she saw what Pete was talking about. The Miami coach was pacing up and down in front of the team's bench, his jacket already off and his shirt stained with nervous sweat. Pat stood calmly at the end of the Cougars' bench, a smile on her face as she exchanged pleasantries with the officials.

"You show them you're ready to play from the get-go, and let *them* be nervous." Pete removed her hands from Sherry's shoulders. "Confidence, rookie. We're here to win, and we don't care who or what we have to run over to do it. Got it?"

"Got it." Sherry nodded, much more relaxed than she had been just moments before.

"Good." Pete smiled. "Because I want that trophy. Not so much for me, but for Coach and Kinsey. They've earned it."

Sherry smiled, thinking how true her friend's words were. "Then let's make sure they get it," she said with determination.

"That's the spirit."

"And now the starting line-up for the Missoula Cougars." The arena announcer's voice boomed over the crowd's cheers. He had already announced the starters for Miami, and they waited impatiently at center court for the Cougars to be introduced.

"Starting at forward, Valerie Jensen." The announcer waited for Val to trot onto the court. "Starting at low post, Antonia Jessep." Again a pause while Tonie joined her teammate. "Starting at high post, Terry Peters... Starting at guard, Diane Sunndee."

Pete trotted out to her teammates, slapping high-fives with the others.

"Starting at guard, Sherry Gallagher." The announcer had to shout to be heard as the arena reverberated with cheers for the rookie player. "And the Cougars' captain, Kinsey Donaldson."

Hearing her name announced, Kinsey looked up in surprise at Pat standing in front of her.

"I told you if we made it this far, you'd be here as one of us. I meant it." Pat pulled Kinsey to her feet, pushing her out onto the floor to join the other starters. Even though she'd made the suggestion to the team on several occasions, they had never voted in another captain. Kinsey was the only Cougar whose uniform bore the capital "C" designating that honor.

The announcer made his final introduction. "Coaching the Missoula Cougars — Pat Calvin."

Pat waved to the crowd, acknowledging the chants of "Kodak, Kodak, Kodak". It was apparent that many Missoula fans had made the trip to Denver to support their team.

After the singing of the national anthem, the Missoula starters trotted over to shake hands with their opponents.

Kinsey walked back to the bench, a huge smile on her face. All the pain and frustration over her early retirement had been wiped away by her coach's unanticipated gesture.

Sherry stretched her hand out to the Miami player she would be playing against. Feeling the player's damp skin, she grinned. "Good luck," she said as she looked into the player's eyes. She was startled to see nervousness tinged with fear looking back at her. Releasing the clammy hand, she went over to Pete. "You were right," she said. "She's as nervous as a cat on a hot tin roof."

"Hmm." Pete grinned. "Sounds like a good title for a book."

Sherry swatted the other guard's arm. "It's the best I could come up with under the circumstances."

Pete laughed. "Of course, she's nervous. She has to guard the Rookie of the Year. Now that you know that, show why you are. Hey, huddle up," she called to Val, Tonie, and Terry.

"Don't you want them over here?" Marcie asked when she saw the Cougars gathering on the court while the Miami players huddled around their coach.

"I've said all I can to them," Pat told her assistant coach. "It's up to them now."

"I want that trophy," Pete told her teammates. "I've earned it, and I want it. This team has nothing on us. We're faster. We're smarter. We're the better team. I don't give a shit what they come out playing. I don't care how many different defenses they throw up against us. I don't care how many fancy plays they've designed to confuse us. We're going to play *our* game, not theirs. If you see something new, slow down and take your time to figure it out before you make a stupid mistake. If we control the ball and we play the game that got us here, we can't lose." She smiled at the four determined faces looking back at her. "Let's go win us a trophy."

CHAPTER SEVENTEEN

Waiting for the officials to make their final preparations before the opening tip-off, Sherry bounced on her toes at mid-court. She took a quick glance over to the Cougars' bench, grinning when she saw Pat was watching her.

Pat winked at her point guard, mouthing the words "good luck".

"You ready to kick some butt?" Pete asked, trotting up to Sherry.

Sherry turned her attention to her teammate. "Yes."

"Good." Pete grinned. "Then let's get to it." She held up a fist, tapping it against Sherry's knuckles when the point guard raised a fist in return. The officials blew their whistles, and the game was on.

Sherry took her position approximately six feet behind the center circle with her back to the Cougar basket. Pete took up a position several steps off to her left but closer to mid-court. Tonie stood inside the circle, her head moving from side to side, looking over her shoulders to make sure she knew exactly where Val and Terry were as they jostled for position outside of the jump circle.

The official held the ball up, ready for the toss. Tonie crouched, her thigh muscles tight, her eyes fixed on the ball. The ball left the official's hand, rising straight up between the two players.

Tonie surged off the floor, her arm stretching as far up as it could reach. She felt the Miami player's body brushing against hers as both players focused on the ball. Tonie's fingers grazed the leather surface first and, with a flip of her wrist, she sent the ball flying over the outstretched arms of the players surrounding the circle.

Sherry reacted instantly when the ball headed in her direction, snatching it out of the air before the player guarding her even knew it was there. She kept control of the ball for just a second before passing it off to Pete, who had started her run toward the basket as soon as Tonie controlled the tip. Spinning around after the ball left her hands, Sherry ran for the end of the court, her guard trailing behind.

The quick movements of the Cougar guards caught the defense by surprise, and Pete and Sherry found themselves heading for their basket with only one Miami player anywhere close to them.

Sherry eased up when she reached the top of the key, content to let Pete score the first points of the game. Her defender had other ideas and rushed past her to try and catch the other guard.

Approaching the basket, Pete glanced over her shoulder to see the Miami player charging at her. Picking up her dribble, she swung the ball behind her back, sending it back in Sherry's direction and out of reach of their sole defender. Sherry caught the pass at the free-throw line and popped into the air, launching the ball for the basket.

Swish.

Miami 0 Cougars 2

"Yes," Pat hissed. She knew from watching Sherry all season that if the point guard made the first basket she attempted, she was much more relaxed than if she missed. With Sherry's first points on the board, Pat could put one worry about the game behind her.

Sherry grinned at Pete, who was trotting back up court to play defense. "Nice pass."

"Anything for you, rookie," Pete said with a smile.

Sherry's responsibility switched to guarding the Miami player who put the ball into play. She hustled to the end line. With arms held out to the sides, she tried to distract the player just enough that she would not make a good pass. The Miami player faked a pass to Sherry's left, then quickly snapped the ball past her on the right.

Sherry went for the fake. "Damn," she grunted when the ball zipped by in the opposite direction. Frustrated with herself, she turned to follow the Miami player up court.

Miami moved the ball around the 3-point arc, patiently waiting for an opening.

Tonie followed her player through the key, tripping when her feet became tangled with a Miami player trying to maneuver on the crowded part of the floor. She could only watch as her player caught a pass and laid it off the backboard for an easy lay-up.

Miami 2 Cougars 2

Pete grabbed the ball as soon as it dropped through the net. Stepping out of bounds, she looked for Sherry.

Sherry ran in a wide arc, crossing within a few feet of Pete, catching Pete's pass, then sprinting down court, her defender trying to keep pace. The other Miami players dropped back quickly, setting up their defense at the Cougars' end of the court.

Sherry slowed at the 3-point line, looking for the best way to get the ball to the basket. Tonie was planted near the bottom of the key, her strong legs keeping her defender from gaining position on her. Terry and Val were exchanging positions at the top of the key, trying to confuse their defenders by running them into one another. Pete took a lazy run through the center of the key, dragging her defender into the maze of bodies.

Terry broke free, raising her arm to alert Sherry to her situation as she cut for the basket. Sherry flipped a pass, aiming it to drop into Terry's arms a step or two from the end of the court. Terry leaped for the ball. Grabbing it, she banked it off the backboard, and it fell into the basket.

Miami 2 Cougars 4

The teams continued to trade baskets until time was called to allow for the television network carrying the game to run the obligatory commercials.

"It looks like both teams showed up to play tonight," the announcer said. "Does that surprise you?" he asked his companion.

"Not at all. We have the two best teams in women's professional basketball here, and I expected nothing less from them."

"Well, I'm a little surprised that neither team has shown any signs of championship game jitters. After all, for many of the players, this is the first game of such importance that they've played in. It will be interesting to see if the teams can maintain the intensity of the first few minutes."

"Let's get back to the action..."

Following Pat's instructions during the timeout, Sherry backed off a few feet when she guarded the inbounds pass. The coach wanted to keep the Miami players guessing what kind of defense they would face each time they inbounded the ball.

The Miami player tossed the ball to her teammate, and Pete closed in to slow her down as she ran up the court. Sherry followed her player across mid-court and kept a close guard on her as she maneuvered up the side of the court, looking for a screen from a teammate. Pete's player lobbed the ball to a teammate at the bottom of the key.

Tonie saw the ball floating in her direction and dropped away from her player. She jumped up, knocking the ball off its intended path.

As soon as Tonie made her move, Sherry left her player. She sped toward the loose ball, grabbing it out of the hands of a Miami player and wrapping her arms around it so it could not be snatched back. She waited for the Miami players to run down court to set up their defense. Once she was left with only her defender to worry about, Sherry started her dribble. She trotted to mid-court, looking to Pat for a play. Pat held up her right palm, her fingers spread out. Sherry passed the same hand signal to her teammates, continuing her dribble up to the 3-point line.

Val moved to the corner of the top of the key, working to keep her guard to her back. Tonie was doing the same at the bottom of the key. Pete started a cut across the key, her defender closely matching her step for step. Val took a step to her left, planting her feet to establish position just as Pete brushed past her. Val stood her ground when the guard following Pete ran into her.

The instant Pete was free, she turned toward Sherry. The ball having already covered half the distance to her, she reached out for it. The Miami players converged on Pete, so Pete snapped the ball back out to Sherry.

The point guard pushed up into the air, catching the ball and releasing it in one smooth motion as she hung in the air.

Swish.

"Time," the Miami coach called to the officials.

"Sherry Gallagher is putting on a show tonight!" the announcer screamed into the microphone. "She is a perfect 6 for 6 from the 3-point line and has helped to give the Cougars a 14-point lead."

"Miami has to do something to shut her down, or they won't have any chance in the second half."

"Sherry!" Pat yelled to be heard over the noise of the crowd and the music blaring from the arena speakers. "They're probably going to come out double- and triple-teaming you. They need to shut you down until halftime. The rest of you, be alert. If Sherry has three players hanging on her, two of you should be open. Pete, take over point," Pat instructed the veteran player. "Let them focus on Sherry while you get the ball in play. Sherry, they'll try to get you frustrated and making stupid fouls. Don't let them. Just keep them occupied until the half."

Sherry nodded.

"Okay." Pat glanced up at the scoreboard. "Four minutes to the half. Nothing fancy. Bring the ball up, work for the open shot. No stupid fouls. Got it?"

"Got it!" the Cougar players yelled back.

"Let's go, then." Pat sent the players back out onto the court.

Switching roles with Pete meant Sherry would inbound the ball. As she trotted to the end line, her defender looked around in confusion. Sherry used the player's uncertainly to get the ball in to Pete.

Pete started up court, loosely guarded by a Miami player who kept glancing over toward Sherry. Sherry diverged from her normal route up the center of the court, trotting over to within a few steps of the sideline. Pete's guard became concerned when she saw the distance increasing between herself and Sherry. She glanced over her shoulder to see if any of her teammates were moving out to help guard the rookie.

Pete saw her defender's attention straying. Taking advantage of the player's lapse, she quickened her steps. The quick move left her defender several steps behind her.

Terry's guard moved out to help play prevent against Sherry, leaving the post player alone at the top of the key. Pete snapped the ball to Terry.

As Terry turned for the basket, Tonie's defender rushed to fill the gap left by her teammate, who was now double teaming Sherry as she ran in a lazy figure-eight pattern near the sideline. Terry bounced the ball to Tonie. Unguarded, Tonie threw the ball up to kiss the glass and drop into the basket.

The Cougars backpedaled down court, allowing Miami to inbound the ball unguarded. Pete and Sherry stopped at mid-court, waiting for the ball to reach them before they picked up their players.

The Miami guard dribbled past the center strip, switching hands so her body would be between the ball and her defender, Pete. Pete fell into step with the player, putting on just enough pressure to make the guard work at getting the ball up court.

Sherry was backpedaling, watching both her player and Pete's. Val was surprised when her defender released, running past her in Sherry's direction. At the same time, the player Sherry was guarding put on a burst of speed, running for the key.

"Watch out." Pete yelled, seeing the pick being set up.

Sherry spun around to follow her player, increasing her speed as she did. She didn't see the pick until she had turned completely around. By then she was running at full stride. She slammed into the Miami post player, the force of the impact knocking the smaller guard to the floor.

Pete ran toward Sherry, surprised that the officials hadn't stopped play. Now unguarded, the Miami player that had been Pete's responsibility stepped across the 3-point line and shot a 12-foot jumper.

"Time!" Pat screamed, concerned about Sherry, who was still sitting on the floor, dazed after her collision. "How can you not call a foul on that?" she yelled at an official when he came near enough to hear her.

Lizzie trotted out to check on Sherry.

The official shrugged. "Nothing to call, Coach."

"Nothing to call!" Pat stormed. "What about an illegal pick?"

Marcie and Kelley called the Cougars over to the bench, doing their best to keep themselves between Pat and the official.

"Back off, Pat." Marcie pushed the irate coach off the court. "We don't want you to get thrown out. She'll be fine."

Pat looked out on the court to where Lizzie was helping Sherry to her feet.

"You sure you're okay?" the trainer asked.

"Yes." Sherry frowned. "She just surprised me."

"I'll say. Are you dizzy at all?"

Sherry shook her head, both to answer the question and to clear out the cobwebs that had gathered there during the last several seconds. "I'm fine."

"Okay, then let's get you over to the bench before Coach goes nuts."

Sherry walked toward the sidelines. She thought about trotting but didn't think it would look too good if she stumbled on her shaky legs. "Damn. What's that gal eat for breakfast?" she mumbled, rubbing her shoulder.

"Bricks," Lizzie snickered. "Sit down." she instructed, having noted the player's unsteady steps.

"Is she all right?" Pat asked, her eyes focused on the player.

"She'll be fine, but I want her to sit out the rest of the half."

Sherry struggled to stand. "I can play."

"Sit," Pat ordered. "Wendy, you're in. Let's just get through this half," Pat said, sending the Cougars back out on the court. "No retaliation," she called out to her players before taking a seat next to Sherry. "You okay?" she asked, softening her voice so the fans sitting behind the bench couldn't hear.

"I'm okay, Coach." Sherry smiled. "I just wasn't expecting her."

"Need to expect the unexpected." Pat grinned. "Only way to avoid it."

"And if I don't want to avoid it?"

"You still need to expect it." Pat placed her hand on Sherry's leg, giving it a quick squeeze as she stood up to watch the play on the court.

Sherry watched the coach for a minute before turning her own attention back to her teammates. It wasn't long before the buzzer sounded, ending the half.

Miami Surf 43 Missoula Cougars 58

"Thoughts?" Pat asked her assistant coaches. The three women were standing off to the side of the locker room, letting the players get settled before addressing them.

"Things are going well," Kelley said.

"Miami will come out with some new looks," Marcie said, studying a sheet of paper she had written notes on during the first half.

Pat nodded. "I agree."

"And they'll going to be gunning for Sherry." Marcie frowned. "That may be a problem, Coach."

Pat nodded again. Sherry had come a long way since showing up for tryout camp, but she was still a rookie, and Pat was unsure how she might react if Miami kept up the pressure on her. "We'll just have to keep a close eye on things," she told her assistants. "Let's see if Pete can keep her grounded."

"All right," Marcie agreed. "I'll talk to Pete when we're done here."

"Good." Pat turned to face her players. "Feels good, doesn't it, ladies?" she asked. "We've got half the game behind us, and we've got a nice lead."

Many of the players smiled and shouted out their assessment of the Cougars' good fortune.

"And that's good." Pat raised her hands for quiet. "But believe me, the second half will be a whole new ballgame. And Miami isn't going to roll over and play dead. We need to tighten up our defense; they were getting too many easy shots near the end of the half. I want to see you all over them, whether they've got the ball or not. Guard your player tight. No more easy passes. No more open shots. Get on them." Her voice was rising as she made her points. "Get into their damn uniforms if you have to, but don't give them one second of rest. And what happened to our rebounding? Did we all of a sudden become flatfooted? Terry, Tonie, you were letting players half your size take the ball away from you." Pat knew she was exaggerating, but she wanted the players to know she had seen them dogging it as halftime approached. "I don't care if we have a 100-point lead, you keep playing like that and Miami will snatch the trophy out from under your noses."

"Won't happen, Coach," Tonie stated. "I'm grabbing every rebound this half," she declared to her teammates. "And what I miss, Terry will grab," she challenged the other post player.

Terry smiled. "I'm right there with you."

"That's more like it." Pat grinned. "Okay, any injuries you big lugs have been hiding from me?" Her question was answered by a group shaking of heads.

"Lizzie?"

"Nothing I know of, Coach." The trainer looked up from re-wrapping Pete's ankles. "Worst we have is Sherry's run-in with the wall," she said.

"Sherry?" Pat asked, as the players snickered.

"I'm good to go, Coach." Sherry stuck her tongue out at her teammates. "By the way, thanks for the warning," she snarled playfully.

"Hey, I yelled," Pete objected defensively.

"Yell louder next time," Sherry grumbled.

"Let's get serious for a minute," Pat told the players. "You all are going to have to be alert out there this half. Most likely, Miami will try to isolate Sherry or box her in. And more picks like that one wouldn't surprise me. Don't let them catch you napping. If you see something being set up, let everyone else know. Val, don't let that gal pull free from you again. It's hard to set a pick if someone is guarding you."

"She won't be setting any more of those," Val said determinedly.

"Okay, we've got another half of ball to play before we can take home our trophy. Are you ready?"

"*Ready!*" the Cougars shouted.

"Let's go then."

"I must say I'm surprised that Coach Calvin has been able to stay focused this season, what with all the controversy spinning around her again," the announcer was saying.

"It is unfortunate that she seems to always have a cloud hanging over her. This year was a little different in that there were two storms swirling around."

"That's right. First was a repeat of last season when allegations were made that she had been using her position as coach to...shall we say, exert undue influence on one of her players."

"Allegations strongly denied by all parties, I might add, including the league office, which has reported all season that no formal complaint had been filed."

"That's true. And then she had to deal with her other outstanding rookie player, Dawn Montgomery, who started the season on somewhat shaky ground. In fact, we aren't the only ones surprised to find her still a member of the Cougars."

"I have to agree. When she purposely took the legs out from under Gallagher at the start of the season, I thought for sure she'd be given her walking papers. But not only is she still here, she's turned her game around and is one of the first players sent in off the bench. Coach Calvin has done a remarkable job with Montgomery."

"If the rumors floating around the league are true, Coach Calvin may not be able to take all the credit for Montgomery's change of attitude. Many believe that she has simply been using the Cougars to better her chances of getting signed by a team in a larger market. After her mediocre play in her college senior year, few teams were willing to take a look at her."

"That's true."

"Looks like they're getting ready to start the second half, so let's switch back to the action."

Pat was curious when Miami started the second half with what appeared to be a standard man-to-man defense. It wasn't until Sherry stepped inside the 3-point arc that Miami collapsed another player to help guard her. The strategy worked better than Pat would have anticipated. Confronted with the unending pressure, the point guard was getting frustrated, and her accuracy was beginning to suffer. Slowly, Miami reduced the difference in the score.

"Time." Pat called out when Miami scored, narrowing the lead to only 8 points.

The Cougars trotted over to their coach. Sherry stood with her hands on her hips, breathing hard. Trying to break free of the persistent double team was wearing her out.

"Wendy, go in for Sherry," Pat told the player on the bench.

"I'm good, Coach," Sherry protested.

"Take a breather," Pat said. "We have lots of game left. Pete, take the point. Good job on boxing out on rebounds," she told the post players. "We need to put up some points. Pete, Wendy, Val, if you're open at the arc, shoot. Even if we don't make them, we'll force their defense to come out and open up the key. Okay, let's go."

Miami Surf 82 Missoula Cougars 87 — Time remaining: 3:57

Sherry dribbled up court, her second defender waiting at the 3-point line. She snapped the ball to Pete off to her left and made a cut toward the right sideline. Pete dribbled to the top of the key, dropping the ball off to Val and then running around to the left and up the side of the key.

Tonie battled with her defender, trying to get free at the bottom of the key.

Val spun around, passing the ball back to Pete.

Tonie side-stepped away from her defender, leaving herself momentarily open.

Pete snapped the ball to Tonie.

Tonie grabbed the ball, spinning toward the basket. Leaping into the air, she banked the ball off the backboard. The ball bounced on the rim, tapping the backboard before dropping back onto the edge of the rim and falling away from the basket. Tonie sprang back into the air, nudging the ball back toward the basket as her defender tried to gain position. Tonie dropped back to the floor, her foot coming down on top of her defender's. Unable to hold the player's weight, Tonie's ankle rolled, buckling the leg and taking Tonie to the floor.

Few of the Cougars noticed the ball drop through the basket. They were too concerned with their teammate clutching at her ankle in obvious pain.

"Damn," Pat muttered. She'd seen the same thing happen many times before and knew the post player was done for the game. "Dawn, get in there."

After several minutes, Lizzie, with the help of Kellie, was able to help Tonie to the sideline.

"She's done," Lizzie told Pat.

The player grimaced. "Sorry, Coach."

"You did your job." Pat smiled at Tonie. "Now rest up for the celebration."

Miami put the ball into play. Sherry blanketed the player dribbling up court until she passed off to a teammate at mid-court. The Miami player dribbled down the side of the court, watching to see if anyone came free under the basket.

Dawn, struggling to maintain position on the Miami post player, was shoved in the back. Stumbling forward, she glimpsed her player as she stepped out to the edge of the key — arm raised high, asking for the ball. Regaining her footing, Dawn raced out to retake her defensive position just as the ball reached the player.

The Miami player spun toward the basket, squaring up for a shot. Dawn jumped with the player, her long arm swatting for the ball as it left the Miami player's hand. She made contact with the leather. The ball flew over the Miami player's head, heading for the sidelines.

Sherry ran for the loose ball, leaping into the air as she reached the edge of the court. Airborne, she managed to get her hand on the ball, flicking it back toward the court.

Dawn drove an elbow into her defender's side, charging past her.

Sherry's quick reflexes saved her from injury. Pulling her legs up under her, she cleared the row of metal chairs at courtside, falling into the lap of a fan in the first row of seats. "Thanks." She smiled at the man who had cushioned her landing. Leaping to her feet, she jumped back over the chairs and onto the hardwood.

The Miami player Dawn had elbowed was charging toward her, bent on revenge. She raced after Dawn, intent on taking her down. Leaving her feet, she lunged for Dawn.

Dawn reached the ball. Grabbing it, she spun around, twisting her body as she zipped a pass over to the side of the court.

Sherry caught the ball in full stride, running for the other end of the court.

Dawn laughed as the Miami player flew past her, hitting the court and sliding all the way to the sideline. She casually started trotting after the rest of her team.

For the first time in the second half, Sherry was leading a fast break toward the Cougars' basket. And it felt good.

Sherry made it to mid-court before any of the Miami players reached top speed. Cutting for the top of the key, she bounced the ball between her legs, switching hands. She changed direction again, running straight for the basket. After one long stride, she picked up her dribble, cradling the ball in the palm of her right hand. Another stride, she planted her foot, pushing her body off the floor. Twisting in mid-air, Sherry placed her back to the basket. Swooping her hand up over her head, she tossed the ball up to kiss the backboard before it dropped through the net. Returning to the hardwood, she waited for the Miami defenders to reach the end of the court.

The players on the Cougars' bench were on their feet, as were many of the fans. The Rookie of the Year was back in the game.

Miami Surf 89 Missoula Cougars 103 — Time remaining: 0:12

Sherry dribbled the ball at mid-court, one eye on the game clock. After her fast break, she had led the Cougars on a scoring run that quickly put the game out of reach for Miami. With each bounce of the ball, she could feel the excitement growing inside her, and she couldn't wait for the final few seconds to tick away.

The Cougar bench was standing, counting down the seconds.

"You did it, Coach." Marcie stood beside Pat. "You've done one hell of a job with this team."

Pat smiled, wrapping an arm around Marcie's shoulders and reaching for Kellie with her other arm. "*We* did a hell of a job." She grinned. Pat was bursting with pride over her players and their accomplishment. They had won her the prize she wanted, something that, regardless of the rumors and unfounded accusations, could never be taken away from her. But as she stood there watching Sherry smiling as she bounced the ball between her legs, Pat knew the championship was not the only reward she could return to Missoula with. The love of the point guard was within her grasp, and she was determined not to let it slip through her fingers.

When the clock showed a single second to play, Sherry heaved the ball as high over her head as she could.

The buzzer sounded. The Cougars were the champions.

As the Cougars ran for their bench, the coaches and the rest of their team rushed onto the court to meet them.

Grinning, Pat walked along the front of the scorers' table to accept the Miami coach's congratulatory handshake. She turned to return to the Cougars' celebration.

Sherry saw Pat heading for the team, many piled in a tangle on the floor. Without thinking, she trotted toward her coach, leaping up and wrapping her arms and legs around the surprised woman. "We won!" she shouted. "Baby, we won!"

"Um, Sherry." Pat sucked her lower lip between her teeth, not quite sure what to say or do.

"Oh, shit." Sherry saw the troubled look on the coach's face and unwrapped herself, dropping back to the floor. "Shit, I'm sorry," she muttered, her neck and cheeks flushing with embarrassment.

"Don't be." Pat smiled at the mortified woman. "Go on, celebrate with the team."

Chuckling, Pete watched the exchange between the women. When Sherry turned away from Pat to rejoin her teammates, Pete raced for the coach and leapt into her arms. Mimicking Sherry's excitement, she tightly wrapped her arms and legs around Pat, squeezing hard.

Pat laughed at the veteran player's antics. "Pete, what the heck are you doing?"

"Well, I thought if Sherry could mug the coach in front of twenty thousand fans and who knows how many watching on TV, then I should get to share in the fun. Although, I'm not sure how my hubby will take this." She giggled.

"Get off me."

Pete smirked. Leaning in, she plastered a smacking kiss on the coach's cheek. "We won!" she yelled, loud enough for fans sitting several rows away from the court to hear.

"But somehow I don't think you're as happy to have me in your arms as you were to have Sherry," she whispered in Pat's ear. Disentangling herself from the coach, Pete ran back to her teammates.

CHAPTER EIGHTEEN

A day after the championship game, the victorious Missoula Cougars returned to their hometown early in the evening, their airport arrival welcomed by thousands of faithful fans. Even after they managed to board their bus, they continued to be surrounded by celebrating Missoulians. Many followed the bus into town in their own cars and pickups with horns honking and banners waving all the way to Cougar Arena.

It was late by the time Pat finished her last interview with the press and began tidying up her office before leaving for home.

Mac walked into the office. "We need to talk," she informed her coach, her tone all business.

"I know."

"Be in my office first thing in the morning."

"All right." After Mac left, Pat sat behind her desk, staring at the trophy placed prominently in the middle of it. *Well,* she thought, *my coaching career is over, but at least I have that.*

Winning the championship really didn't make up for all Pat felt she had lost. She thought about the sleepless nights spent wondering what kind of professional career she would have enjoyed had she been able to continue playing. No, the trophy did not make up for all those missed games, but it did ease some of the pain. And there was one thing that could assuage it even more.

Smiling, Pat stood, gathering up her keys and wallet. Tomorrow she would meet with Mac and do whatever was necessary to make sure that a future with Sherry, the truly good thing to come of the just-ended season, could be possible.

Pat nervously wiped the palms of her hands on her jeans before knocking. Even as her knuckles rapped on the door to Mac's office, she knew she could just open the door and enter her boss's office. Under the circumstances, she thought it best to wait for the invitation.

"Come in, Pat," Mac called through the door.

Pat's clammy hand twisted the cold knob. Pushing the door open, she walked through.

"Coffee?" Mac asked, holding up an empty mug. "I just made it. And I bought fresh sweet rolls on the way in."

"Thanks," Pat said as she closed the door, "but I'm not sure I could keep it down."

"Understandable." Mac poured coffee into the mug.

Pat accepted the ambiguous response as confirmation of why the owner had called her in. "Have a seat." Mac carried the mug of steaming coffee to her chair behind the desk. "We'll be here a while."

Pat blew out a long breath, dropping into one of the plush leather chairs in front of the desk.

Mac took a sip of coffee. "First, I want to congratulate you on an outstanding season."

"Thanks." Pat smiled tensely. "It was a great bunch of gals to coach."

"Some rocky bumps along the way."

"A few."

"Kinsey was unfortunate." Mac paused for another sip. "But you handled it well. Having her at the game helped a lot."

"She deserved it."

"Dawn caused some problems."

"She played hard at the end."

"She did." Mac took another sip. "We'll talk more about her later."

"All right." Pat wasn't sure what there was to talk about concerning the player she felt had been a disruptive influence for the team, especially with her ongoing relationship with the owner's niece. *But what does it matter? When we're done here, Dawn and the rest of the Cougars will no longer be my responsibility.*

"Let's talk about Sherry."

Pat swallowed, hard. She had been expecting the topic, but it still delivered a powerful punch to her midsection. "I broke my word to you," she said, seeing no reason to hide the truth. Her future was already decided, and the best she could hope for was to save Sherry's career or at least make sure she still had the opportunity for one if that was what she wanted. "I told you I would never see Sherry outside of the team. I did."

"How often?"

"Once."

Mac sipped from her coffee mug, listening to Pat's explanation about the night she had called Sherry and the two had driven to Salmon Lake.

"We kissed," Pat said, finishing the story.

"I see." Mac stood, carrying the mug back to the coffee pot for a refill. She stood for several minutes looking out the glass wall of her office to the court below where Sherry was practicing free throws. Occasionally, the point guard would glance up in the direction of the owner's office.

"Did Sherry know you were coming here?"

"No. Why?"

"She's down there." Mac nodded toward the arena. "Looks to be concerned about what could be going on up here." The owner smiled before turning around to face the just-as-anxious coach. "Relax, Pat." She grinned, leaning against the glass. "I'm not firing you."

"You're not?"

"No. Just how would it make me look if I fired the Coach of the Year? Congratulations, by the way. They made the announcement this morning."

In spite of the timing of the news, Pat smiled. "Thanks. That's nice."

"It sure is. And I'm not going to have people questioning whether I've lost my mind by firing you on the day you get that honor. But..." Mac pushed off the glass wall. She poured coffee into a second mug and placed a sweet roll on a plate. Adding a fork, she handed the plate and mug to Pat. "Here, you look like you could use this."

Pat placed the plate on the edge of the desk, deciding her roiling stomach hadn't calmed enough to even give the pastry a taste. Instead she leaned back in the chair, nursing the hot coffee.

"But," Mac repeated as she sat, "I can't let what you did go unnoticed. It needs to be dealt with. And this is coming strictly from me." She emphasized. "I don't give a damn what the league office has to say. As long as they let the likes of Palmer coach, what they think about you they can shove in a sock and flush it, for all I care. But you signed a contract with *me,* and you gave *me* your word. And you broke it. *That* I can't let pass."

Pat nodded. She didn't have to respond; there was nothing she could say. Mac was right. She had violated the terms of her contract and had broken her personal word to the owner. Those statements were true.

"You're young, Pat." Mac continued. "Too young to be a coach at this level, many would say, and several have. And I'm not immune to affairs of the heart, believe it or not. But being the owner of a professional sports team presents its own special challenges. And in order for the organization to function, I must have complete faith and trust in the people I put into positions of authority. You broke that trust, and I can't let it slide. We'll get past this, but for now I'm placing you on unpaid disciplinary leave for thirty days. There's bound to be some fallout over this with the press, but I think, as you may have already realized, that once you go public with your feelings for Sherry you're going to have a lot of that to deal with."

Pat looked at Mac in disbelief. "You accept this?" she asked, not even caring about the loss of pay or the public humiliation that her suspension would cause.

"Pat, you're in love. Sherry's in love. There aren't too many people who have spent the last several months around the two of you who don't know that. Unless I've been endowed with some super powers in the last few minutes, I know of no way I can stop the two of you from loving each other. Now the question is...how to make it possible for you to be together and still stay a part of the Cougars. Because, believe you me, I have no intention of not having the Coach of the Year and the Rookie of the Year back in uniform next season."

"I, um..." Pat stammered, her eyes blinking rapidly as she fought back the tears. She had never expected Mac to endorse the relationship growing between herself and Sherry as long as they both were employed by the Cougars. And to hear Mac say they were going to work out a plan to keep them both with the team...well, that went way beyond any hope she'd had when she first entered the office.

Sherry was still shooting free throws, even though she had long since passed the magical number of one hundred. She was just too nervous and anxious to stop. Catching a movement inside the corridor at the end of the court, she turned to check it out. She was pleased to see the coach emerging from the dark hallway, although she was surprised at the relaxed look on her face.

Pat skirted the court, choosing to climb a few rows up into the seats instead.

Sherry let the ball drop from her hands, hurrying over to stand on the sideline in front of Pat. "Hi," she said uncertainly.

"Hi, yourself." The coach patted the seat next to her, grinning when Sherry used the seats between them to climb up to her.

"Meeting with Mac over?" Sherry asked, taking the offered seat.

"Yes."

"Did she..."

"No. She didn't fire me."

"Then I'm refusing to sign the new contract," Sherry said stubbornly. "If we can't both work for the Cougars, then I won't. And I might as well go tell her right now."

Pat reached out to stop the player from moving. "Hold on," she said, grasping Sherry's arm.

Sherry looked at Pat, then down at the hand resting affectionately on her arm. She raised her head to look into the coach's eyes, her own filling with tears. "Pat?"

"Listen to me, okay?" Pat asked softly. Sherry nodded, placing her hand on top of Pat's. "Mac isn't going to fire me, but she is suspending me for a month."

"That's not fair." Sherry pulled her hand back, again beginning to rise.

"Sherry, sit down." Pat chuckled, reaching over for Sherry's hand. For good measure, she took control of both of the guard's hands, holding them tenderly between her own. "Listen." She looked into Sherry's eyes. "Please?"

Sherry nodded, enthralled by the feel of the warm hands surrounding her own.

"Mac has every right to suspend me. Truth is, I wouldn't have blamed her if she had fired me. I broke the terms of my contract, and I broke my word to her. And," she said, placing one finger against Sherry's lips to stop her impending protest, "I'd do it all over again if I had the chance." Sherry smiled against her fingertip. "So I'm suspended, and *you are* going to sign a new contract, just not the one you were thinking."

"Huh?"

"Marcie has accepted the coaching position at her alma mater. She resigned after the game yesterday."

Sherry frowned at Pat, confused by the seeming change in subject.

"That leaves a position open on my staff. Mac, on Pete's recommendation and with my agreement, is going to offer you that position."

"Assistant coach?"

Pat nodded.

"I can't do that. I don't know anything about being a coach. I'm a player, Pat, nothing more. I'm just going to tell Mac no thanks. I'll leave basketball. I'm sure I can get a job doing something. Anything. That is, I mean, if you want me around. Because—"

Pat leaned forward, pressing her lips against Sherry's to stop the woman's babbling. "You're not listening," she chided, pulling away long moments later.

"Sorry." Sherry sighed, reaching up and running a fingertip around her still tingling lips. "What were you saying?" she asked absently.

Pat chuckled. "I've watched you this season working with Pete and Marcie to learn all you could about your position and the game. And I've watched you turn around and pass on what you've learned to Wendy and Amie. Not only did you work to improve your play on the court, but you worked to help them improve theirs. That's what a coach does." She grinned. "And you're a natural."

"So..." Sherry mulled over the explanation, not at all convinced by Pat's endorsement. "I go from player to coach?"

"No."

"Huh?"

Pat's grin widened. "That is so damn cute."

"What?"

"The way your nose crinkles up when you say that."

"Say what?"

"Huh."

"Huh?'

"That's it." Pat laughed, pointing at the center of Sherry's face. "*That* is just so damn cute."

"Pat!" Sherry cried out, infuriated yet charmed, grabbing the offending finger. "Will you tell me what the hell you're talking about?"

"You still play." Pat chuckled as the guard kept a tight hold on her finger. "Sherry Gallagher, player slash coach."

"Doesn't that leave us right back where we started?"

"Um. Okay. Maybe it should be: Sherry Gallagher, coach slash player."

"I don't see a difference."

"Look, there's plenty of coaches in the league and at the college level, and even the high school level, that have their partners, wives, husbands, whatever, as their assistant coaches. You being a member of the coaching staff puts you a step above being just a player. And you remain on the roster and play; you'll do most of your coaching on the court, because Mac absolutely refuses to give up her Rookie of the Year now that she's got one. And she doesn't want to fire the Coach of the Year, either."

"Is that why she didn't fire you?" Sherry asked seriously. "I heard the news just before I left the apartment. You deserved it." She smiled lovingly. "I'm so proud."

Pat smiled back. "As I am of you."

"So you and Mac came up with this little plan all on your own?"

"Pete actually gave Mac the idea."

"I'll have to remember to thank her at Marcie's going-away party."

"Now that you mention it, I guess I should."

"Brat." Sherry swatted the coach's arm, relaxing back in her seat. Suddenly, the end of her world seemed so much further away.

"And you'll be pleased to know you won't have Dawn to deal with in your first year as coach slash player."

Sherry was a little surprised by the news. After all they'd put up with through the season, it seemed strange to be releasing her now that she was showing some signs of a turnaround. "Didn't Mac offer her a contract?"

"Yes. But Dawn turned it down. She signed this morning with Los Angeles. Seems that's why she's been working so hard. She approached Coach Buttram after she graduated but was told she'd have to improve her court behavior and she'd have to prove it by playing a year on another team, if she could find one to sign her."

"Which she managed to do by bedding Mandy?"

"Seems so."

"And speaking of Mandy..." Sherry snickered. "She's not going to be too happy to have me sticking around."

"Probably not, if she was going to be here." Pat laughed. "But she's headed for L.A., too. It seems they really are in love with one another. Boy, I hope they know what they're in for."

"Huh? Are they crazy?"

"Damn, I love that look."

Sherry stared at Pat.

"We can say that now," Pat said softly.

"We can?"

Pat nodded. "Yes."

"Good, because I've been waiting to say this for a long time. I'm in love with you, Pat Calvin," Sherry whispered, relieved to be speaking the words that had been burning her tongue for months.

"I'm in love with you, Sherry Gallagher," Pat whispered back.

After several heartbeats of just enjoying the sound of the declarations echoing in their thoughts, Sherry asked, "Now what?"

"First, you have to go up and talk to Mac. She's a little anxious to have your signature on a contract."

"Okay. And then?"

"Well," Pat said timidly, "if you don't have any plans for later, I thought we could go to dinner."

"Dinner? Like in a date, dinner?" Sherry teased, only half joking.

"Yes."

"You mean a bona fide date? One where you actually walk up to my door and pick me up?"

"Yes."

"And we go to a restaurant without any cares that someone might see us? A really, real date?"

"Yes, Sherry, a real date," Pat growled playfully.

"Can we hold hands?"

"Yes."

"Can you kiss me?" Sherry asked shyly.

"You mean like this?" Pat cupped Sherry's face and gently pulled the woman she loved toward her. This time when she pressed their mouths together, she took her time to explore the soft lips with her tongue before sliding it inside the warm, wet mouth that opened willingly for her.

Sherry sighed contently, her hands instinctively slipping behind Pat's head, pulling her closer.

It was lack of oxygen that finally separated the women who had waited so long to express their love for each other.

Pat rested her forehead against Sherry's. "That was nice."

"Yes, it was." Sherry smiled. "Can we do it again?"

"Later." Pat grinned, laughing at the pout forming on the guard's lips. "You need to go talk to Mac, and I need to go home and wash the pickup. Can't be picking up my girl in a muddy truck."

"Your girl, huh?"

"If you want to be."

"Oh, I want to be. I really, really want to be." Sherry placed a quick peck on Pat's lips as she stood. "I'll go. You go. And I'll see you when?"

"How's five? And I thought if dinner goes well, we could take in a movie afterward."

"Oh, I love the movies." Sherry clapped her hands together happily, jumping over the back of the row of seats at courtside. She used the cushioned seats to bounce down to the court. "But, Pat," she turned to face the coach, "I should warn you — I like to sit in the back row and snuggle."

"Works for me."

Pat paid for the movie tickets, then held open the door into the multiplex lobby, waiting for Sherry to walk through before she followed. "You want anything?" she asked as they passed the refreshment counter.

"No." Sherry shook her head, rubbing her tummy. "After that dinner, I'm stuffed."

"You should be, with what you ate." Pat laughed. She led her fuming date to the back of the lobby, handing their tickets to a teenaged boy who wasn't bothering to hide his unhappiness at being on duty.

"Down there." The boy pointed off to his left. "Second door on the right. Enjoy the movie," he said, his voice lacking any inflection.

"Goodness." Sherry snickered as she followed the boy's directions. "I hope the movie isn't as boring as he made it sound."

"Don't think I'll be noticing." Pat grinned, pulling open the door.

"What?"

"Oh, nothing. Come on." Pat grabbed Sherry's hand, yanking her inside the theater.

They walked up the narrow corridor at the side of the theater, a high wall blocking their view of everything but the large screen. Rounding the end of the wall, the women were happy to see most of the seats were empty. They mounted the steps leading to the back of the theater and settled into the two middle seats in the very back row.

"Think it'll stay this empty?" Sherry asked.

"Let's hope so." Pat slipped her arm behind Sherry's head to drape it over her shoulders. Sherry leaned into the embrace, sighing happily. The lights dimmed, and the seemingly endless commercials and previews began.

Pat stretched her legs out over the seat backs in front of her, twisting slightly to be closer to Sherry.

Sherry turned until she was facing Pat, her legs curled up and resting on top of the coach's. "Does this hurt?" she asked, mindful of Pat's injured leg.

"A little." Sherry withdrew her legs. "No," Pat said quickly, placing her hand over Sherry's legs to hold them in place. "If it gets too bad, I'll tell you."

"Promise?"

"Yes."

Sherry snuggled as close to Pat as she could manage with the armrest poking up between them. Pat's hand moved down Sherry's back, gently rubbing the fabric against the skin underneath.

Sherry curled her body even more, arching her back into Pat's caress. Her own hand explored the body under her, and she heard a sharp intake of breath when it moved up Pat's side to within inches of her breast. She pulled away from Pat just enough to be able to look into her eyes. "Pat?"

Even in the capricious light reflecting back at them from the movie screen, Pat could see the look of desire on Sherry's face.

"Take me home," Sherry whispered.

Pat wasn't sure she could. Her need for the woman in her arms was so great at that moment, she felt as if all the blood in her body had settled in one overheated and throbbing bundle of nerve endings. She was sure if she even tried to stand her useless legs would collapse beneath her and she would end up falling flat on her face.

"Okay," she whispered.

Sherry untangled herself from Pat, then stood and waited.

Pat took a few moments to try and control her racing heart but eventually gave up when it refused to slow with Sherry present. On shaky legs, she let Sherry guide them back down the steps in the darkness.

They walked to the front of the theater, to the door at the bottom corner of the screen which would let them exit the building directly into the parking area. It was only a few more minutes before Pat's pickup was driving out of the lot.

Pat and Sherry walked arm-in-arm up the cement walk from the driveway to the front door of Pat's modest three-bedroom house.

It took Pat only a moment to insert the key in the lock and open the door. "Welcome." She smiled at Sherry, reaching behind her to flip on the living room lights.

"I'll sightsee tomorrow," Sherry said, forestalling the obligatory tour. "Tonight, I'm only interested in the bedroom." Her voice was husky with desire.

Pat pushed the door shut and slid the deadbolt in place. "This way." Her heart was beating so fast she was sure she'd pass out before they made it halfway down the hallway. "Do you...?" she asked, reaching for the light switch in the bedroom.

"No," Sherry answered. The moon was full, and the room was filled with a soft, golden glow.

Pat let her hand drop, following Sherry to the middle of the room. The lack of lighting posed no problem for her as she knew the room's layout by heart. Her king-size bed took up most of the room except for a chest, six drawers high, where she stored her numerous sweatsuits and workout clothes. A second, smaller dresser occupied the wall next to the closet, and an overstuffed chair that was seldom used sat in the corner between the two windows. There was a door leading into the bathroom, but otherwise the walls were uninterrupted, even by art.

Sherry didn't bother looking around the room, not caring how it was furnished. She did, however, care about the woman standing beside her. Turning, she placed her hands on Pat's waist, guiding the woman backward until her legs bumped the end of the bed. With a gentle shove, she pushed Pat down to sit in front of her.

Pat sat, her knees slightly spread and her hands pressing down into the mattress, her eyes following every movement Sherry made as she untied her shoes and kicked them off.

Sherry stepped between Pat's legs. Leaning over, she placed a tender kiss on the woman's lips, then stood up. Pulling the polo shirt she wore over her head, she held it out to her side for a moment before allowing it to fall from her fingers to the carpeted floor.

Pat gulped, her body surging with pent-up passion.

Sherry moved to take off her sports bra. Bending her right arm at the elbow, she pulled it free first, then repeated the motion with her left. Slipping her fingers under the elastic band at the bottom of the bra, she slowly inched it up over her breasts before lifting it over her head and dropping it to join her shirt.

Pat sat motionless, entranced by the exposed skin highlighted by the moonlight, her tongue licking dry lips and chest heaving with her short gasps of breath.

Sherry slid down the zipper of her khakis. Slipping her hands inside the waistband, she pushed the material down her thighs, taking her underpants with them.

Tentatively, Pat reached out, placing her hands on Sherry's hips, pulling her close. She turned her head, nuzzling her cheek on the bare skin of Sherry's belly. Using only the tips of her fingers, Pat traced her hands up Sherry's sides and around her back. She pulled the woman closer. With her ear pressed against the silky soft skin, Pat could hear the heart underneath beating at a tempo that matched her own. She inhaled deeply, wanting to absorb all of what was Sherry. She could smell the light trace of herbal soap Sherry had used to wash her body hours earlier. And a hint of the shampoo she used on her hair, which smelled like strawberries freshly picked off a mountain slope. And she could smell the sweet aroma of Sherry's desire coming from between her legs.

Sherry curled her arms around Pat and placed kisses on the top of her head. "Let me undress you?" she asked as Pat kissed her stomach, causing the muscles there to twitch uncontrollably. She reached behind her, entwining her fingers with Pat's as she unwrapped the arms that held her. "Sit back, love."

Pat reluctantly pulled away. She had a tremendous need to press her legs together to relieve the pressure building in her groin but was prevented from achieving any relief because of Sherry's position between her thighs.

Seeing the effect she was having on the woman who would soon be her lover, Sherry took her time as she freed each button of Pat's shirt and then pushed the garment off Pat's shoulders and down her arms. She tugged the tight tank top out of Pat's slacks, then lifted it off as Pat raised her arms. She smiled, seeing the proof of what she'd long ago guessed. "I love a woman who feels confident enough to go bra-less," she murmured, gazing hungrily at the inviting breasts. "Lay down," she said softly, directing Pat by pressing her fingertips on her shoulders.

Pat was on fire. Just the thought of Sherry's skin touching hers was almost enough to fire the orgasm she was trying so desperately to hold back.

Sherry stepped out of the pants pooled around her ankles, flipping them out of the way before crawling onto the bed. Holding her body above Pat's, she smiled down at the woman. Slowly, ever so slowly, she lowered her body until their nakedness met.

"Oh, god," Pat moaned, unable to contain her release any longer.

With Pat convulsing beneath her, Sherry needed her own release. She grabbed Pat's hand, guiding it between their bodies. Spreading her legs, she groaned, "Inside, please."

Led by instinct, Pat slid three fingers into Sherry, pressing her thumb against the throbbing clit at the same time.

That was all Sherry needed. Her release was instantaneous, an explosion started by the fingers she held in a vise grip. "Pat," she cried, rocking her body to force the fingers deeper inside her.

Pat felt a second orgasm building. She wrapped her free arm around Sherry, pulling her down onto her hand. Her fingers curled inside her lover, exploring and probing the smooth, slick walls they encountered. "I'm gonna come again," Pat groaned.

Sherry's lips latched onto Pat's earlobe, sucking and running her tongue over the heated flesh. "Come for me, baby," she urged, her own orgasm not yet subsiding.

"Oh, god." Pat's hips bucked when a hot tongue dove inside her ear. Wave after wave of red hot lava rushed through her body, and all she could do was hold on to Sherry and scream. It was several moments before the room was quiet.

Pat lay exhausted, her body rippling with aftershocks.

Sherry lay boneless on top of her lover, her legs pressed together trapping Pat's hand inside of her. "I love you," she whispered.

"Mmmm," was all Pat could manage, a smile spread across her face.

"I want to feel all of you," Sherry said, disappointed that Pat still had her slacks on. "But I don't want you to move." She was not ready to release the fingers inside her.

"Not sure there's any way to get my pants off like this," Pat said with a chuckle.

Sherry felt the laugh. Twisting her head, she rested her chin on Pat's breastbone. "I don't suppose we could stay like *this* forever?"

"Don't think so. Want me to..." Pat wiggled her fingers.

Sherry clamped down harder on Pat's hand. "If you do, I'm going to come *again*."

"Really?"

"Yes," Sherry moaned.

"No sense in wasting a good thing. Besides, I'm not sure I'm done yet. And if you come, I'm pretty sure I will, too."

"Really?"

Pat smiled. Just seeing Sherry naked and lying on top of her was causing her to tremble with need. She felt the heat growing between her legs and knew it would only take the sound of Sherry's cries when she released to set free her own desire. She wriggled her fingers again.

"More," Sherry moaned, easing the pressure she was using to hold Pat inside of her. "I'm almost there."

"Not yet, love," Pat whispered, shifting positions. She slowly pulled her fingers free, stopping all movement whenever she felt Sherry's release start. "Hold it, baby," she murmured.

"I can't," Sherry groaned, thrusting her hips forward, attempting to drive herself back onto Pat's hand.

With her fingers pulled out of Sherry, Pat shifted again. She scooted out from under her lover, rolling Sherry on to her back and spreading her legs. Resting her body on her elbows, Pat placed a knee against Sherry's clit.

Sherry screamed. The sensation of the rough material of Pat's pants rubbing on her throbbing bundle sent bolts of lightning through her, setting off tiny explosions all through her body. Her hands clutched at Pat, fingers digging into the soft skin of her lover's back. "Harder," she cried.

Leaning down to capture a nipple between her teeth, Pat drove her knee against Sherry's clit. Hearing Sherry's screams and feeling the body under her jerking sent Pat over the edge.

The women held on to each other as their orgasms detonated.

"Take off your pants," Sherry said when later the women snuggled together preparing to sleep.

Pat sat up, swinging her legs over the edge of the bed. She pulled first one foot and then the other up to remove the shoes she still wore, then stood, unzipping her pants and letting them drop to the floor. She slipped off her panties, then fell back on the bed, reaching for the blankets folded over the end of the mattress.

Sherry snuggled against Pat, her hand finding a breast and playing with it. "You're a remarkable woman."

"I am?" Pat cupped a hand on Sherry's buttocks, pulling her on top of her.

"Oh, yes!" Sherry squealed, not expecting the move. "I've never had orgasms like that. And never that many."

"Well, then, I'd say we're both remarkable women." Pat placed a second hand on Sherry's bottom, squeezing the firm rounds of flesh. "Because I've never had multiple ones either."

"I'm glad." Sherry smiled, snaking a hand down between their bodies.

"What are you doing?"

"I think I've got one more in me tonight," Sherry said, slipping her hand through the patch of fine, curly hair she had been prevented from exploring until now. "What about you?"

"Oh," Pat moaned, her body already reacting to her lover's touch. "I think I could give it a try."

"Good." Sherry's fingers slid into Pat's wetness. "You feel so good," she sighed.

"Don't make me wait too long," Pat groaned.

"I won't, baby." Sherry's fingers moved lower until they found the opening they were seeking. "I love you, Pat," she murmured, driving her fingers inside. Pat's hips bucked, thrusting up to meet Sherry's hand. Sherry body reacted to Pat's release. Slipping to the side of her lover's body, she rubbed her clit on Pat's hipbone.

Pat's fingers dug into the skin of her lover's buttocks, pulling her against her. She cried out Sherry's name as another orgasm exploded inside her.

CHAPTER NINETEEN

Waking in Pat's arms, Sherry smiled. "'Morning."

Pat grinned. "More like afternoon."

"Really?" Sherry rolled her head to peer out the window, squinting when the bright sunlight glared in her eyes. "Ugh." She turned away from the window, rolling onto her side and snuggling into Pat. "I love waking up with you," she murmured, squirming into a more comfortable position.

Pat sighed, kissing the top of her lover's head. "I love you."

"Can we stay like this forever?"

"If you want." Pat smiled, running her hand down Sherry's side. Relishing the feel of her lover's skin, she took her time to explore every nook and cranny her fingers came into contact with. "You're so soft," she murmured.

"You're not so bad yourself," Sherry said, her tongue darting out to pull a well-placed nipple into her mouth.

Pat moaned. The sensation of Sherry's lips on her skin reawakened desires she thought had been satiated the night before. She rolled onto her back, pulling Sherry with her and groaning when her lover's hand squeezed her other breast.

Sherry sucked and licked the aroused nipple in her mouth; reaching down between her legs, she felt for Pat's thigh. Raising the muscular leg off the mattress, she rubbed against it in a slow, steady rhythm.

It was some time before either woman was able to continue the conversation.

Sherry's fingers sifted through Pat's hair. "What are those?" she asked, gesturing toward the pair of suitcases on the floor next to the closet.

"Suitcases."

The lovers had remained in bed most of the day, getting to know each other.

"I know that." Sherry swatted Pat. "I mean, what are they doing there?"

Pat lifted her head to see the objects in question. "Doesn't look like they're doing anything." She chuckled, dropping her head back onto Sherry's lap where it had been resting.

"Pat." Sherry frowned, but her eyes twinkled at her lover's playfulness.

"Every year after the end of the season, I go down to a place in the Bitterroot Valley. It's back in the mountains; I usually stay a couple of weeks. It helps me unwind and rejuvenate for the next season."

"What's it like?"

"It's a lodge, but they also have private cabins you can rent. I usually get one of those. You can cross-country ski or snowshoe or rent a snowmobile. The cabins have hot tubs, which are great on clear nights when the stars are out. And they come with a small kitchen, or you can eat at the lodge; it has a really nice dining room."

"What do you do?"

"Some snowshoeing or just walking. Watch the animals. Most mornings and evenings you can see deer and elk and, once in a while, a moose or bear will wander through. I do some reading. But mostly, I just enjoy the scenery."

"Sounds nice. When are you going?"

"Tomorrow."

"Oh."

Hearing the disappointment in her lover's voice, Pat rolled her eyes up to look at Sherry. "Come with me?"

"I don't know, Pat. I've got so much to do here. My lease is up at the end of the month, and I need to find someplace better to live now that I know I'll be hanging around for a while."

"I know of a nice three-bedroom house you could share," Pat said, rolling onto her side to be able to look at her lover while they talked.

Sherry knew what Pat was suggesting. "You sure you're ready for that step?"

Pat smiled. "Lately I've been doing a lot of thinking about getting myself a roommate."

"You have, have you?"

"Yes."

"Have you had any particular kind of roommate in mind?"

"I have a couple of requirements, but nothing too fancy. Someone who can cook, because I'm lousy at that, and clean, because I hate to do that. Interested?"

"Well, the cooking I might do once in a while, but only if someone else washes the dishes. But the cleaning. Uck. Sorry, I'd have to pass."

"How about if I keep my maid service?"

"Any benefits in it for me?"

"I only own one bed."

"Hmmm." Sherry grinned. "I might be talked into trying it out."

"Good." Pat rolled onto her back. Her arms wrapped around Sherry, pulling her lover on top of her. "Now will you come with me?"

"I don't have any clothes for being in the snow."

Pat glanced at the clock on top of the tall chest of drawers. "No problem. Stores are open for a few more hours. We can get everything you need."

"I don't know, Pat." Sherry frowned. "That's a lot of money and—"

"Have you forgotten you just signed a double contract with the Missoula Cougars? I think a few hundred dollars are well within your budget."

"Oops." Sherry snickered; she had indeed forgotten. "But it's probably too late for me to get a room, don't you think?" she asked, not wanting to assume that Pat meant for her to stay in the same cabin.

"You won't need a room, love." Pat hugged Sherry. "I want you with me. Forever."

Sherry melted into the embrace. "I want that, too."

"Then you'll come?"

"Yes."

"Good." Pat smacked Sherry on the butt, pushed her off to the side of the mattress, then hopped off the bed.

"Ow." Sherry rubbed the stinging flesh. "What was that for?"

"Get up, lazy bones!" Pat shouted from the bathroom. "We have shopping to do. Can't stay in bed all day."

Sherry looked out the window at the fading sunlight. "We just did."

"I'm taking a shower," Pat singsonged.

"Oh." Sherry leaped up. "I'm coming, love."

EPILOGUE

"Okay, all strapped in." Pat gave a final tug to the straps securing Sherry's snow boots to her snowshoes, then stood up. "Now before you try to walk..."

"Oof," Sherry grunted as she fell into a mound of soft snow. "Guess I should have waited for the rest of the lesson, huh?" She looked up at Pat standing over her.

"Could have saved you some trouble." Pat chuckled, reaching down to pull Sherry to her feet. She brushed snow off her lover's new winter jacket and insulated snow pants. "Here." She picked up a pair of ski poles leaning against the side of their cabin. "Let's get these adjusted to your height," she said, untwisting one of the poles and pulling the end out. "How's that?" she asked, handing the pole to Sherry.

Sherry placed the pole tip on the ground. "What should it feel like?"

"Comfortable." Pat untwisted the second pole. "Not too high, not too short."

"But juuussssttttttt right."

"Yes, my little bear." Pat kissed Sherry. "Here." She handed her the second pole. "Try that. They're real easy to adjust, so play with them until you figure out what's right for you."

"Okay."

Pat grabbed the second pair of poles, adjusting them to her preferred length. Slipping her gloved hands through the loops, she wrapped her hands around the pole grips. "Now when you walk, just walk naturally. Only thing you have to remember is that snowshoes are wider than your regular shoes. So just spread your legs a bit. And I know you know how to do that." She leered at Sherry.

"Pat!" Sherry cried out in mock horror. "We're in public."

"Baby, there isn't another human being for, what?" She glanced around at the next closest cabin. "Maybe fifty feet."

"You are so bad," Sherry grumbled, laughing.

"Ready to give it a try?"

"Yes. Where are we going?"

"Down there." Pat pointed with a ski pole. "Then we'll head up that road. It's mostly level for the first mile. By then, you'll be a pro at snowshoeing, and the hills won't bother you."

"Okay." Sherry adjusted the pack on her back, then took a first tentative step. The poles made balancing on the wide shoes easy, and after a few steps she was comfortable enough to look at Pat instead of her feet. She smiled. "This is fun."

"Told you so. Biggest thing is when you try to turn or back up. You have to be careful not to put one snowshoe on top of the other. That's when you get in trouble."

"I'll try to remember."

"If you don't," Pat laughed, "you'll be picking your butt off the ground again."

Sherry blew Pat a kiss. "I think I'll let you do that."

"Gladly."

The women walked in silence for several minutes, the sound of freshly fallen snow crunching under their shoes the only noise disturbing the peace.

"It's beautiful out here," Sherry said as they made their way between the snow-covered pine trees.

"Yes. I love being out like this." Pat sighed. "It's nice to finally have someone to share it with."

Sherry turned to look at her lover, the melancholy in her voice reflected in her eyes. "How come you don't ask your friends to join you anymore?" she asked, knowing Pat had grown up in Missoula and the town was full of her friends.

Pat stopped. Leaning on her ski poles, she took a few minutes to think about Sherry's question. "Do you realize that we never talk about basketball when we're together?" she finally said. "Why is that?"

Sherry shrugged standing beside Pat. "I don't like to. When I'm on the court, I'm 200 percent into the game. But when I'm away from it...I guess I look at basketball as something I do, not as who I am."

"Exactly." Pat nodded, beginning to walk again.

Sherry reached out, placing a hand on her lover's arm, stopping her. "I'm sorry, Pat. That must be hard."

Pat sighed, smiling sadly. "Seems like since I was named head coach, all anyone wants to talk about is basketball. The rest of who I am just started to slip away. It just got to be easier to do things by myself. That was one of the first things that drew me to you." She looked at Sherry. "You never once talked about the game when we were away from it. With us now both being coaches, that may not be possible," she said wistfully.

"Let's make a pact." Sherry grinned. "When we're with the team, we talk basketball. When we go home, we don't. Deal?" she asked, reaching out a gloved hand to Pat.

"Sweetheart," Pat accepted the hand, drawing Sherry to her, "when we're home there's only going to be one thing on my mind."

"What's that?" Sherry asked, leaning into Pat, her lips inches from her lover's.

"You." Pat pressed their lips together.

Mickey was born and raised in Southern California. She has lived in New Mexico and Washington state and, for the past several years, in Western Montana. A lifelong history and nature enthusiast, Mickey has explored many of the locations she uses in her stories. She is also an amateur photographer and enjoys photographing the natural beauty of Montana as well as recording remnants of life in the frontier.

Mickey has plans for several more books and looks forward to the day she can spend all her time writing. Visit Mickey's website at mickeyminner.com

LaVergne, TN USA
03 September 2010
195786LV00007B/135/P